A
―――――――――――
CANDLELIGHT REGENCY SPECIAL

Candlelight Regencies

- 216 A GIFT OF VIOLETS, *Janette Radcliffe*
- 221 THE RAVEN SISTERS, *Dorothy Mack*
- 225 THE SUBSTITUTE BRIDE, *Dorothy Mack*
- 227 A HEART TOO PROUD, *Laura London*
- 232 THE CAPTIVE BRIDE, *Lucy Phillips Stewart*
- 239 THE DANCING DOLL, *Janet Louise Roberts*
- 240 MY LADY MISCHIEF, *Janet Louise Roberts*
- 245 LA CASA DORADA, *Janet Louise Roberts*
- 246 THE GOLDEN THISTLE, *Janet Louise Roberts*
- 247 THE FIRST WALTZ, *Janet Louise Roberts*
- 248 THE CARDROSS LUCK, *Janet Louise Roberts*
- 250 THE LADY ROTHSCHILD, *Samantha Lester*
- 251 BRIDE OF CHANCE, *Lucy Phillips Stewart*
- 253 THE IMPOSSIBLE WARD, *Dorothy Mack*
- 255 THE BAD BARON'S DAUGHTER, *Laura London*
- 257 THE CHEVALIER'S LADY, *Betty Hale Hyatt*
- 263 MOONLIGHT MIST, *Laura London*
- 501 THE SCANDALOUS SEASON, *Nina Pykare*
- 505 THE BARTERED BRIDE, *Anne Hillary*
- 512 BRIDE OF TORQUAY, *Lucy Phillips Stewart*
- 515 MANNER OF A LADY, *Cilla Whitmore*
- 521 LOVE'S CAPTIVE, *Samantha Lester*
- 527 KITTY, *Jennie Tremaine*
- 530 BRIDE OF A STRANGER, *Lucy Phillips Stewart*
- 537 HIS LORDSHIP'S LANDLADY, *Cilla Whitmore*
- 542 DAISY, *Jennie Tremaine*
- 543 THE SLEEPING HEIRESS, *Phyllis Taylor Pianka*
- 548 LOVE IN DISGUISE, *Nina Pykare*
- 549 THE RUNAWAY HEIRESS, *Lillian Cheatham*
- 554 A MAN OF HER CHOOSING, *Nina Pykare*
- 555 PASSING FANCY, *Mary Linn Roby*
- 570 THOMASINA, *Joan Vincent*
- 571 SENSIBLE CECILY, *Margaret Summerville*
- 572 DOUBLE FOLLY, *Marnie Ellingson*
- 573 POLLY, *Jennie Tremaine*
- 578 THE MISMATCHED LOVERS, *Anne Hillary*
- 579 UNWILLING BRIDE, *Marnie Ellingson*
- 580 INFAMOUS ISABELLE, *Margaret Summerville*
- 581 THE DAZZLED HEART, *Nina Pykare*

The ARDENT SUITOR

Marian Lorraine

A DELL BOOK

Published by
Dell Publishing Co., Inc.
1 Dag Hammarskjold Plaza
New York, New York 10017

Copyright © 1980 by Marian L. Horton

All rights reserved. No part of this book
may be reproduced or transmitted in any form
or by any means, electronic or mechanical, including
photocopying, recording or by any information storage
and retrieval system, without the written permission
of the Publisher, except where permitted by law.

Dell ® TM 681510, Dell Publishing Co., Inc.

ISBN: 0-440-10256-1

Printed in the United States of America

First printing—July 1980

The ARDENT SUITOR

CHAPTER ONE

Andrea stood leaning against the white pillar on the back terrace and watched with benevolent amusement as her brother and sister played at the game of tennis in a not particularly proficient manner. Their general ineptitude did not measurably interfere with their enjoyment, however, as they had wisely commissioned a pair of willing young servants to retrieve their errors and thus were spared the tiresome part of the game. She had come to call them for refreshment but was reluctant to distract them.

It had been more than six months since Andrew had been home and Chloe as usual followed him around like a little puppy, for she had always looked upon him as a veritable god. When they were younger, this credulous hero-worship was quite touching and seemed perfectly harmless. But Andrea had hoped it would run its course, for Drew was not exactly desirable material for an idol. Not that he was any worse than other young men of his class and affluence, but his attributes of exceptional beauty, wealth, and a devil-may-care, engaging affability combined to charm almost everyone with whom he came in contact.

Andrea was the only person she knew who had ever called him to book for anything, and as a consequence they had a sort of adversary relationship. It was not that they did not love each other dearly—they were twins, after all—but they never thought so well of one another as when they were apart. There were several reasons for their disharmony, not the least of which was Andrea's ability to best her brother at almost everything. He had long since reconciled himself to her supremacy and, in fact, took advantage of it, going off to play soldier while she handled all their financial and estate affairs. A great-uncle who was a colonel in the Army had recommended him to Field Marshal Wellington and he had become one of the popular young staff officers who, in addition to being trusted aides, were known for their gallantry and expertise in the social graces. Because of Drew's happy experience in the service, where he found the pageantry, privilege, and esprit de corps much to his taste, he decided to remain in the Army for a while longer to sit out the occupation in Paris, which, after Waterloo, had once again regained its international appeal and was the mecca for a great many of the fashionables. Now he was home on leave to celebrate his and Andrea's birthday.

Drew knew his twin greatly disapproved of his high-stepping mode of living, and he did not like to be constantly reminded (not as much by her words as by her critical attitude and penetrating looks) that his sensibilities were not all that well-refined. He was not given to introspection and saw no fault in being a dashing young blade. It was no blame to him if silly young women were disappointed in their aspirations. Even without a title he was ruthlessly pursued and was not averse to an occasional dalliance with one of the reigning beauties, who inevitably found herself abandoned if she presumed too much.

Actually, Andrea did not overly concern herself with the dashed hopes of most of these young women whom she felt left themselves open to insult by their forward ways. She *did*, however, fault Drew in one particular instance, when he misjudged the sensitivity of a sweet young girl, who probably would never recover from her trusting infatuation. After their breakup she retired to her country home and never received another suitor. It was her type of personality that a man of Andrew's stamp would find difficult to understand and appreciate. And that was what worried Andrea, especially about Chloe's blind devotion to him. He adored her, of course, but as he would a puppy or a kitten, not as someone who had complicated feelings. He thought she was a pretty little widgeon like her mother, though that was not quite the case. She was sweetly affectionate and had an enchanting little face and figure, but there was more depth and sensitivity beneath this simple facade. She desperately needed to love and be loved, for she possessed a dependent nature and would surely languish in a void.

For this reason Andrea had been gratified by the deepening attachment between her sister and their neighbor and longtime friend, Jonathan Hanley, heir to his uncle Viscount Paxton. He loved her and understood her and she was responding to his sensitive courtship in a totally satisfactory manner. She was only seventeen, however, and Drew had arbitrarily decided that during the coming spring Andrea and Lady Jane should take her to London for the Season to make her debut. He disregarded Jonathan as a suitor, seeing him more as a fixture than as a prospective brother-in-law. As a doting brother, he imagined an exalted position for his lovely young sister. It was this kind of callous presumption that infuriated Andrea, since she felt with all her intuition that this young couple was ideally matched. She distrusted the influence Andrew wielded over Chloe, for already the child was being seduced by promises of instant popularity, glittering affairs, and beautiful clothes. It was not an unnatural reaction. Andrea had enjoyed an exciting Season herself, but she never had been an impressionable girl and, she had to admit, she worried about throwing Chloe, with her trusting nature, into a world ruled by insincerity and cynicism. In his usual harebrained way, Drew had heedlessly interrupted a budding romance. Having created, with a complete lack of perception, a disruptive situation, he would now proceed to take himself off to his own superficial world, leaving his twin to try to minimize the undesirable consequences of his interference. Andrea experienced one of her frequent urges to throttle her exasperating brother, feeling a helpless anger because she knew that she could not refuse to comply with his direction if Chloe should truly wish to be presented to the *ton*.

The two players decided to take a break from their

exertions, as it was a warm afternoon, even this first day of November, for southern Devon enjoyed a milder, more benign climate than other sections of England. The estate was situated between Exeter and Torbay not far from the coast and Andrea was rarely tempted to go to London, a long journey of more than two hundred miles. In fact, she had not been there for almost two years. It was not that she did not enjoy a limited stay to visit the theaters, museums, and shops, but that she was kept busy looking after their three extensive properties and taking care of (or at least supervising the lives of) her stepmother and half-sister, both of whom gratefully accepted Andrea as the head of the household in Andrew's absence.

"Come, refresh yourselves," Andrea said good-humoredly, "and then you can go change. Chloe, you look the veriest gypsy."

"Oh, Andy, do I? It *is* warm today and I *do* try so hard so that Drew won't totally despair of me."

Her brother rumpled her hair and protested, "Here now —what a thing to say. Have I ever given you cause to complain about my forbearance?"

"Oh, no, dear Drew. But it would be surprising if you did not feel a little vexed with my clumsiness, especially when Andy plays so well."

"Well, I do not," he assured her, "so don't tease yourself." He reached for a glass of lemonade and a biscuit and lounged on one of the benches while Andrea served Chloe and herself.

"Is Mama up from her nap yet?" Chloe asked.

"I believe so," Andrea told her. "I expect she will be down in a minute."

On cue, the fourth member of the household made her appearance and came to join the party.

Andrew jumped up to pull out a chair for her, saying, "So, Ladyjane, you have had your beauty sleep and must put the rest of us in the shade. You look angelic as always."

"My dear Andrew, you are such a flirt," his stepmother chided. "No wonder you are so popular with all the ladies."

"The married ones, my dear. I am very discreet with young debutantes."

"Dreadful boy. You are a shameless scapegrace," Lady Jane reproved indulgently.

"He's learned his lesson—I hope," Andrea remarked caustically.

"Speaks the voice of the puritan," Andrew said irritably, with an offended expression. "Must you always cut at a fellow?"

"Sorry," Andrea apologized lightly, for she knew she was just being snippy because of the resentful thoughts that had been going through her mind.

Andrew left then to dress for the evening and Chloe tagged after him, chattering away, trying to soothe his ruffled feelings.

"Andrea," her stepmother scolded mildly, "can you not be a little more charitable? That happened more than two years ago, and he does feel properly guilty."

"It doesn't show."

"You must give him some credit, dear. He is not so careless now."

"Who knows what he is up to when he's away? It's not as though we can keep tabs on him."

"We would have heard if he had gotten into any scrapes. Your aunt Henrietta would feel it her duty to inform us," Lady Jane remarked innocently.

"You're right, of course, love," Andrea admitted with a rueful face. "I will try to hold my tongue."

Her stepmother noticed her preoccupied air and asked, "What's bothering you?"

"Drew wants us to take Chloe to London for the Season."

"Oh, no!"

"My reaction precisely."

"You know how much I dislike being obliged to be sociable. My nerves and constitution simply will not bear it. I'm afraid I could not possibly go. Drew must not ask it of me. I would much rather remain here."

Andrea listened in wonder to this steady progression toward a state of panic and she moved to put her arm around the tiny woman's shoulder. "Hush, dear, it will be all right. We'll think of something."

What a strange brood they were, Andrea mused. Lady Jane positively grew terrified at any thought of having to go to London. One would have thought she would have recovered after all these years but her natural shyness, combined with her repressed memories of humiliation suffered all of fifteen years ago, kept her properly cowed and she called upon the standard protestation that her indifferent health, which was merely conveniently fragile, would not permit her to join in any of the amusements of the *ton*. This excuse was only evoked when it seemed she would be importuned to take her place in society, for she did not have any objections to visiting in a general, informal way and thoroughly enjoyed an occasional journey to Bath, which was no longer frequented by the fashionables. In London it had been brought home to her just what role she actually played in her husband's life and the shock had destroyed her self-confidence and ability to live with the demands and deceits of high society.

Lady Jane had been only eighteen when Lord Carleton Wycliff had marched into her life. His first wife, Eugenia, had died giving birth to twin babies and for two years after her death he had retired to his properties in Devon. Then, trying to erase his pain and loneliness, he began to spend most of his time in London. With his boyish personality, good looks, and large fortune he was quickly accepted into the top echelon of society and became a favored companion of the Prince of Wales and his crowd. Lord Wycliff found himself welcome in the most elegant drawing rooms and, it must be admitted, the more fashionable boudoirs. But after a time, recognizing that his eligibility was too much of a lure, he decided to remarry to protect himself from the grasping, demanding ladies who had set their caps for him. He chose the young, innocent, dutiful Lady Jane Minton, daughter of the Earl of Sanborn. He congratulated himself on this inspiration, for in addition to serving the purpose he intended, he had provided a mother for his children and an instrument for his pleasure when he was in Devon. He never really intended that she should join him in London or any of his other fashionable haunts. She had but a limited claim on his life, and he only vaguely explained this to her before they were married. She certainly had no idea of the implications of his descriptions of their life-style that would necessitate his prolonged absences.

When Chloe was two and the twins were eleven, Lady Jane decided she might be pleased to spend a few weeks in London to refurbish her wardrobe, take in some of the entertainments, and perhaps visit with a few of her girlhood friends. She summoned her courage during the Christmas holidays and timidly informed her husband that she was thinking she might like to join him in town that spring.

He looked at her oddly and asked quizzingly, "Really, my dear? That surprises me. I had thought you were content here."

"Oh, I am, my lord, and I should not like to be away for long or on a regular basis, but Lady Retford has been asking me to come for some time, and now that the children are older and are so sturdy and well-cared for, I thought I might enjoy a short diversion. I do not mean to be a charge upon you in any way."

"Sweet little puss she is," thought the Lord approvingly. "Might not be a bad idea to show her off as long as she doesn't expect me to dance attendance on her." "All right, then," he told her, "I shall direct your coachman to hire a pair of outriders to escort you—before the first of April—to give you a chance to order some new clothes for your engagements."

And so, in the last week of March, in a cold, wind-driven rain, Lady Wycliff arrived at her husband's townhouse in Queen Anne's Gate. She had no particular wish to be involved in the fashionable parties and contented herself with attendance at the smaller soirées, the theaters, concerts, and day visits with some of her old friends and with some of the Marchioness's acquaintances. Her husband was out most evenings but occasionally accompanied her to the lesser receptions. She was perfectly happy with these arrangements and remained unaware of her lord's liaisons.

Had Lord Wycliff realized the depth of the festering resentment lodged in one lady's breast, he would have taken precautions to protect Lady Jane, for he was not an insensitive man and had no wish to subject his wife to any public humiliation. However, he unhappily misjudged the quiescence of the situation. The widowed Countess Craycraft, who once had thought she would be the next Lady Wycliff, maliciously enlightened Lady Jane one evening on her husband's unfettered life-style and cruelly charged that he had bought a wife to suit his convenience.

The shock of these revelations so unnerved and crushed the young woman that she fled London immediately and never accompanied her husband in public again.

Andrea had learned the history of this painful interlude after her father died and Lady Jane and she had grown to be good friends. Lord Wycliff had returned home permanently after suffering a heart attack in London. As soon as he had sufficiently recovered, the Prince's physician advised him to retire to his estates because his weak heart would not permit him to continue living the high life he had been accustomed to for the last fifteen years or so. With a careful regimen and the attentive supervision of his family, he enjoyed a pleasant two years in the salubrious environment of Devonshire and concentrated on putting his affairs in order. He soon recognized the special aptitudes of the twins and proceeded to instruct Andrea in the finer points of managing the estates and finances because it was obvious that Andrew was not yet ready to accept heavy responsibilities and wished to indulge his more undisciplined, venturesome nature in a less pastoral atmosphere.

Lord Wycliff lived until the twins had reached their majority and he saw his depositions put into effect, which included buying a commission in the Army for his restless son as soon as he took his degree at Oxford, and then, within the month, with no warning and no pain, he slipped away peacefully in his sleep.

After Andrew left for the wars, the relationship between Andrea and Lady Jane changed subtly, for there were only ten years between them, after all, and they were closer than that in spirit. They often had intimate discussions and shared the education and guidance of Chloe, especially since, in recent years, Andrea's strong personality established her as a natural leader and both mother and daughter willingly accepted her principles and direction.

One evening when they were alone Andrea and her stepmother caught themselves both admiring and studying the portrait of the first Lady Wycliff. "She was very beautiful," Lady Jane remarked without envy. "You and Andrew look very much like her."

"It gives one a strange feeling, you know," Andrea said meditatively, "to look up there and see yourself and yet know it was someone else whom you should have known and never did and that you were actually responsible for her death. I often wonder what she was like."

"She must have been truly remarkable, Andrea. She was the only woman your father ever loved."

Andrea turned her head slowly and met her stepmother's eyes.

"It is true," Lady Jane repeated softly. "You must have known your father did not see me in exactly the same way."

"Well, of course, as I grew older, I knew that the relationship between you was one of accommodation and respect though not without affection. I didn't know if it had always been only that."

"Yes, I shall tell you of it now because we are friends and I should like to explain," and Lady Jane revealed the mercenary motives that led to her marriage and hesitantly described her subsequent mortifying enlightenment about her purely servile yet benevolent relationship with her husband. "But," she admonished as she finished, "I should not like you to hold it against your father. I was a perfect gudgeon and, more than anyone, I have to blame my father."

"So you might!" Andrea exclaimed indignantly. "But I cannot relieve *my* father of some responsibility in the matter. It is infamous that men are so intent on indulging their egos and manipulating others to satisfy their passions and ambitions that they treat women as mere pawns. Father certainly set a terrible example. It is no wonder Andrew is so heedless."

"Perhaps he will find a woman someday who will be able to tame him," Lady Jane offered hopefully. "Your father was a faithful husband when your mother was alive."

"It's hard to credit, considering his later deceits," Andrea demurred inclemently.

"No, I believe it," Lady Jane insisted. "She had a strong character and possessed the necessary charm and determination to keep him interested and satisfied. But, all in all, my love, I have not been unhappy. I have discovered that many people who marry for love end up with a great deal less than I have had. You and Andrew and Chloe have been worth any slight I may have suffered." It was a generous statement that persuaded her stepdaughter to embrace her affectionately.

Later Andrea drew her brother into a discussion of the matter and was shocked that he had been well aware of his father's unfettered life-style. He, naturally, had not been so isolated from the lax morality of society as the two girls had. He was inevitably enlightened by his school friends when he was at Westminster and Oxford and could not remain ignorant when he paid occasional visits to his father in town. In obvious admiration, he unwisely remarked, "He was quite the fellow in his day."

"Drew! I had hoped you would deplore such treatment as he dealt Ladyjane."

"I do, Andy," her brother assured her hastily but sincerely, nonetheless. "And do not be afraid I shall ever follow such a course. I am determined to remain a bachelor."

"Well, I do think that is a little drastic."

"I do not believe I have the temperament to be a good husband," Andrew confessed candidly.

Andrea looked at him in disgust and then said musingly, "If Father was as much of a rake as they say, it does make one wonder if we have other brothers and sisters, doesn't it?"

"None that could be claimed, I expect. He was careful in that respect. I know his feelings on the subject because, some years ago, after he learned of my dalliance with the innkeeper's daughter, he took me aside to explain the rules, and I have since been circumspect, I assure you."

"What a revolting admission. It is tantamount to being corrupted by your own father."

"That's coming it a little strong, my love. It was his duty to keep me out of trouble."

Andrea was less than amused by her brother's frank confidences and suffered a strong desire to vividly vilify the male animal, who seemed to have a deplorably excessive egotism and little or no sensibility for the sensitivities of the female of the species. She sustained this mood for several hours and unconsciously nurtured a liability of suspicion that would make it difficult for her in the future not to question every gentleman's credibility in affairs of the heart.

CHAPTER TWO

After an unusually peaceful visit, for the twins had seemed determined to try to avoid coming to cuffs, Andrew prepared to leave for a few weeks but promised to return for several days at Christmas before he rejoined his comrades in France.

To please Chloe he dressed in his uniform, a whim which, even without her persuasions, would have been an irresistible posture on his part. He was not required to wear it when he was off duty, but, considering the splendor of the raiment, it was no wonder that the proud young man enjoyed parading in the decorated scarlet tunic, white culottes, and knee-high polished black boots, all molded to his slight but muscular and well-proportioned figure.

Andrea had to admit that her brother was certainly the handsomest man she knew, with his dark eyes and hair, finely chiseled features, and dazzling white teeth. She necessarily felt a twinge of embarrassment to be so admiring of her own image. But so it was, and their personal beauty could not be denied. The twins looked very much like their mother and even more like their grandmother, who had been the daughter of a Spanish grandee. In fact, Andrew, in proper attire, could serve as a model for the spectacular bullfighters and Andrea, with a high comb and lace mantilla, could easily be mistaken for a noble señorita. While they looked very alike, they differed greatly in personality. Andrew had inherited his father's easy, lighthearted approach to life. Andrea, with her indomitable spirit, quickness, and lightning changes of mood that flashed across her expressive face, grew to be much akin to her mother in temperament, which is probably the reason she had always been her father's favorite. He could never look at her without remembering his beloved Eugenia, and he had become almost querulously demanding of her time those last two years he spent at home.

Finally, with a good deal of fanfare and words of caution and affection, Andrew gaily took his leave to hurry to join the fashionables in the pre-Christmas festivities in London.

Andrew had kept the lease on his father's townhouse in Queen Anne's Gate because it was in a convenient location and served very well for temporary lodgings in London. He could have done with a less grand establishment, but he did not have to scrimp financially and he permitted himself the luxury of a permanent town residence. An old couple and their widowed daughter kept the place in order, and he had never had cause to complain of their supervision of the property. After refreshing himself and giving instructions to the staff, which now included his coachman and valet, and after looking over his correspondence, which had accumulated considerably the last few days since there was a frantic step-up of social activities and all eligible young men were much in demand, he took himself off to the clubs to see who was in town.

Several of his fellow officers were on leave and soon they formed a close-knit group strutting down the streets in their scarlet tunics, gallanting the ladies in the parks or to the shops and bookstores, eyeing the actresses in the theaters, and doing the pretty at the balls, assemblies, and other social affairs.

One afternoon at White's Andrew ran into the Duke of Kensington. He greeted him heartily. "David! When did you get back? I thought you were going to your seat for a few months."

"I was," the tall, slender, sandy-haired gentleman with a square jaw and aquiline nose replied as he returned the handclasp. "But when I got to London, I found my grandmother in residence on Grosvenor Square and so I remained in town, since my purpose was to see her in the first place."

"How long are you remaining?"

"Her Grace plans to go to celebrate Christmas at the estate in Dorset and I will escort her. I expect she will wish to return to London before the Season, however, as she still likes to be where there is action, and she never misses a chance to keep tabs on all the main actors," the man replied with a crooked grin.

"Have you decided what you are going to do?" Andrew asked curiously.

"Yes. I am going to sell out and look about for a wife," his friend replied ruefully.

"My God! Are you serious?"

"Yes, my grandmother has convinced me that it is time I looked to assuring the continuation of our house. She wishes me to beget *several* heirs so there will be no possibility that my second cousins will inherit. They belong to a branch of the family with whom she has had a longstanding feud and the thought that one of them might succeed me fairly sends her into apoplexy."

Andrew burst out laughing and reminded, "That is what becomes of being a Duke. Not having a title, I am not so pressured. Besides, I have nothing against my cousins and my ladies have their own fortunes. Do you have anyone in mind?"

"No. I am finding it hard to give serious attention to the matter. I thought I would wait to see what the Season has to offer. Have you any suggestions?"

"Not I! I mean to stay clear myself. But you'd better not let it get about that you are ready to throw your handkerchief. There are several ladies who have kept themselves available hoping to land you, including your two young widows."

"No damaged goods for me, my friend. Those two are definitely off the list."

"They aren't going to take it too well, I'm afraid, considering what lengths they have gone to to secure your affection," Drew quizzed.

"They should have been less agreeable—not that I would have had them in any case," the Duke stated bluntly.

They sat at a table and called for a bottle of brandy and spent an hour discussing some of their memorable exploits and diversions in Wellington's service. Suddenly an extraordinary thought struck Andrew and he pounded his fist on the table, nearly upsetting their glasses. "What a numbskull I am! I *do* have a suggestion. I don't know why it didn't occur to me when you posed the question. No importunities or toad-eating, you understand, but the fact is, I have a beautiful young sister who is going to make her debut this spring. She is the sweetest, most adorable little lady any man could hope for. I wish you will at least wait until you've seen her."

"Well, if she's coming to town, that's easy enough," His Grace commented agreeably.

"Right! When I go back for the holidays, I shall insist that Chloe be presented."

"I thought you said she *was* going to be."

"So I have instructed, but I suspect Andrea is not committed to the scheme and very well could ignore my wishes."

"Andrea?"

"My twin sister," Drew reminded.

"Oh, yes, I forgot. What does she have to say about it?"

"Quite a lot, I'm afraid. She is the most redoubtable female I have ever encountered, and she has ruled the roost ever since she was eighteen when my father decided to turn over the management of our affairs to her."

"That sounds like a damnable thing to do to his heir," the Duke protested in surprise.

"Oh, I had no objections. She is much more competent on that score, and it left me free to follow my inclinations. But she has developed into a termagant and is always prosing on about sensibilities and responsibilities and any number of other tiresome subjects until it nearly drives me mad, and I can't wait to take off," Andrew expounded revealingly.

"A moralist, is she?" the Duke asked in amusement.

"Yes, by God, and I can tell you it makes a man damned uncomfortable!"

"You make her sound like a prime candidate for ape-leader," David prompted helpfully.

"That she is—no doubt about it," Andrew agreed fervently.

Both men sat in thought for a few moments and then the Duke asked, "When are you off for France?"

"Right after Christmas. Why?"

"I thought I might pay my respects to your family while I am at Kensington Castle. It is but a day's ride from your estate."

"That's a famous idea," Andrew approved. "I shall tell Andrea and Ladyjane, my stepmother, you might do so, though I shall warn them it was an indefinite proposal and you will not be committed if you should change your mind."

"Good. We'll leave it at that."

And so, for the next few days, the gentlemen shamelessly flaunted their bachelor status and raised the hopes of several ladies, including the two young widows who once again found themselves in competition for the attentions of the very eligible Duke of Kensington. In a reckless moment he had also been pleased to amuse himself casting lures to the dazzling Lady Carrington, who, famous for her charms and notorious for her conquests, was, at the moment, the mistress of one of David's old rivals—which intrigued him into trying to tempt her to transfer her favors. He was in a fair way to succeeding and cynically expected to easily accomplish the coup after the holidays.

And then, a week before Christmas, the two scapegraces and the Dowager Duchess left the glitter of London to repair to their estates for the Christmas celebrations with their families, their tenants, and servants. Andrew traveled to Kensington Castle with the Duke and his grandmother and remained overnight before continuing on to Devon.

At Wycliff Manor Andrew received his usual warm welcome, especially from Chloe, and he good-naturedly put himself out to please all the ladies during his ten-day stay.

He postponed bringing up the subject of a possible visit from the Duke of Kensington because he knew it would throw Andrea into one of her huffs, and because he faintly regretted his initiation of the scheme. During the past week, he had finally become aware that Jonathan and Chloe were very much in harmony with one another. Jonathan obviously adored Chloe and guided her gently and considerately, and Chloe seemed to be responding to his determined but subtle courtship even to the extent of seeking his approval rather than her brother's as she had always done previously. Thus it was with a sense of reluctance that Andrew brought himself to the point of telling Andrea of his conversation with the Duke.

"Andy, do you remember David Newbury, who is now the Duke of Kensington?"

"I know who he is, of course, but I've never met him. I believe he was out of the country, or at least out of town, the year I went up to be presented by Aunt Henrietta. In fact, I believe I recall something about his missing the Season that year because he was tired of being chased by a very determined young lady."

Andrew let out a bark of laughter and admitted, "It's very probable and sounds like something he would do. He's been a very slippery fellow."

"You've mentioned him often in your letters as if he were a good friend of yours."

"He is. I've gotten to know him pretty well these last three years, as he was also one of Wellington's men and we hit it off straight away."

"He's older, though, isn't he?"

"Yes, about six years, but we worked together closely and became good comrades."

"Why did you bring up his name just now?" Andrea asked in curiosity.

"Well," Andrew answered casually, delaying the main point, "I saw him in town before Christmas and he told me he is going to sell out."

"So?" Andrea asked suspiciously, beginning to feel the disinclination behind her brother's conversation.

"His situation is different, of course," he stated enigmatically.

"All right, Drew, cut line," Andrea demanded impatiently, waving her hand. "It's obvious you are holding back, so I suspect I am not going to approve but you might as well open your budget."

He got up and began to pace the floor, pausing to look out the window, which provided added misgivings when he saw Chloe and Jonathan walking hand in hand in the garden. He turned to his sister and revealed resolutely, "David's grandmother has been pressuring him to marry and he has decided it is time to think seriously on it."

"Go on," Andrea said menacingly as he paused again.

"Well, he jokingly asked if I had any suggestions and I told him no, but after we talked for a while, I suddenly thought of Chloe."

"That settles it!" Andrea declared grimly, getting up from her desk abruptly. "I will not take her to London. It would be like sending a lamb to the sacrificial altar, especially if she knew you approved his suit."

"Don't jump to conclusions," Andrew cautioned. "There is nothing to say that he would decide in her favor."

"My dear brother, you are a gudgeon. When a man decides to marry and deliberately sets about to look for a wife, what kind of woman do you think he will consider? Love could hardly be part of the picture; it would probably never enter his mind. Chloe would be the perfect choice for such a man. She is beautiful, young, innocent, and impressionable, and he would see her as the ideal foil for his purposes. It would be a case of Father and Ladyjane all over again."

"Chloe would not be importuned. She could make up her own mind," Drew protested.

Andrea tried to explain. "She is young for her age and has a head filled with romantic notions. If you don't foresee the dangers and the heartbreak, I do, and I will not throw her to the wolves."

"Andrea, you might as well hear the rest of it," Andrew continued uneasily. "I expect the Duke to pay his respects to you here in Devon sometime soon. He is at his seat in Dorset and plans to come over before he goes to London."

"At your invitation?" Andrea asked angrily.

"Actually, no, except that I imagine he is interested in seeing Chloe," he replied.

His sister threw him a thoroughly malevolent look and exclaimed vehemently, "My God! You are the most insensible man. Can't you see what's right in front of your face? Jonathan is perfect for your sister. He loves her and would cherish her and devote himself to making her happy. She is young yet, but she is beginning to recognize what he means to her and you blindly step in and try to disrupt this lovely courtship first by enticing her with the bait of a London Season and now by suggesting that one of your disreputable friends look her over as if she were a filly!"

"Draw bridle, Andy," an unfortunate choice of words Andrew regretted immediately. "David is a splendid fellow. He would not allow his wife to be embarrassed or ill-used."

"Are you saying he would be faithful to her?"

"Ah—well, as to that—I say, Andrea—"

"Don't bother to fish for an answer. I understand perfectly," the girl said caustically. "Drew, think for a minute. If I asked the same question about Jonathan, what would you say?"

He sighed, sat down, and looked at her ruefully. "All right. You have made your point."

"Drew, we have all three been good friends, but I know that you and Jonathan are not kindred spirits. Still, you like each other well, and despite the fact that you think him to be too much of a philosopher, I think you will have to allow that he is a lovely man and I have been so pleased that Chloe has begun to recognize his superior qualities. I foresee a happy future for them but he needs a little more time. She is still quite young and really not ready for marriage. But she does need someone she can trust because she has a loving and sensitive nature and would feel things much more deeply than Ladyjane, who had a miserable enough time of it. I am determined the same thing shall not happen to Chloe," Andrea declared adamantly.

"Well, I will promise not to pursue the matter," Andrew submitted. "Perhaps he will not come, anyway. It was a tentative proposal."

"Can't you drop him a note to tell him we are not set up for guests?"

"Certainly not! That would be insulting."

Andrea closed her eyes and clenched her fists. "I have the most dreadful premonition—"

"Don't pull one of your witch's acts," Andrew warned hastily. "It makes my flesh crawl."

"You might at least apologize for rushing the fences."

"Sorry," the young man said curtly.

His sister looked at him in amusement. "You know, Drew, it would be something wonderful if we could ever tell each other we were sorry as if we really meant it."

Andrew laughed in appreciation of her sally, put his arm around her shoulder, and kissed her brow. "My dear Andy, we do use each other ill, do we not? But even so, you are my other self, you know—my better half."

"Yes, I know," Andrea replied impishly, "just as you are my worse."

Drew grinned and playfully cuffed her under the chin, acknowledging the hit. "Serves me right. I should have known better than to give you an opening."

They did not mention the sensitive subject again and, as usual, seemed to deal better with each other after their battle so that it was an unhappy group of ladies who had to see their gentleman off again for another long absence. They decided to make an excursion of it and escorted him to Torbay where he was to board the ship that would take him to France. They enjoyed a luncheon at one of the inns in town and then Andrew affectionately bade them all farewell, teasing each of them with light pleasantries and telling Andrea half-apologetically, "I trust you, Andy, to—uh—see that everything goes well."

"As usual, you wretched man. If you can't sleep at night, you'll know I am raining curses on you."

"My God, Andrea! Not long ago, if you said something like that, you'd be burned at the stake," Drew exclaimed. "Do you have to be so gothic?"

"People who know better shouldn't provoke me," she replied uncompromisingly.

Her long-suffering brother just shook his head, saw them to their carriage, and ordered their coachman to escort them safely back to the Manor.

On the ride home Lady Jane asked, "What was all that double talk about, Andrea? I couldn't make any sense out of it."

"Oh, just one of our normal disagreements—nothing may come of it," the girl answered noncommittally and gave a warning look so that her stepmother would not press her.

Later that evening, when Chloe sat dutifully practicing at the pianoforte while Jonathan patiently turned the pages for her, Andrea and her stepmother had a quiet coze in the corner across the room. Andrea related the particulars of the subject of contention between herself and Drew and was not surprised that Lady Jane was dismayed at the implications.

"Oh, my dear, what possessed him?" she moaned as she looked at the happy, compatible couple. "I had so hoped that nothing would interfere with her chance for happiness."

"I know. Drew was absolutely out of line! You would think that past history might have deterred him but, as always, he goes off on one of his tangents and leaves someone else to pick up the pieces."

"Is that what he was talking about?"

"Yes. He has a guilty conscience and expects me to deal with the mischief."

"My dear, we are all such a trial to you. I feel not a little guilty myself," Lady Jane admitted with a deep sigh. "You must always suppress your own interests to forward one of ours. It is quite shameful when you are such a lovely girl and should have been married long ago and blessed with a home and family of your own."

"Ladyjane," Andrea admonished, laughing at this almost maudlin mood of self-reproach, "you know very well that it has not pleased me to marry, but if it ever should, then I shall do so. You are not to presume that I am irretrievably on the shelf. I assure you I am not the least worried."

"You are the most amazing girl, Andrea. You have such strength and self-confidence, and I did not mean to imply you are without prospects. It's just that I think you should have considered them long before now."

"When Chloe is settled, darling, it will be time enough. Now do not tease yourself about that matter when we have a much more disturbing one before us. It would be too much to expect that we should be spared the tribulation. We must decide how we are to handle it."

"We shall have to receive him," Lady Jane said doubtfully.

"Maybe I could come down with a fever."

"Andrea! Do not joke about such a thing."

The music stopped and they noticed that Chloe and Jonathan were coming to join them, so they postponed their discussion for the moment.

"Well, my friends, do you not think our little lady is turning into an excellent musician?" Jonathan asked, seeking approval for his love.

"She certainly is," her mother agreed.

"How would you know, Mama?" the girl chided good-humoredly, wrinkling her pretty little nose. "You and Andy have been over here chattering like a couple of magpies."

"Oh, dear, we are fairly caught," Andrea said, "but we promise to be a better audience next time, love. I'm afraid we are become regular old gossips. And I for one am feeling the effects of the long day," she added quickly, hoping to ward off Chloe's questions, "so I shall take myself off to bed. Will we see you tomorrow, Jonathan?"

Knowing her well, he read the message in her eyes and replied, "Yes, I intended to ride over for a while in the afternoon. Drew asked me to look at the horses he wishes to sell."

"Oh, yes, that will be good of you. We really don't need such a large stable, and I have finally convinced Andrew we should decrease the number of horses, particularly now since we have two new foals. So I will see you then," she told him and, raising her hand to all of them, made her exit.

The next afternoon Andrea watched for Jonathan and was outside waiting for him so she might command his exclusive company for a few minutes to tell him of the potential trouble that could disrupt their comfortable existence.

He listened quietly to her indignant ravings on her brother's carelessness, her angry disapproval of the Duke's presumptuousness, and her concern about Chloe's susceptibility—all of which was culminated by an expressive, if unladylike, oath.

Jonathan had to laugh at her vehemence. He reminded her, "You said it was not a definite thing."

"He's coming. I *know* he's coming. I can feel it in my bones."

"Andrea! You are positively outlandish with some of your expressions. Sometimes I think there must be gypsy blood in your background."

"Why, Jonathan, what a perfectly intriguing suggestion. It is not beyond the realm of possibility, after all, and would certainly account for the strange turns of mind I have," she reflected interestedly, immediately prepared to accept the theory.

"My God! Now I have corrupted your reason. I should know better than to give you that kind of an idea."

"Don't be a gudgeon. I am as I am whether I have or not, so what is the harm in thinking it? Now let's get back to our problem. Do you know the Duke?"

"Yes, I have met him in town."

"Drew thinks he's a splendid fellow," Andrea said sarcastically.

"So do a lot of people."

"Mostly ladies, no doubt."

"Actually," Jonathan admitted, "*all* the ladies, but a

good many men also. He has only held the title a year—since his older brother was killed in that disastrous Battle of New Orleans. It is understandable that he should wish to put his house in order."

"From all accounts he has plenty of material from which to choose. He doesn't have to cast his eyes on Chloe. Jonathan, I do not mean to put you down in any way, for I am very fond of you, admire you tremendously, and cherish you as one of my dearest friends. But the fact is that Chloe has a little way to go yet. You know how impressionable she is and how her mind is filled with romantic notions."

"Yes, I'm afraid she does have visions of a knight in shining armor," Jonathan acknowledged.

"Is the Duke handsome?"

"Not in the way Andrew is, but, yes, he does present an impressive figure."

"And is Chloe likely to see him as her knight?" Andrea asked.

"Very probably, should he wish her to."

"My God! What are we going to do?"

"Well," Jonathan said, "I expect we shall have to see her through it. We must allow her to grow up."

Not being the least receptive to this conclusion, Andrea nevertheless refrained from stating her objections. She preceded him to the stables, and they turned their attention to the matter at hand.

CHAPTER THREE

The month of January passed and Andrea began to relax, thinking perhaps she had been a little precipitate in her judgments, although her intuition usually did not deceive her. Chloe had not mentioned the subject of her debut and Andrea and Lady Jane were careful to keep it out of their conversations. It was a suspenseful situation, however, because it had likely been discussed during some of their visits with their neighbors who had young girls. Fortunately, however, none of them seemed to be planning to travel to London in the spring. Thus the two cravens were thankful that they had been given a reprieve and hoped the matter would remain dormant.

So, it was with a shock of reawakening that Andrea saw the letter sealed with an ostentatious ducal crest. With distaste she picked it up by one corner from the correspondence tray and carried it to her stepmother to whom it was addressed.

"My love, I'm afraid we were becoming too complacent. The phantom is about to strike."

"Andrea! What a strange thing to say!—Oh, dear," Lady Jane bemoaned, as the letter was dropped in her lap. "Is it from—?"

"Yes."

They both stared balefully at the unwelcome missive, having a mutual reluctance to discover its contents, but Lady Wycliff finally tore it open, quickly read the short message, and then handed it to Andrea.

"The day after tomorrow!" the girl exclaimed. "That is a bit presumptuous."

"But, my dear, he says he will be staying in Exeter and will ride over from there. He is not expecting to be put up."

"Thank goodness! Perhaps he merely means to make a courtesy call and will remain for only a couple of hours."

Lady Jane looked skeptical and remarked, "It seems a long way to come for just a courtesy call."

"I was afraid you would think so," Andrea said with a rueful expression. "He will probably stay in the vicinity for a few days. It may be that he has other acquaintances nearby," she added hopefully and then, with a gesture of annoyance, she surrendered, "Well, we might as well make up our minds to tell Chloe."

"Tell me what?" asked a curious voice from the doorway.

"Come in, love," Lady Jane invited. "We are to have a visitor."

"Really? Who?"

"The Duke of Kensington."

"The Duke of Kensington! Andrew's friend?" Chloe cried delightedly.

Andrea sighed in helpless resignation and thought, "The magic words—Andrew's friend" and realized that she had her work cut out for her.

"When is he coming?"

"The day after tomorrow."

"How exciting! We never get to meet any of Drew's fashionable friends. I wonder what he will be like. Tall and handsome, do you suppose?"

"Naturally—what else?" Andrea remarked drily.

"Andy, don't be a marplot. This will be a famous treat. I can't wait to tell Jonathan. He will have to come to meet him."

"He is already acquainted with him," Andrea revealed dispassionately.

"How do you know?"

"Because he told me. I may as well own up that Drew suggested that the Duke might come to call on us while he is situated in Dorset, but it was not definite, so I did not mention it to you."

"Andy, why should you not?" Chloe demanded reproachfully. "I could have been looking forward to his visit all this time."

"Yes, and making up any number of romantic fancies," Andrea accused teasingly.

Chloe blushed at this reference to her flights of imagination, but she did not take offense and confessed with a giggle, "I know it is very silly, but it can be such fun when one is bored, Andy, so don't scold."

"I am not scolding; however, I am persuaded we should not have permitted you to read all those romantic novels. Still, if you can remember that the fantasies are not the way of the real world, I suppose you won't suffer unduly."

"Well, I don't know how I can forget when you are constantly reminding me, my dearest sister," Chloe quizzed affectionately. "How long is the Duke going to stay?"

"We don't know," her mother informed her. "He says he will be lodging in Exeter."

"But that is fifteen miles away! Why can't he stay here?"

Lady Jane explained, "Andrea thinks he may be just paying his respects and has other acquaintances in the neighborhood."

"Oh," Chloe said with a disappointed face. "Well," she decided, brightening a little, "it will be fun to meet someone new, especially as he is Drew's friend, and perhaps he *will* stay longer."

"Not if I can help it," Andrea muttered to herself with exceedingly unfriendly visions of ways to discourage him.

They all three talked for a few minutes about other things, but Chloe was too caught up with the imminent arrival of so important a guest. She announced she would ride over to tell Jonathan and his mother the exciting news.

"Why don't you ask Jonathan for lunch the day we expect His Grace and then he will be here to help us extend our welcome," Lady Jane suggested.

"Yes, I will, Mama, and the Duke will see that we are not without our distinguished citizens in this remote place," Chloe proclaimed proudly and, in a few minutes, was riding off with a young groom in attendance.

"That was an excellent idea, Ladyjane," Andrea approved. "When it is apparent there is already an attachment, perhaps the Duke will not try to fix Chloe's interest."

"So I hoped," her stepmother affirmed, "though I cannot but think that we may be a little overly emotional about this matter. It is not likely that he should already have a set notion and, if we do not go to London, there will be no opportunity for a further acquaintance."

"I wish I could feel you were right, my love, but I have this uncomfortably persistent sense of foreboding which convinces me we are going to be put to our wit's end," Andrea bemoaned gloomily.

"Well, I don't know if I do, also, or am just persuaded because of the way you go on, but I must own that I do regret that Drew directed him here."

"Yes, and then to have left us with the bright remark that he trusted us to see that everything went well. I could wring his neck!"

"Andrea! You *do* have a deplorable tendency to make indelicate representations. It is quite unsettling. I hope you mean to be civil to the Duke," Lady Jane said dubiously.

"I shall treat him as he deserves," Andrea promised, in a manner that gave her stepmother cause to expect the worst. "And, my dear, do not try to make a lady out of me. You have done your best, but you must know by now I am a hopeless case."

"It is not that you are not a lady, love; it's just that you do have an occasional lapse, which does not do you credit," Lady Jane said affectionately.

"I shall try not to embarrass you, and if I am not provoked, I daresay I shall manage well enough," Andrea demurred with a twinkling eye, "though I shall have to put on a good act."

And so, despite all hopes to the contrary, the red-letter day arrived, and very soon after they had settled themselves to wait expectantly in the drawing room, the little group heard the arrival of a lone horseman. They stood to welcome their visitor, all with varying degrees of anticipation and apprehension.

When the butler announced the Duke of Kensington and the gentleman self-confidently entered the room, Andrea experienced an immediate sinking feeling, for it was plain that the Fates were against her. Why couldn't he be short and fat? No, instead, he must tower over them all and carry his trim, athletic body with an easy grace that Andrea found particularly reprehensible. Looking at his blond hair and tanned face that had laugh lines at his eyes and mouth, she groaned to herself and thought pessimistically, "There's a face of doom if ever I saw one." She glanced at Chloe to see what effect this nonpareil was having on her and was not surprised that the girl was staring like a mooncalf. Andrea had to admit to a wayward thought herself, a weakness that made her furious and bode ill for any kind of casual encounter.

Lady Jane had immediately moved forward to greet him, holding out her hand and saying graciously, "Welcome, Your Grace. We are honored."

"Lady Wycliff?" the Duke asked with raised brows as he gallantly kissed her hand.

"Yes, Your Grace."

"It is hard to tell, you know," he complimented, showing off his perfect teeth and causing Andrea to mutter darkly under her breath, "A Beau yet!"

Lady Jane laughed self-consciously and turned to Chloe, who was standing closest to her. "May I present my daughter, Chloe?"

"Of course—Miss Chloe," fawned the obsequious Duke

as he held the girl's hand for a moment before bringing it to his lips. "There could be no mistake. Andrew has described you perfectly—the face of an angel."

While Andrea decided she was going to be sick, Chloe fell into the trap and blushed charmingly as she thanked him prettily and gushed that they were all delighted to make his acquaintance since Andrew had often spoken of him in his letters.

"Discreetly, I hope," said the gentleman with a rueful smile, another platitude that made Andrea curl her lip. By now she was ready and determined to show him that there was at least one member of the family who did not mean to be a toad-eater and, when Lady Jane directed the Duke's attention to her with the introduction, "This is my other daughter, Andrea," she held out her hand sideways, indicating that she was not receptive to his gallant mannerisms.

At first glance the Duke recognized the antagonism in her face and immediately understood why he had been having a disquieting impression of an unfriendly presence in the room. She was standing before him practically glaring with those dark, expressive eyes and warning him to mind his step.

With a flicker of his eye, he took her hand and tried to turn it but, meeting with resistance, had to exert a fair amount of force to gain his end. "She's a strong little devil for her size," he thought. As he lowered her hand, she snatched it away and he said mockingly, "Miss Wycliff, I knew, of course, that you and Andrew were twins, but, even so, the resemblance is incredible. However, I must say that I prefer the feminine version."

"Must you?" Andrea snapped as she rubbed her hand that was feeling the effects of an unequal combat.

Her undisguised hostility amused the Duke and he replied with a grin, "I'm afraid so," and thought, "So that's it. She thinks I am a damned dandy."

Lady Jane was dismayed at Andrea's uncivil behavior and groaned to herself, "Oh, dear—and she promised," and stepped into the arena and brought Jonathan forward. "Your Grace, I believe you are acquainted with our neighbor and dearest friend, Jonathan Hanley."

"Of course," acknowledged the Duke. "How are you, Hanley? You are making quite a name for yourself. I just recently read your treatise supporting Wilberforce in his fight for a Registry Bill. I believe it helped convince some Members that it is a positive step toward abolishing the slave trade."

"That's encouraging," said Jonathan, who was prepared to accept the Duke's friendly overtures now that he had witnessed the previous introductions. He had hardly kept from laughing during the silent skirmish of a few moments ago and realized now that he had nothing to worry about. Those two were already committed, though it might be some time before they understood what had happened. He was not surprised that Andrea had offered the Duke a challenge because she was not one to hide her antagonisms, but he was surprised that Kensington had accepted it without thinking twice. He could suppose that, because David was so well acquainted with Drew, he almost had a feeling of familiarity. Jonathan tried to ignore Andrea's reproachful look and remarked affably, "I hear you have become a notable art connoisseur these last few years."

"Let us hope so," the Duke responded. "At least, I have been spending a lot of money trusting in my own judgment."

Andrea looked at both men speculatively, for she had not heard of this interest of the Duke's, and it didn't fit with her impression of him; not that one had to be a sober, proper man to appreciate art; it was well-established that Lady Hertford's son, Lord Yarmouth, was one of the most respected art collectors and yet also one of the worst profligate rakes of the age.

The Duke refused Lady Jane's offer of refreshments, admitting that he had eaten a late breakfast from having overslept after the long journey the day before.

"Did you ride or come by carriage?" Jonathan asked.

"Both, actually. I had sent changes of horses and teams

ahead and traded off riding and driving with my coachman."

"Do you remain long in the area, Your Grace?" Lady Jane asked politely.

"A few days, Lady Wycliff. I had hoped to further our acquaintance and meant to try to persuade you ladies to accompany me on an excursion or two as I am not familiar with this part of the country."

"Oh," Chloe blurted out, "Andy thought you might have friends nearby, and we would not see very much of you."

"Did she?" the Duke asked innocently, amused at what he presumed was wishful thinking on Andy's part. "Well, I have not, so I hope I may return with the carriage tomorrow and ask you to show me some of the countryside."

"Oh, yes," Chloe cried delightedly, "for it is especially lovely along the coast. But you are staying so far away and—Mama?" she queried meaningfully, which left Lady Jane no choice but to offer him hospitality.

"Of course. We did not know your plans, Your Grace, but," and here he noticed the apologetic, almost guilty look she involuntarily sent to her stepdaughter, "you must stay with us. It will be quite a treat as we do not often have guests, being so far from town."

David had glanced in the mirror and the sight of Andrea's scowling indignant face decided him to accept the belated invitation, a perverse reaction, for he was not used to finding himself unwelcome. He meant to discover what had so set this girl against him.

"Thank you, Lady Wycliff. I do not wish to impose, but I confess that the prospect of spending more time in the company of three such lovely ladies is too much of a temptation, and I shall allow myself to be easily persuaded." Granting that this little speech, which was meant to be taken lightly, was not very imaginative, David nevertheless was disconcerted when he found himself the recipient of a marvelously eloquent look of scorn. Contrary to his expectations, he began to think that he might find this impulsive visit considerably entertaining, for he was irresistibly drawn into mouthing some piece of nonsense just for the devilment of it. The girl's face was an open book and the expressiveness was refreshingly unlike the bland or affected demeanor of most young ladies. Her Latin bloodline was certainly dominant, and there was a striking contrast between her and the other two, who were typically English.

With interest he observed the varied reactions to his ready acceptance. Chloe seemed delighted and completely undismayed by the undercurrents in the room while Lady Jane was sending pleading looks to her stepdaughter. Andrea stood uncompromisingly with a set face, though she seemed to be engaging in a silent battle with Jonathan, who appeared to be having trouble suppressing his amusement.

The silence was becoming awkward so the Duke took pity on his hostess and suggested, "I will ride back to Exeter to gather up my belongings and, if it will not inconvenience you, I shall keep my valet with me and one horse. The coachman can return to town with the carriage to wait for me there."

Lady Jane once more looked at Andrea and the girl, finally recognizing that the Duke meant to impose his presence on them, said in a barely civil tone, "That will not be necessary. There is room in the stables and no doubt Martin and Thomas will derive a good measure of vicarious pleasure from the privilege of hobnobbing with the coachman of a Duke."

David was beginning to become angry, but he controlled his temper as he thought, "It's true. This girl does rule the roost around here and with an iron hand it seems." Deciding that any token demurral on his part would not be well-received, he said amiably, "As a matter of fact, my driver will be grateful for lodging as he is an old friend of your coachman and had been hoping to see him."

"Then it is settled," Lady Jane remarked in relief.

"Yes. I shall leave shortly and return tomorrow morning."

"But we could send Thomas," Chloe objected.

"No, thank you, Miss Chloe. I shall go myself. It will give you time to adjust to being saddled with an unexpected guest," the Duke teased, wishing he were in a position to see Andrea's face.

David then took his leave, particularly from Chloe and Lady Jane, for Andrea remained well away from him. He promised to be back for lunch the next day.

As soon as he was out of sight, Chloe ecstatically began enumerating all the wonderful attributes of their visitor and the worst suspicions of the other three were confirmed. Andrea decided she could not bear to listen with any degree of indulgence or equanimity. So she left the group to direct the housekeeper to prepare rooms for the Duke and his servant and then went for a long ride. She was forced to endure further superlatives at dinner but retired early to her room, professing a headache. She slept uneasily and so did not feel refreshed in the morning and uncharacteristically remained in bed until almost nine o'clock. Finally she admitted she was just trying to put off the inevitable and got up, dressed, and went downstairs for a cup of coffee.

"How is your headache, Andy?" Chloe asked sympathetically, coming into the breakfast room to join her sister.

"It's better, love, but I did not sleep well and so played the lazyboots."

With an air of excitement the younger girl asked, "What do you think we should plan for the Duke this afternoon?"

Accepting the fact that she was going to have to participate, Andrea replied unenthusiastically, "Well, since he will have spent a good part of the last few days on horseback, I suspect we should just allow him to have an easy time of it and perhaps drive him around the estate in the open carriage. We can show him the view from the Point since it is such beautiful weather today."

"Yes, that sounds perfect. I hope he will not be bored," Chloe said doubtfully. "There is so little to see here, actually, and he is used to a more exciting, entertaining life."

"Well, Chloe, we are not too deeply obligated, and he will have to be satisfied with our country pleasures. He is, after all, as he remarked, an uninvited guest."

The younger girl caught the annoyance in her sister's voice and asked hesitantly with a puzzled expression, "Andy, don't you like the Duke?"

"No, darling, I don't," Andrea acknowledged freely.

"But why? You don't even know him."

"Just call it one of my fancies, Chloe. You know I often have these odd presentiments, and I experienced one the moment he walked into the house."

"How strange of you, Andy. He doesn't in any way look like a villain and he remained the perfect gentleman even when you were so uncivil."

"Little you know about gentlemen, my love. He was every bit as rude to me but in a much more subtle way."

"Well, if he was, you provoked him to it," Chloe declared defiantly, adding shyly, "and—I like him."

"Yes, I know," Andrea commented drily, "but, my dear, I think it would be more seemly if you did not make it so obvious."

Chloe blushed at this light reprimand and knew it was deserved so she replied meekly, "Yes, Andy, I will try to be more the young lady."

Sometimes Andrea felt almost frightened by the intensity of her love for her sister and she put her arm around her. "I am not scolding, darling, but you are such an infant, and I cannot bear to think of you being hurt. Do try to remember that the Duke is a man of the world just as Father was."

"Of course, Andy," Chloe said, although she did not fully understand the implication, having only a vague notion that it had something to do with other women.

They went to find Lady Jane and caught up with her in the dining room, where she was directing the placing of some greenery. She loved to work with plants and spent a lot of time in the greenhouses where she was cultivating all sorts of unusual and out-of-season specimens. She always managed to provide some kind of flower or showy foliage for the various vases and urns around the house.

While they were admiring the cheerful effect of the budding forsythia mixed with some early daffodils, they heard the carriage approaching and went into the hall to wait for the Duke's appearance.

In a few moments the butler admitted him and Andrea immediately assumed control and directed the servants to take his baggage.

"We have placed you in Andrew's quarters in the old wing, Your Grace. I think you will be comfortable there and will find everything you need," Andrea informed him coolly.

"Thank you, Miss Wycliff," the Duke answered soberly, waving his man to follow the footman. "I will go to change now if you will tell me the plans for the afternoon," he prompted, looking at Chloe.

"Oh, we thought you might be tired of riding, my lord Duke, and we had only decided on a short tour around the estate in the carriage," the girl answered brightly.

"Good. I would be pleased to see the property, but I did drive the chaise today, so I am agreeable to horses if you prefer."

"Oh, well, Andy—?" Chloe said uncertainly, turning to her sister.

"Then we will ride, Your Grace. It is a pleasant day for it," Andrea decided.

They all satisfied themselves with a light lunch and proposed to ride out about an hour later. "Your Grace, while we change into our riding habits," Lady Jane suggested courteously, "please feel free to investigate the house and the stables. We will try not to be too long."

The Duke expressed his thanks, promised not to be impatient, and found his way to a surprisingly well-stocked library. Someone here was interested in art, he discovered, finding several art histories he had not seen before. There were also some rather good small landscapes on the walls and even—yes—there was the Goya Andrew had bought on his recommendation. This room and possibly others would bear further investigation. He forced himself to postpone this pleasure and went out to the stables to await the ladies.

Presently they joined him, and David's sincere admiration showed in his eyes and his manner as he complimented them on their appearance. Chloe in blue and Lady Jane in yellow looked charmingly English, but Andrea in her stark black and white presented a striking image of her Spanish ancestors.

He moved to help Lady Jane onto her horse while the grooms assisted the other two and then they followed Andrea's lead.

The terrain was varied in this section, and they rode through a small woodland where the tenants were permitted to hunt and set traps. Then they passed the cluster of farms and the dairy and, in the distance, across the fields, saw grazing sheep. Jonathan's home, which was only a little over two miles from their own, was pointed out beyond a small stream, and then they turned east to ride to the crest of the Babbacombe Downs, where they could get a wide view of the sea and the coastline.

The Duke was properly impressed and asked if they often came here.

"Oh, yes, Your Grace," Chloe replied eagerly, "either here or down on the beach where we take off our shoes and walk in the sand when the weather is warm."

"Chloe," her mother chided lightly, "do not tell tales."

David laughed and protested, "No, Lady Wycliff, it is no great matter. I could wish I might join you. Do you suppose we could look for a warm enough day?"

"Certainly not," Andrea denied sharply. "It is only early February." And, turning her horse, she directed, "We had better head back. It still gets dark fairly early and we are some distance from the Manor."

A note had been sent to invite Jonathan and his mother to dinner but Mrs. Hanley begged off with an apology because she had come down with some sort of plague—

47

some infection and was confined to her room for a few days. However, Jonathan did come, for which Andrea was properly thankful since it made conversation much easier.

During dinner the Duke turned the discussion from generalities to his special interest and remarked, "Earlier today I was examining your library and noticed a collection of art histories and some fine paintings. Who has an interest in that area?"

"Oh, that's Andy," Chloe informed him, "and she has been making me study about some of the old masters."

"Do I detect a slight disinclination?" David asked quizzically.

"Only a little, really. It is not that I don't enjoy looking at paintings, but I don't have an artistic eye and I can't appreciate them like some people."

"That's all right, darling," Andrea allowed, trying to avoid being questioned. "You more than make up for any lack in that field by your very great understanding of music."

"I shall look forward to a demonstration later," the Duke said dutifully and then, refusing to be deterred, remarked to Andrea, "I have seen the Goya before."

She looked hard at him for a moment and then attested, "Of course, you are the friend who recommended the purchase to Andrew."

"Yes. Do you like it?"

"I do, rather," she admitted, "but I have the feeling that I would rather not be painted by him. He is not as kind to the sitter as our English artists. Of course, that is pure vanity rearing its head, I know, for Gainsborough, Romney, and the others always made everyone attractive and cannot be considered great artists in the true sense of the word, I suspect."

"They did have a tendency to romanticize their subjects," the Duke agreed, "but they have left a valuable legacy, nevertheless. Are you particularly interested in any special period?"

"Not really. I have not had much opportunity to study the field deeply, you understand, except for a few trips to London and to the homes of friends. However," she added thoughtfully as if it had just occurred to her, "I seem to have a partiality for paintings that make dramatic use of light and color and landscapes rather than religious themes and especially portraits that reveal character or emotions." She stopped abruptly, not having meant to carry on a lengthy conversation with her sworn enemy.

The Duke was delighted with her observations, which showed considerable sensitivity, so he ignored her withdrawal and promised agreeably, "Then I shall have to arrange for you to see a particular group of paintings when you come to London. They may not be in England long. Do you know the story of King Joseph's baggage train?" He looked around the table and Jonathan answered, "We heard something about it being left behind after the battle of Vittoria and that it caused a riot among our own troops."

"Yes—well—along with everything else, the clothes, food, money, jewels, and so on, there was a collection of art works that we later determined were stolen from the Royal Palace in Madrid. Wellington took charge of them and sent them to his brother for safekeeping in England. I was assigned to see that they were stored properly until they could be returned to the House of Borbón after the war. The Duke has been trying to persuade the King of Spain to advise him how he wants them returned but has not yet received an answer. As a result they are still in London. It is a tremendous collection although some of the great masterpieces by Rubens and Titian were passed over. Still, there are some magnificent paintings, including several remarkable portrait studies, one of Pope Innocent X and another entitled, *A Spanish Gentleman*." *

In spite of herself Andrea was interested and acknowledged, "I should be grateful for an opportunity to see them, Your Grace, if it should be convenient."

"I can arrange for it, I'm sure, but you must come soon for I am doubtful how long they will remain in the country."

"I have no definite plans to go to town at the moment,

my lord Duke, so I will have to take my chances," Andrea replied uncooperatively. She signaled Lady Jane, who immediately suggested they retire to the drawing room and that the men might remain for their port if they wished.

"I will join you, Hanley," David said agreeably, "but it is not a rite with me."

"Then I am for joining the ladies," Jonathan decided promptly, which gave Andrea another reason to pull caps with him. Why the devil didn't he contrive to keep the man occupied? she wondered.

In the drawing room the Duke stood before Lady Eugenia's portrait, which had been done by Reynolds, and he turned to Andrea. "This is your mother?"

"Yes."

"You and Andrew are very like her but there is a difference. I believe you look more truly Spanish."

"We favor our grandmother, actually."

"Is her portrait in the house?"

"In my sitting room," Andrea replied unhelpfully, and looking squarely at him, she defied him to pursue the subject.

Of course he could not, and swearing to himself, he vowed to bring that little lady down off her high horse. For the moment he retreated, however, and asked Chloe, "Will you play for us now, Miss Chloe?"

"Yes, Your Grace," the girl answered pleasantly. "Do you have a preference?"

"Well, I must confess that I am not a good critic but my ignorance does not interfere with my enjoyment, and so I will ask you to choose."

"Then I shall play Jonathan's favorites," she said and began with some of Haydn and Handel's works and then launched into one of Beethoven's sonatas.

David thought, "The girl is very good, it seems," and looking around the room, he realized that, like Andrew, these three were intensely devoted to the lovely Chloe. Her mother, of course, was listening with an obvious pride; Andrea was a figure of complete absorption with a little smile hovering around her mouth; while Jonathan revealed himself quite openly as he gazed lovingly at the performer and turned the music sheets for her.

David's eyes went back to Chloe and he mused, "She really is an exquisite little thing and seems to have a sweet, uncomplicated personality. Andrew was right. She is a lovely lady and would make a fine wife—except for one thing—she isn't interesting like her sister." His thoughts were interrupted when the music stopped, and he heard Andrea exclaim, "Chloe, my love, that was perfectly beautiful. You have never played better."

"You know I have been practicing, Andy," her sister told her as her face glowed with pleasure for she knew she had done well.

"Yes, and it shows. Jonathan is right. You are becoming extremely proficient."

"Permit me to congratulate you, Miss Chloe," the Duke said, adding his compliments. "It is a pleasure to be entertained by one so talented."

"Thank you, Your Grace," the girl answered demurely. "I like to play, and I have an excellent teacher and strict taskmasters to strengthen my resolve to work hard."

"You do them credit and I am sure you would be in great demand by the London hostesses to perform at their parties."

"My lord Duke," Andrea admonished severely, "I beg you will not prejudice my sister with unrealistic ideas of the discernment of the audiences at the so-called musical soirées. You and I both know that these gatherings serve merely as showcases for the fashionables, most of whom have no artistic appreciation and are extremely discourteous to the performer. I would not permit Chloe to be exploited at such affairs. She will play for serious music lovers only."

Andrea's vehemence intrigued the Duke and he smiled at Chloe. "You have a fierce champion, I see."

The girl laughed gaily and went to hug her sister. "Yes, Andy is extremely biased, but I confess I agree with her. I really do not like to play for people who only feel obligated to listen."

"Yes, I understand, but there are many who can appreciate a good performance, and I hope you will not deny them merely because there might be others present who cannot."

"Well, perhaps, when I have more confidence, it would not matter so much, but whisperings and restlessness do bother me a little and make it harder to concentrate," Chloe told him candidly.

It was getting late and Jonathan decided to take his leave, promising to return the next day to join in whatever project they had in mind.

"Well, we have several options," Andrea told him. "We will discuss them and be ready to ride out when you come —eleven, I think, would be about right." When Jonathan had gone, she noticed that Lady Jane was looking a little tired, and she felt done up herself from not having slept well the night before, so she suggested, "I am sure the Duke will excuse us if we leave him to his own devices. I believe he is anxious to explore the library anyway."

"My dear Miss Wycliff, I beg to be acquitted. I admit to an interest in some of the books I saw this morning, but not to the extent that I would deprive myself of such pleasant company." This banality generated the response he expected, and he almost laughed aloud at the withering glance with which he was favored by that expressive face.

Recognizing the danger signs, Lady Jane hurried to forestall Andrea's retort and agreed, "I beg you will excuse us, Your Grace, but please do feel free to ask the servants if you require anything." Gathering up her daughters, she marched them off to their rooms.

The next day they rode to the small village of Widecombe that was situated in the wide valley of the East Webburn River just within the forbidding wilderness of Dartmoor Moors and visited the fourteenth-century church with pinnacled tower that was known as the "cathedral of the moor." Chloe informed the Duke that every September a fair was held in the town, and there was even a song about it. He looked properly impressed and then asked if they might ride a little deeper into the moors. They wended their way around a cluster of farms and paused at the top of a rise that gave a good view to the west.

"Andrew has spoken of this area. We were once encamped in a wild barren area, and he remarked that it reminded him of Dartmoor," the Duke told the others.

"He has reason to remember it well," Jonathan said. "He and his cousin Jeffrey were lost in there overnight once and were lucky to be found. Andrea and I fortunately saw them take off and so were able to sound the alarm when they failed to return after a couple of hours. Now, if we go in at all, we are careful to follow marked trails. It is best to admire them from a distance."

"Yes, and it is a beautiful sight when the heather is blooming," Chloe added, happy to be able to remark about another natural phenomenon.

Andrea had been sitting quietly with a pensive attitude and she was brought to attention when the Duke asked, "Miss Wycliff, were you always a comrade of these adventurous fellows?"

"Usually," she answered without elaboration.

"Yes, and it worried Mama to a frazzle," Chloe tattled. "I was always left behind but Andy was a regular tomboy."

"Well put, my dear," Jonathan confirmed, "especially when that scamp Jeffrey was here."

"Jeffrey—that would be Retford's heir?"

"Yes, the Earl of Stockwell."

"Of course—I am well acquainted with him," David commented, "but I have not seen him since I returned from the continent."

"Well, he will likely show up here anytime. He often comes to stay for a while," Chloe remarked offhandedly with a sideways glance at her sister.

The implication was intriguing and strangely disturbing and David searched Andrea's face for some sign of interest but was met with a blank look and a turn of the head as she began to ride back the way they had come.

That evening Lady Jane and the Duke played backgammon while Andrea read and Chloe entertained on the pianoforte until, once again, the ladies left him and retired to their chambers.

The next morning it was decided that they should take the carriage to Torbay to eat a picnic lunch and then drive down to the beach area. Once again Chloe was delighted to inform the Duke of interesting local distinctions and led him to the spot where William of Orange landed in 1688. She reminded him that only a few months ago the harbor had played host for a very short time to the vanquished Napoleon when he was in custody on the *Bellerophon*, which came to Torbay before being ordered to Plymouth.

The Duke smiled indulgently at her eager propagandizing and teased, "I believe you are quite proud of your Devon."

"Yes," she admitted, blushing a little. "Of course, I have not seen very much of England, but I am sure that we are exceptionally favored here."

"I will agree with you, Miss Chloe, and I have seen almost all of Britain," the Duke assured her and was rewarded with a brilliant smile.

Jonathan was not with them on this excursion but had invited the Duke to a tour of his property and an afternoon of fishing the next day. Andrea was thankful to be relieved of their guest's disquieting presence and took the opportunity to visit a few of the tenants. After driving leisurely around the estate in the open carriage for an hour or so, she stopped to sit on a large stone by the stream, amusing herself throwing pebbles and watching the ripples in the water as she thought about the letter she had received the day before. It had only confirmed her worst suspicions, but she felt a curious disappointment. She had almost begun to think she had misjudged the Duke. He had been extremely pleasant even in the face of her incivility and had not singled out Chloe for any special attention. Andrea had almost let down her guard. Now she had to face the fact that he was, after all, a man like her father, and as she had promised, she vented her anger by raining curses on her brother. While indulging in this ill-natured, wholly unprofitable exercise, she heard a horse approaching and in surprise recognized the Duke. He dismounted and came to stand beside her.

Without looking at him, Andrea remarked ungraciously, "I thought you were fishing."

"I was, and I brought some lovely trout for our dinner. Jonathan came back with me and he will join us tonight."

She seemed unusually quiet with almost an air of sadness and David told her, "I came to look for you because I have wanted to talk to you alone."

"What about?" she asked curtly.

"I have been puzzled about your attitude toward me. It is obvious you meant to dislike me before ever I came. Will you tell me why?"

"That's just it—you came," the girl answered, turning those dark, accusing eyes on him.

She looked away again as he said ruefully, "Andrew has been indiscreet, I see."

"If I am to keep this household on an even keel as he expects," Andrea threw at him, "then I should be properly informed of his whimsical machinations."

"Do you disapprove of me as a suitor?"

"Unequivocally," she replied succinctly.

"Why?"

"I should think you would be able to work that out for yourself—your reputation preceded you. And I can't believe that Drew actually sent you here to look Chloe over as if she were a piece of goods on the market."

"That's a harsh appraisal, my dear," David objected, taken aback by her bluntness.

She ignored his lapse into familiarity and challenged, "Why *did* you come?"

"All right, Andrea. I understand you have reason to feel a certain skepticism, but I resent your presumption that *I* would treat my wife shabbily."

"You might not be obvious about it, but it would be all of a piece," she charged.

Becoming angry himself, David felt like shaking her but

controlled the impulse and limited his reprisal to telling her that she had a lot of cheek to make such statements before the fact.

"After the fact would be too late, my lord Duke," she retorted sharply.

They glared at each other and he taunted unwisely, "I do not think Chloe finds me so objectionable."

"Oh! of all the insufferable coxcombs! Do you feel so set up with yourself because a young impressionable child whose head is filled with romantic notions stares at you like a mooncalf? She hasn't the least conception what life as a Duchess would involve. Not only that—she needs someone who would cherish her and encourage her in her music, which is really an important part of her life. And, moreover, you can't have failed to notice that Jonathan is deeply in love with her."

"Yes, I've noticed, but she seems to look upon him as a sort of older brother."

"So she was accustomed to but has been gradually changing her attitude toward him. The affair was beginning to come along very promisingly before you showed up here."

"If she is so easily won over, not much can be said for her constancy," the Duke remarked drily.

"You don't understand at all, do you? She is still a child. But," Andrea added sarcastically, "I suppose that fact would fit in nicely with your plans, would it not?"

"What are you insinuating, you little termagant?" David demanded angrily.

Warming up to the battle, she accused, "Just that it would be convenient to have a compliant young bride who would not have the temerity to interfere with your— diversions. I always suspect older men who have scandalous reputations when they turn their eyes on girls barely out of the schoolroom."

"Older men!" the Duke exploded. "Let me inform you that I am far from considering myself in that light."

"So *you* may be. But the fact remains that you are almost twice as old as Chloe. In fact, you are old enough to be her father!"

This exacerbating comment earned her a thoroughly malevolent look and David objected testily, "That is coming it a little strong."

"Are you trying to tell me that you could not have been a father at fifteen?" Andrea demanded indecorously.

"My God! That is the most indelicate remark I have ever heard from the mouth of any respectable female," David expostulated in shocked disapproval.

"You can't be serious!" an undaunted young lady scoffed unbelievingly. "It is certainly hard to credit but, if that is true, I do humbly beg your pardon. I had no idea you had been so sheltered." She paused and then deliberately turned the knife. "Nevertheless—I ask you—does the shoe fit?"

The Duke looked at his attacker with a vengeful eye and countered ungallantly, "If this is an example of your idea of a scintillating conversation, it is no wonder that you have reached the age of twenty-six still unmarried."

The spiteful gibe had the unfortunate effect of adding fuel to the fire and goaded Andrea to proclaim boastfully as her eyes flashed belligerently, "So! *Now* you mean to try to humble me. Well, Your Grace, you will have a hard time of it because I am not without prospects and, if you can stand there looking at me and suppose I have not had offers, some still standing, by the way, then you do not have much respect for the discernment of your sex—or are blind!"

Thinking that he had never seen a more alluring creature in his life, David let his eyes roam over her insolently and then remarked slowly with an insinuating note, "I am not blind."

If Andrea had not realized she had asked for this treatment and therefore expected it, she would have been thoroughly shaken, but she managed to say caustically, "That was very well done, Your Grace—an excellent performance, in fact. And, I might say," she added provokingly, "right on cue."

"You are a tongue-valiant little witch," David fumed, furious with himself for giving her yet another weapon.

"I suppose you would rather I had come to offer for *you*."

"It would certainly have been more seemly," she acknowledged commendably, causing the Duke to feel a moment's elation, but then ruined the effect when she continued, "or for Ladyjane for that matter. She is only four years your senior, after all."

This outrageous suggestion stunned the Duke for a moment, for he had not yet learned to anticipate her audacious manner of expressing her positions. He was consciously struck by the ridiculousness of this unseemly sparring match. "All right, Andrea," he submitted as he had to laugh, a surprising reaction that Andrea found unsettling. "You win. There is no besting you in an argument, it's plain to see. And I'm sure I must be mad, but the truth of the matter is that I find myself quite agreeable and so I ask you, my dear—will you marry me?"

For the first time in her life Andrea was struck dumb. She stood staring at him incredulously, thinking the violence of their exchange must have overset his reason. And then, the anger began welling up in her again and she fairly spat at him, "How dare you! How can you have the temerity to indulge in such mockery! You are easily satisfied, my lord Duke. If not one, why not the other?" she raved, beginning to pace back and forth.

"Stop working yourself into a passion," David said. "You are deliberately misunderstanding. I may not have done that very well, but it was a novelty and well beyond my experience."

"Was it, Your Grace? That is hard to believe considering how glibly it rolled off your tongue."

"You know very well I have never proposed to a girl before in my life. If I had, I would not be doing so now," he proclaimed unthinkingly.

"Well, my lord Duke, *that* is the last time you will be able to make that high-flown claim," Andrea advised triumphantly and planted herself firmly in front of him with narrowed eyes, her nose and chin in the air.

It was more than David could stand and against his better judgment he pulled her into his arms and kissed her as he had been wanting to from the first moment he saw her. She fought furiously, finally breaking away after he loosened his hold when she reached behind him and yanked vigorously at his hair.

He got himself under control and tried to apologize. "Andrea, I am sorry, but if you had any idea how you can provoke a man, you would not hold that impulse against me. And I *do* want to marry you, my love, truly I do. Don't you understand?"

"No! No, I don't. How can you be sure of such a thing when you have only known me for three days? It is absolutely unreasonable and I will not listen to you. A woman would be a fool to marry such a man as you."

"Don't start that again," he warned with a set face and an angry glint in his eye. "You don't know what you're talking about."

"The devil I don't! I admit for a couple of days I was beginning to think you might be the splendid fellow Andrew advertised, but the letter I received yesterday soon put me to rights."

"What letter?"

"From a friend of mine in London."

"One of the tattlemongers?"

"Call it what you like. Any denials or excuses?" she inquired, almost hopefully.

"I don't know. Of what am I accused?"

"Of being a womanizer for a start, my lord Duke—a man who is not satisfied with one mistress, or even two, but at least three and God knows how many more of the demimonde."

"At thirty-two I am supposed to have been a monk?" he asked defensively. "At least you know I have no favorite."

"Have you not?" Andrea queried sharply, disappointed by his tacit admission. "Don't let Lady Carrington hear you say that. She will have your liver and lights. I am informed you just came from a week in London, where you managed to detach her from Lord Carlson. I must tell you she is not happy that you left her immediately and is threatening to punish you. I wonder if you realize what you have gotten yourself into. It makes one doubt your perception unless, of course, you are besotted. The woman is a maneater, and once she digs in her claws, it has been well-documented that she does not let go until she is pleased to do so."

"Don't be absurd," David said angrily, feeling extremely put out that she had checked up on him and no doubt had learned all the lurid rumors from some scandal-mongering woman. "That was just a diversion."

"They mean nothing, of course," she said sarcastically. "You don't realize how strongly I feel about deceptive relationships. It is quite a mania with me. If you think I would consider marrying a man for whom I feel such contempt, you are certainly wide of the mark. I can't believe you actually put it to the touch."

"That makes it plain enough," a deeply offended gentleman said stiffly, cursing himself for imagining that he had found his love and that she would know it as well as he. He had certainly been taught a lesson and the next time he proposed to a girl, he would make sure she was not a viper-tongued little witch.

"I hope so," Andrea retorted uncompromisingly, turning on her heel and climbing into the carriage.

David mounted his horse and followed her back to the Manor. They were both still seething when they entered the house and without speaking to anyone they went directly to their rooms to change for dinner.

Jonathan had been a witness to their return and ruefully concluded that their private meeting had obviously produced results contrary to what he had hoped for. He had the uneasy feeling that things were bound to take a turn for the worse and resigned himself to the prospect of having to follow Andrea's tumble into the inevitable bumble-bath.

At dinner it was evident that the combatants had gotten themselves under control as far as their outward behavior was concerned but their rather pointed snubbing of one another could hardly be overlooked, although Lady Jane did her best to ignore it. Chloe seemed puzzled and glanced at Jonathan for reassurance. He smiled and winked at her conspiratorily and received such an affectionate smile as a reward that he thought his heart would leap across the table. It was unfortunate that at that moment the Duke was engaged in deliberately charming his hostess for, if he had witnessed the intimate little exchange, he might not have been so intent on forwarding designs that were bound to lead to considerable grief. However, he was already deep into following the course of action he had hit upon when he was imagining all sorts of harassments that would cause Andrea to regret her cavalier treatment of his suit. Rather than taking the time to get himself in a more rational frame of mind that would have allowed him to recognize his blame and the humor of the affair, he had found it more consistent with his mood to vent his anger on the girl who had rejected him so unceremoniously—almost gleefully; on Andrew for setting him on the wrong track with his totally deceptive description of his twin; on his grandmother, who had pressured him excessively so that he reacted imprudently and managed to make a complete Jack Pudding of himself; and on the turns of Fate that made him a Duke, a title he was finding to be more of a liability than an asset. He decided that, at least at the moment, the thing that the disdainful Miss Wycliff wished to avoid at all costs was the obligation of taking her sister to London for the Season, so this was the very object he was determined to achieve. He knew just where to attack and was telling Lady Jane about the beauty of the Royal Botanical Gardens at Kew in the spring and was tempting Chloe with assurances that there were many excellent musical programs to be attended during the Season. He teased her about what a sensation she would be at the balls, for always the gentlemen compete furiously with each other whenever an Incomparable like herself appears on the scene, but he hoped that she would grant him special consideration as a friend of the family, if for no other reason.

While all of this cajolery was being shamelessly proffered and relentlessly continued after they had all retired to the drawing room, Andrea, because of a determined effort to suppress her desire to smash something, developed an excruciating headache which almost made tears come to her eyes. Jonathan failed to note her distress because of his preoccupation with the little charade that was being enacted, which he found not one whit amusing, since Chloe predictably was being easily swayed by the Duke's blandishments. He said irritably, "For God's sake, Andrea, what the devil did you do or say that put him in such a temper? I would have sworn that he had no intention of courting Chloe and tonight he is attacking with deliberate intent."

They were sitting together on the couch. Lady Jane was nearby working on her tambour frame, to which she always applied herself industriously whenever her nerves were on edge, while Chloe played the pianoforte with a determinedly attentive Duke giving every appearance of being completely enchanted with the performer as well as the performance.

Andrea put her hand over her eyes and winced with pain. Lady Jane asked anxiously, "Andrea, are you unwell?"

"Dreadfully," came a trenchant reply.

"My dear," her stepmother said, dropping her work and coming to sit beside her. "Whatever is the matter?"

"Nothing bilious, love. It's just that my head feels as if it were going to explode. I expect it is because I have been so tense and angry and have the most fierce desire to fly out at somebody," she said darkly as she glanced balefully at the Duke.

Jonathan suggested, "Let's go into the library so that at least you won't have to watch your antagonist at work. You can explain to me just how you managed to set him off."

"All right. I am probably near the popping-off point anyway," Andrea agreed miserably, and they went across the hall leaving Lady Jane to chaperon.

In the library Andrea began to pace the floor and said reproachfully to Jonathan, who was standing calmly, watching her with a not particularly sympathetic expression, "Well, you don't have to look as though you thought it were my fault."

"Isn't it?"

"I didn't ask him here!"

"Andrea, stop being evasive. Something happened this afternoon and, since it concerns me deeply, I want to know what it was."

"We came to dagger points!"

"That's obvious, but why?" Jonathan pressed.

"He asked why I disliked him and I told him."

"Told him what?"

"That I took exception to his coming to look Chloe over as if she were a piece of goods. He, in fact, admitted it was true and asked why I disapproved of him as a suitor. I remarked on his scandalous reputation and told him that he was old enough to be her father!" Andrea confessed unrepentently.

"My God! No wonder he is on his mettle."

"And then he cut at me, and I got even angrier and—and—I told him I had information from London about his recent amorous activities there and that a woman would have to be a fool to marry a man like him and that I held him in the greatest contempt and—now he means to get back at me in some nefarious manner."

Jonathan expressed his skepticism. "I'm sure that's not the whole story, my dear Andrea, but I suppose I shall have to settle for an abbreviated version. However, I must say that this was a devil of a time for you to lose your usual excellent perception because, before tonight, he showed very little interest in Chloe and now, as a result of this afternoon's hostilities, he is bent on making mischief."

Andrea sat down at the desk with her head in her hands and said contritely, "I'm sorry, Jonathan. I don't know how this got so out of hand. It's becoming a nightmare."

Looking at the pitifully abject figure, Jonathan regretted having added to her distress with his criticisms and went to take her hands in his. "It's all right, Andrea. I expect that some kind of imbroglio was inevitable from the moment he walked in the door. We'll just have to muddle through."

She let out a deep sigh. "I suppose this means we will probably have to go to London."

"I'm afraid so," a not too pleased gentleman agreed reluctantly. "With Andrew as a forerunner, Chloe was ripe for being beguiled and, now that Kensington has pushed the door open a little wider, it would likely prove unwise to take a stand against it."

Andrea narrowed her eyes and declared passionately, "I think I will make a stuffed image of that hateful man and thrust pins in it every day!"

Jonathan burst out laughing. "Andrea, how *do* you conceive of these bizarre inspirations?"

"I have read of the voodoo rites in Jamaica," she answered with a sheepish grin.

"Well, I beg you to dispense with the dramatics and try to act with discretion as a proper chaperon should."

"Are you coming, too?" she asked hopefully.

"Yes, of course. I have to protect my interests, after all."

They had left the door open and looked up as they were joined by Chloe and Lady Jane, followed by the Duke, who had been somewhat piqued when he had discovered his audience had dwindled.

"Andy," her sister said solicitously, "Mama says you have another headache. You are not usually so bothered. Perhaps you should see the doctor."

Andrea's face softened as she looked affectionately at the sweet girl and assured her meaningfully, "Don't worry, love. I expect it is because I have been cursed with some plaguey affliction which will no doubt disappear in a day or two."

Chloe accepted this explanation at face value but Lady Jane looked dismayed. Meanwhile, Jonathan was having a hard time keeping his countenance, and the Duke found himself caught between amusement and vexation for once again being the victim of a consummate setdown. It was certainly the first time he had ever been characterized as a "plaguey affliction."

"My God!" David told himself. "That is the most outrageous, abominable, backbiting female I have ever known, and if she thinks I am going to back down, she has sorely misjudged her opponent." Aloud he said, "Speaking of disappearing, Miss Wycliff, I have just been telling your mother and sister that, much as I have enjoyed my visit here, I feel I must return to Dorset, as my grandmother is anxious to journey to London, and I regret that I must leave tomorrow."

"Now that you have done your damage," Andrea thought malevolently, but she commented with apparent civility, unless one took notice of the deliberate inflections, "Of course, my lord Duke. No doubt your *grandmother* misses the pleasures of town, and I am persuaded we *should* have been gratified you were able to spend these several days with us for I am sure you have been neglecting your other interests. I do hope you won't discover your *affairs* to be too frightfully complicated."

"Nothing I can't handle," he responded significantly, thereby digging a deeper hole for himself.

Knowing Andrea's undisciplined instinct for having the last word, Jonathan could imagine lamentable results if this tongue-fencing were to continue. He placed a warning hand on her arm and, turning to the Duke, asked, "When do you plan to leave?"

"Not too early. I hoped to persuade the ladies to join me for breakfast and to get away before noon. I intend to make the trip in two stages, as I have no set schedule and must anticipate another long drive within the week."

"Well, then, I shall take my leave of you now and wish you a safe trip," Jonathan said cordially as he put out his hand.

David shook it firmly and replied, "Thank you, Hanley," and added with a crooked grin—(that made Andrea say to herself, "If I were a man, I would call him out!")— "No doubt I shall see you in London shortly."

"So it appears," Jonathan acknowledged curtly, thereby

relaying the message of a lessening of his friendliness. He turned to the others and bade them good night, leaving in a not too amiable frame of mind.

After the ladies had retired, David went outside to walk about the grounds, trying to unravel the confusion in his mind. He had antagonized Jonathan, alienated Lady Jane, angered Andrea, and charmed Chloe. If anyone of these accomplishments had been desirable he might have felt some consolation, but, since every one of them was contrary to what he actually wished, he felt a sense of frustration and self-reproach that he had let his emotions rule his head. He decided he would no doubt regain his reason once he had conquered his passion for a captivating dark-eyed, dark-haired little vixen. "Damned fool!" he swore at himself and went in to bed where he lay awake several hours unable to reconcile himself to his rejection. Unconsciously he committed himself to a continuing program of provocation.

In the morning he was joined by all three ladies and, even though Andrea had very little to say, they enjoyed a pleasant farewell breakfast. Shortly before eleven his hostesses stood at the door to wish the Duke godspeed. He thanked Lady Jane for her hospitality, and Chloe especially for making his stay so pleasant. Then he moved to Andrea, and with his back to the others and a challenging light in his eyes, he said quizzically, "Miss Wycliff, I am anxious to be enlightened about those—uh—standing matters we discussed, and I look forward to seeing you in town. You *are* coming, aren't you?"

"You devil!" Andrea fairly hissed between her teeth.

"Witch!" David countered softly and then, bowing gallantly, he went out to mount his horse and waved jauntily as he turned down the drive.

CHAPTER FOUR

As the departing Duke disappeared around a curve, Andrea breathed a sigh of relief, even though she knew she would have to deal with the aftermath of his mischief-making eventually. She contrived to postpone this necessity for the moment by announcing that she had been neglecting her accounts and would have to work several hours at her desk; she would then make plans to spend a few days at each of their other two properties in North Devon, having missed her normal round at the first of the year. She requested a footman to send word to the steward that she was ready to go over their business and she would be pleased to see him sometime after noon when she would have had a chance to organize her figures.

The housekeeper also appeared at this moment to ask Lady Wycliff if she might confer with her on some domestic matters, and Lady Jane immediately closeted herself with this lady, happy to escape a private interview with her daughter, which she wished to avoid as much as Andrea.

Andrea turned to Chloe, "Well, love, what are your plans for today?"

Her plans for the day having been successfully foiled (she had hoped to broach the subject of her debut but found herself outfaced), the disappointed young lady said disconsolately, "I think I will ride over to see Mrs. Hanley, for she is still not up and about, and then I'll stop by the Gatlings. I haven't seen Betsy and Clara for almost two weeks. They are probably going to be miffed that we did not invite them to meet the Duke."

"I doubt he would have appreciated being advertised as a prize, Chloe. It would have been too gauche," Andrea demurred.

"I know, but I don't think that will weigh with them."

"Well, I'm sure you can make your peace, darling, but do take someone with you and come back before dark."

"Honestly, Andrea, I am not a child!" Chloe declared huffily, and tossing her head, marched up the stairs.

Andrea stared after her sister with a sinking heart. Chloe's defiant attitude was definitely out of character. She usually accepted Andy's well-meant counselings good-naturedly, but now it seemed the child had been enlightened by the Duke's honeyed words and had begun to see herself as a desirable young woman, a discovery that induced her to take exception to any kind of patronizing and to resent the calculated maneuvers which denied her a hearing. Andrea realized they were going to have to take a different approach, or they might have an open rebellion on their hands. The hard fact, no matter how much they fought it, was that they were going to have to go to London and they would all have to accept it with as much grace as possible. Andrea decided to ride over to discuss it with Jonathan later in the afternoon. With a resigned air, she went to the library to concentrate on ordering their affairs for several weeks absence.

When Andrea joined Lady Jane for a light luncheon, she told her of Chloe's unnatural behavior and concluded, "I suppose we are going to have to recognize she is ready to try her wings. It is unfortunate that the Duke's visit should have precipitated this awareness, but I suppose it had to come sooner or later. Jonathan has already told me that we must allow her to grow up and must stand by to see that she doesn't get badly burned."

"But she is such an innocent, Andrea—as much as I was, I'm afraid," Lady Jane remarked ruefully.

"I know. She sees everything through a rosy glow, and I sometimes wonder if we have protected her too much. She has had such a pleasant, untroubled life up to now, that perhaps it will be best that she be exposed to the real world. And, my dear, I hope you are going to conquer your antipathy to spending some weeks in town because I am counting on you to help me checkmate the Duke."

"Andrea, you know I—"

At this moment the butler announced the arrival of the steward and Andrea pushed herself away from the table saying, "Think about it, love, and we'll speak of it later."

After two hours of checking the books, agreeing on certain actions to be taken to correct a few problems among the tenants, and deciding on a program of land rehabilitation, Andrea made arrangements with Mr. Jones to visit the other properties to confer with the managers who were subordinate to him. Andrea made a practice of showing herself occasionally at the other estates to assure her people of her concern and to make a point of reaffirming her confidence in Mr. Jones's supervision. He was an extremely able and knowledgable man who ran the estates with a firm but fair hand. His methods in both human and business matters had proven extremely successful as all the operations were profitable, or at least self-supporting, and provided a comfortable living for a number of workers and their families.

It was nearly three o'clock when he left and Andrea prepared to ride over to meet with Jonathan to discuss his recommendations about the forthcoming journey to London.

Upon arriving at Hanley House, Andrea asked the butler if the patient was well enough to receive another visitor. He assured her that Mrs. Hanley had improved considerably and would no doubt be pleased to see Miss Wycliff.

When she was admitted to the bedroom, she found a rather bored lady sitting on the chaise, restlessly turning the pages of a book. Andrea had to laugh, for it was obvious that she had had quite enough of this forced inactivity.

Katherine Hanley was a tall, vigorous woman with a delightfully facile mind, who always had some project in the works. It was from her that Jonathan had inherited his intellectual proclivities. She was an inveterate book collector and an author in her own right, though she concentrated on histories, particularly of the British peoples and their customs. Before the war with France she had traveled extensively with her husband. Several of Jonathan's very early years had been spent on the continent. Recently, however, she had contented herself with occasional journeys to Ireland and Scotland, and on several short trips had persuaded Andrea to accompany her.

She looked up with pleasure when the girl entered her room and exclaimed, "Andrea, my dear, I am so glad to see you. I am becoming deucedly blue-deviled and am thoroughly out of charity with that blasted doctor who insists that I play the invalid for another day or two." She then cautioned Andrea as she moved closer to greet her affectionately, "No, no, don't come too near. I am sure I am perfectly well, but I should not wish to pass on this nasty disorder which I managed to pick up somewhere."

"Very likely from one of the tenants' children, if I am any judge," Andrea said flatly.

Mrs. Hanley gave her a sheepish smile and then remarked quizzingly, "Jonathan tells me you have been confronted with something of a problem."

"Yes!" Andrea admitted vexatiously. "Was Chloe full of praises for the Duke when she came this morning?"

"Actually, she said very little about him and guarded her answers when I asked leading questions, which I found more disconcerting than if she had been quite open about it."

"I know. I have the same feeling, and I am persuaded His Grace was indulging himself in an irresponsible flirtation just as Andrew has been wont to do. Chloe is so wrapped in cotton wool that she was taken in like a little goose."

"It's only natural, my dear. She has not had much contact with the glamourous elements of our society except through Andrew's eyes, which we have to decry as a somewhat specious representation."

"Yes," Andrea agreed, "and he is definitely in my black

books for his infelicitous meddling. As far as the Duke is concerned," she added with fire in her eyes, "I have been wishing I could blow him off the face of the earth."

Having been advised by her son of his opinion on the true but unrealized inclinations of the two antagonists, Mrs. Hanley eyed her young friend speculatively. It was not like Andrea to take such a militant stance though, of course, the circumstances were certainly provoking. She said warningly, "Andrea, I do think you should trust Jonathan's judgment in this matter. He will not allow it to get out of hand."

The girl lowered her eyes and allowed humbly, "I know he thinks I have been precipitate and have aggravated the situation, so I came today to ask for his counsel. Is he at home? Perhaps he could join us."

"I'll send for him," Mrs. Hanley complied promptly.

In a few minutes the gentleman appeared and queried dubiously, "Does this summons mean I am to participate in a strategy meeting?"

"Yes," Andrea owned up with a meek expression. "In fact, we are appointing you director."

"I wish I could count on that, my dear Andrea, but I'm afraid I have to mistrust your good resolution not to cook up some harebrained scheme."

"Jonathan! How can you be so unfair! I am not the imprudent one in the family."

"That point is open to question, my girl, seeing as you have injudiciously established a discordant relationship with the Duke just as you have with Andrew. You will have to admit that you never back off in any contest of wills."

"Well, I shall try to control myself," she promised, not denying the charge. "Did you see Chloe this morning?"

"Briefly," he answered noncommittally.

"Well?" Andrea demanded.

"She seemed a little embarrassed and didn't stay long; no, she did not mention the Duke or going to London."

"I was treated to a little coldness myself. I believe she thinks we all mean to fob her off and is priming herself for one of her rare but effective withdrawal maneuvers to get her way."

Jonathan grinned. "She is a spoiled little minx and knows she has us all under her thumb. We might as well let her have her head."

"Yes, so I have concluded. So, this evening, since I leave for North Devon in the morning, I thought, if you are agreed, I would tell her that we will remove to London within the month and prompt her to work on Ladyjane while I am gone."

"All right. It would suit me to locate in town for a while to do some research and make contacts with my friends from the universities. I believe my lady mother is ready for a change herself."

"Yes, dear, I am. And your Aunt Clarissa has been begging us to come these many weeks. You know how put-out your uncle becomes when you neglect him for any length of time. He has such a strong sense of family and has been quite possessive of you since your father died. You really should contrive to spend more time with him."

"Well, we shall make a party of it and all go together," Jonathan decided. "When did you think of leaving?"

"I thought maybe about the second week in March. We none of us have a proper wardrobe for an extended Season and will need several weeks to be outfitted," said Andrea.

Jonathan smiled at her purely feminine reaction and teased, "I believe you are looking forward to this excursion after all."

"One must look at the pleasant aspects of any venture however disagreeable it might be in other ways," Andrea retorted primly, but with a sparkle in her eyes.

"Of course," he agreed soberly.

She made a face at him and then declared jokingly, "I had better leave now or I will be late and would likely be censured, since I had warned Chloe to return before dark and received a cut for my presumption."

Jonathan escorted her to the stable where her groom awaited her with the horses. She asked him to check in on the household the next week or so while she was away.

When she arrived home, she heard Chloe practicing so she went directly to Lady Jane's sitting room, hoping to find her in a cooperative frame of mind.

Immediately on seeing her, her stepmother began sidestepping. "I am so glad that Katherine is on the mend. Chloe said she is nearly recovered."

"Yes, and, as can be expected, she is becoming quite resty. In fact," Andrea noted with intent, "she is looking forward to a stay in London."

Lady Jane had hoped to put off any discussion of this subject and was at a nonplus at the prompt attack.

Andrea took pity on her and went to take her hands. "Ladyjane, I have talked to Jonathan, and we have agreed that there is nothing for it but that we shall have to present Chloe."

"Oh, dear," lamented her stepmother. "I know it is my duty to accompany you, but do you think you could manage without me?"

"Darling, I may be twenty-six, but, being unmarried, I do not think it would be acceptable for me to serve as sole chaperon. We would have to impose on Aunt Henrietta's hospitality and, while I know she would be delighted to have us, I confess I believe we would be more comfortable in our own establishment, to say nothing of my desire to be relieved from a frightfully awkward position."

"Oh, of course, I forgot about Jeffrey."

"Yes, I love him dearly, but not as a suitor, and he is determinedly persistent. I'm afraid it would give rise to speculation, especially since both his parents are in favor. Not only that, but I should like to have some control and complete cognizance about who should call on us as we could not do if we were guests at Retford House."

"You always have your arguments so well-prepared," Lady Jane bemoaned, "that it puts one quite on the defensive."

"You *must* try to forget that unpleasantness, love. All of that happened years ago and it is no longer of any interest to any of the *haut ton,* even to those who might remember it. You will not have to show yourself at many affairs. I can handle that. I just need you in the house."

Lady Jane sighed resignedly. "I will try to reconcile myself, Andrea. After all, Chloe is surely more my responsibility than yours."

"I do not mean to bring that up to you, my dear. I feel naturally obligated myself, so do not think I am prodding you on that account. What say you to our taking only a few clothes with us and splurging on elegant new wardrobes? I see no reason for us not to profit from this sacrifice," Andrea tempted, with a mischievous eye.

"Well, I must allow we have rather neglected that department, and it is true that Chloe will have to be completely outfitted. Her schoolgirl clothes are not at all appropriate."

Relieved that her stepmother seemed to be taking a positive approach, Andrea left her with the suggestion that they reassure their recalcitrant charge at dinner and put her back in a happy frame of mind.

An hour later all three ladies sat down at the maleless table, and after the butler had served the first course, Andrea remarked conversationally, "I drove over late in the afternoon to see the Hanleys, Chloe, dear, and was pleased to discover that Mrs. Hanley was feeling much better. In fact, she is looking forward to a holiday, and Jonathan has agreed to escort us all to London."

"Andrea!" her sister squealed in delight and rushed around the table to embrace her fiercely. "I felt sure you were not going to take me, and I was all set to write to Aunt Henrietta."

"Without telling us?" her mother asked sharply.

"Oh, no, only if you refused, and of course, I would have asked your permission," Chloe denied with an offended air.

"All right, love, do go sit down and eat your dinner and we will talk about it," Andrea directed indulgently as she disengaged herself.

"I am so excited," Chloe declared, "that Jonathan is

coming, too! I was afraid I would miss him dreadfully and now it is just perfect! When are we going?"

"In two or three weeks."

"So soon? But I thought the Season didn't start until April."

"My dear, you have no idea what one must go through to prepare for a London Season, particularly when one is to make a debut," Andrea told her. "We shall certainly have to go several weeks early to make arrangements and to order all our new clothes. In fact, I must warn you that, in the beginning, we are going to be fully occupied with our shopping, fittings, and other tiresome details. You are going to have to resign yourself to a very uneventful life because you will not wish to neglect your music for all that time. The social engagements will have to be put off until we are ready to be seen."

"Andy, I will be good, I promise you. Do you think I might have a sky-blue ballgown? Jonathan says I look best in that color."

Andrea laughed and said, "Yes, I agree with him. And on my way through Exeter tomorrow I will stop at a bookshop for the latest copies of the *Belle Assemblée* and send them back to you so you may see what the newest fashions are and maybe choose one or two you would especially like to have copied."

"Mama, did you hear?" Chloe bubbled, clapping her hands. "We are going to be *so* diverted! And I know you must be pleased to be going to see your old friends. You have been rusticated too long. In fact, I can't recall you ever going to London," she remarked wonderingly.

"No, I am not comfortable in London, my dear."

"But why? At least for a short while?"

"Chloe," Andrea interrupted, "why do you not take your exuberant spirits out on the pianoforte and leave Ladyjane and me to discuss the humdrum particulars? When you are ready to retire, I shall come to your room and we will have a long coze."

"All right," Chloe agreed cheerfully. "I know you are

putting me off, but you will see how amiable I mean to be—and I shall send Maria to tell you when I am in bed." With a happy laugh she left the others at the table and went dutifully to the pianoforte, which soon sent lovely little melodies throughout the house.

"Thank you, Andrea," Lady Jane said softly.

"You know," her stepdaughter ventured musingly, "I have been thinking we should tell Chloe something of your difficulties, for you of all people have cause to be wary of the malicious talebearing that one must learn to expect in society."

"Oh, dear, Andrea, no doubt you are right, but I am such a coward and have not had to think of all that for such a long time."

"I will tell her if you will permit me," Andrea offered.

"Well, if you really think we must, I believe you would do it better, my love," Lady Jane accepted gratefully.

"I'll tell her tonight when we are having our little chat. Now I had better see to my packing for I mean to leave early in the morning. Do not expect me to return for at least ten days because I will not be able to visit the other estates again before summer, and I do not want to hurry this trip."

As she promised, Andrea went to Chloe's room and settled herself at the foot of her bed with a pillow propped up against the bedpost. The girl was still in high gig and looked very much the child, sitting with her knees drawn up in her girlish nightgown and hair tumbling down her back.

"Now, there are some things I want to discuss with you seriously, Chloe, but I see you are still in transports, so I will listen to you first as I know you are bursting with questions and confidences."

"Oh, yes, but nothing in particular—just everything. You know, like going to Almack's and seeing all the sights and meeting new people and going to balls and . . . and . . . I wondered if I might have some very fashionable grown-up gowns and . . ."

"Well, darling," Andrea broke in, "if we talked about all that we would be up all night and I have to leave early in the morning, so I think we will each consider those things for the next few days. And then we can all put our heads together when I get back. But, about the last, yes, I'm sure Ladyjane will permit you to have gowns more suitable for a young lady." She paused for a moment and then commented meaningfully, "I know you suddenly have a desire to be considered grown-up, but I must warn you that, if you wish to be treated as an adult, you must act like one."

The girl blushed and hung her head. "You are vexed with me because I behaved so rudely this morning."

"Yes," Andrea replied. "You thought you were not going to get your way and acted the spoiled child, never once considering that we might have some good reason for not wishing to commit ourselves to this scheme."

"Andy, I am sorry. You know I did not mean to cut you and I will not be so uncivil again, I promise you."

"Well, darling, at least, if you will try very hard, it will be to your credit. I expect you will run aground once in a while because growing up is very difficult. You must remember that, even as a young lady, you will need advice and that we are all of us your very best friends."

"Of course, Andy," the girl agreed with a puzzled expression because she could not understand why her sister was making so much of her little sauciness.

Andrea smiled and said, "Now I will tell you what this is all about," and she very candidly described the circumstances of their father and Lady Jane's marriage and the contretemps that gave her mother such an aversion to being obligated to reappear in society. "She was really so deeply crushed that she still cannot bring herself to conquer her scruples."

"Poor Mama," Chloe sympathized with tears in her eyes. "All these years she has hidden away because of her embarrassment."

"Well, yes, more or less. And so, I must tell you, our trip to London hinges entirely on whether or not we can persuade her to go, for we cannot go alone and I am unalterably opposed to sending you to Aunt Henrietta—at least for another year or two. You are very young and it is not imperative that we go this Season."

"Andy!" her sister began to object until she noticed the raised brows and the warning look and realized she was being tested. With a determined effort, she said reluctantly, "Well, of course, I would be disappointed, but I understand what you mean and I would not wish to cause Mama any distress."

"Chloe, my love, you are a darling and I will tell you that I believe Ladyjane has nearly reconciled herself, so I leave you to keep her on the right track, but you must not tease her about being sociable or she will back off. Then, when we get her to London, we may be able to coax her into our entertainments little by little. I am hoping that we can use this excursion to help her come out of her shell. It will be our secret project."

"Oh, Andy, that will be such fun! And I will be very diplomatic and she will not know we are plotting."

Andrea laughed and applauded. "Very good. And now I had better go to bed so I will be ready on time tomorrow." She got up, went to kiss her sister, and received a bear hug in return. As she started to leave, Chloe said tentatively, "Andy—"

"Yes?"

"I should like to ask you something."

"What is it, love?"

"Are all men like Father?"

"A good many are, I'm afraid," Andrea answered frankly.

"Is Andrew?"

"Yes, Chloe. He is quite the man about town and behaves scandalously with the ladies, but at least, he is not married."

"And—the Duke?"

"A prime example, actually," Andrea informed her sister ruthlessly. "I have had word from London that he has three known mistresses, two of whom hope to marry him, but he keeps them all dangling."

"Is that why you dislike him?"

"Yes, especially since he is looking for a wife to give him an heir now that he has such a grand position, and came here to look you over on Andrew's recommendation."

"Andrea!" Chloe exclaimed with a shocked expression. "That is a terrible thing to say!"

"It is true, nevertheless."

"Well, I wish you hadn't told me."

"You asked, and being able to accept these unpleasant truths is one of the adult responsibilities I was telling you about."

"Oh, dear, it is so disillusioning," Chloe said, suddenly disenchanted. "Why are men like that?"

"For one thing, in this permissive age it is too easy for them to stray, and many men do not have the necessary moral strength to discipline themselves. Men like Father and Andrew and the Duke who are handsome, charming, and wealthy are always sought after by ladies of loose morals. They just take advantage and, generally, have an unadmirable, cynical outlook on life. Moreover, many of them are not in love with their wives and often have married merely to ensure succession or for material or social gain or, as Father did, to protect themselves from a more demanding connection."

"Oh, dear, you make it all sound so mercenary and unromantic," Chloe moaned regretfully.

"So it often is," Andrea remarked unpromisingly and went to the door.

"Andy—do you think Jonathan—is like that?"

"Jonathan is different, love. He is a man of great character and sensitive nature."

"Yes, so I think, too," Chloe said with satisfaction as she slid under the covers. "Good night."

When she closed the door, Andrea thought that the girl at least showed some perception and wondered how long and how much of a shock it would take before Chloe realized that she cared deeply for Jonathan.

* * *

When Andrea arrived home late in the afternoon after an absence of ten days, she was immediately pounced upon by Chloe, who obviously had been impatient for her return.

"Andy! I am so glad to see you. Mama and I have been having a famous time looking at the magazines you sent, and I can't wait to show you some of the things we have decided on."

"All right, love, but do let me settle in and then we will talk about everything."

Following her sister up to her room, Chloe continued chattering, "And we received a lovely thank-you note from the Duke and beautiful little gifts. Mama's is a delicately carved ivory fan and mine is a perfectly exquisite little dance cardholder on a ribbon. We have just been all of a flutter wondering what yours is. I was so surprised when the package arrived because I had no idea he would send anything, but Mama says it is perfectly proper for a gentleman to show his appreciation of hospitality in such a fashion."

"Yes," Andrea agreed reluctantly, "so long as the gift is not too expensive or intimate," and she experienced a wayward anticipation about the elegantly wrapped package she saw ostentatiously displayed on her dressing table. She suspected it contained some provocative object, and she could hardly restrain herself from grabbing it and tearing it open to discover just how insolent he had contrived to be.

However, she resolutely ignored the temptation, which required no great firmness of spirit on her part since she was well aware that Chloe would not allow her to procrastinate for very long. She occupied herself redoing her hair and then, putting a light shawl around her shoulders, started to move away.

"Andy, you are the most provoking girl!" Chloe accused, stamping her foot. "How can you not want to open the package? Do stop teasing!"

Andrea had to laugh and scolded as she picked up the

gift. "You are a forward little minx, but since you are so impatient, we will see what the Duke thinks I deserve." She uncovered a velvet box and opened the catch, revealing a pair of large, simple, dangling gold earrings."

"Oh!" Chloe exclaimed, "how unusual. They almost look like—" and she stopped, suddenly aware of the innuendo.

"Yes, my dear, they do—and they are—gypsy earrings," Andrea acknowledged, feeling amused and pleased in spite of herself.

"How famous!" Chloe cried delightedly, perceiving the joke. "They *are* beautiful, and I hope you won't be miffed at the Duke for he is not the only one who sees you so."

"Has Jonathan been maligning me?" Andrea asked with a wry face.

"I am not going to tell tales. But do put them on, Andy."

"Not now, love. Someday, when I am properly dressed. They require a certain style," her sister demurred.

"May I take them to show Mama?"

"Of course. Where is she?"

"In her room. She is resting because she has been feeling a little low."

"Because of our forthcoming trip?" Andrea asked quickly.

"Maybe, but she has not put forth any objection and sometimes almost seems to be looking forward to it," Chloe replied.

"Then you have been doing a good job," her sister commended. "Come, let's look in on her."

Lady Jane was sitting before her mirror while her maid pinned up her hair, and she saw the two girls as they entered. "Andrea! I didn't hear you return. How was your trip?"

"I only just got back, Ladyjane, and everything is to rights, so we may have an easy mind. Mr. Jones, as always, is up to the mark and deals extremely well with any problem. I have decided to increase his salary, for we would be in very bad loaf if he should ever decide to leave our service."

"Mama," Chloe interrupted, "do see what the Duke

sent Andrea. Isn't it droll?" she asked with dancing eyes.

"They're lovely," Lady Jane remarked appreciatively. "I wonder wherever he found them?"

"That *is* a poser," her stepdaughter mused thoughtfully. "Do you suppose he has a gypsy dancer in tow?"

"Andrea!" both of the others exclaimed with shocked expressions.

"All right," said a shamefully amused voice, "I'll give him the benefit of the doubt and write a pretty thank you. Now show me your favors."

Chloe ran to her room and brought back the ornate silver filigree dance cardholder and Lady Jane displayed her ivory fan. Looking at their little cache, Andrea remarked that she was of the mind that these gifts were none of them just tokens and bordered on the extravagant, which made her question the propriety of keeping them.

"I do not think it is of too great an importance, Andrea. If it were just one of us, it would be different, but, in this case, I think we might accept graciously," her stepmother reassured her.

"Well, if you say so, Ladyjane, I will not scruple, but if anyone should ever ask how I came by these earrings, I'm afraid I shall be obliged to give a devious answer. Now tell me what you two have been up to while I was away."

Once again Chloe ran out and came back with the copies of the *Belle Assemblée*, which had several pages turned back and had obviously suffered from excessive examination. Andrea became quickly caught up in Chloe's enthusiasms because she did love pretty clothes and found herself exclaiming over some of the new designs and remarking favorably on the shorter skirts, which were so much more practical and of easier care. They all were so engrossed with this pleasant occupation that they were surprised to be called for dinner and reluctantly put aside their lists of fancies and requirements which had grown to alarming proportions.

"Well, I shall have to write to Mr. Barnstable to ask him to be sure we have plenty of ready funds because we are apparently going to dig deep," Andrea remarked. Seeing a couple of chagrined faces, she reassured them, laughingly, "Do not worry. We have more than enough blunt and can easily afford to dress ourselves elegantly. Besides, we owe it to ourselves for I am persuaded we have become quite dowdy."

At dinner they addressed themselves to the problems endemic to a prolonged stay in town, and Lady Jane said she had already sent word ahead to have the rooms on the third floor redone for the two girls, "for I presumed we would move into the house in Queen Anne's Gate."

"Yes, we might as well," Andrea agreed. "It would be much simpler than trying to establish ourselves in a rented property, and we really do not need a larger place because I am sure Aunt Henrietta will insist on our holding Chloe's ball at Retford House. Have you written to her of our coming?"

"Yes, I posted the letter a few days ago, and I have been dreading a reply ever since because I am sure she will try to persuade us to stay with them," Lady Jane admitted.

"I shall write also emphasizing our intention to be private and ask for her to arrange to have a pianoforte installed in the first-floor drawing room."

"Oh, Andy," Chloe said gratefully, "I am so glad you thought of that. I never imagined there would not be one. I should be lost without it."

"I do hope you will discipline yourself to practice at least an hour every day."

"I mean to be very good, Andy, for," Chloe explained with a twinkle in her eye, "I know you would not hesitate to pack us up and come home."

"Good heavens! What a bear I must seem!"

"Well, would you not?"

"Yes," Andrea replied with a contrived fierce expression, "and don't you forget it."

CHAPTER FIVE

And so, the next couple of weeks the three ladies continued to make plans for their journey, and there was much communication back and forth with the Hanleys to coordinate arrangements. Finally, it was all agreed they should leave on the sixth of March, proceeding in a leisurely fashion so they might take in some of the more interesting sights along the way.

It was decided to take two traveling carriages to allow for the comfort of the traveler. Lady Jane would companion Katherine Hanley on the first stage of the journey while Andrea and Chloe would ride together. Later they would change positions and so enjoy a diversion. Jonathan had assumed responsibility for making proper arrangements for changing and resting the horses and would occasionally join one or the other pair of ladies inside the carriages instead of riding pillion. A third chaise had been hired to transport the servants and additional luggage, and so it was an impressive caravan that started out on the road to Exeter.

Since there was not a great deal of interest along the first part of the route, they had agreed to make a long first day of it, breaking the journey for a light lunch at Axminster and then settling down for a longer stretch following the road north of Blackmoor Vale to stop for the night at an inn in Shaftesbury. The second morning they stopped at Salisbury to see the cathedral and drove by the Old Sarum Hill site. They continued on to Winchester, arriving in time to explore the cathedral there as well, being entertained by Mrs. Hanley's lectures on its historical importance.

That night at the inn at Guildford they enjoyed a lively discussion about their journey so far. Katherine Hanley commended her friends for their affability in indulging her ruling passion "because most people find such fusty matters exceedingly tiresome, although they think it quite elevating to investigate some other country's ancient ruins. Now that the war is ended, I expect we shall see another exodus."

"Yes," Jonathan agreed, "for, as soon as the Bourbons returned the second time, Paris was overrun with civilians, mostly English."

"Well, I must confess to a curiosity myself," Andrea admitted, "and I refuse to be shamed, for it is all very well for you to decry such an ambition when you have already seen all these things yourself."

"Touché, my dear," Mrs. Hanley said as she laughed good naturedly. "You are right, of course, and," she added lightly, "perhaps we should all consider making the Grand Tour together."

It was raining when they crossed the Thames at Westminster Bridge so their view of the skyline was somewhat obscured. But they could see the church spires faintly through the mist. They pulled to a halt almost immediately since Queen Anne's Gate was across from St. James's Park not far from the river. Jonathan helped the Wycliff ladies out of the carriages and saw them settled in their house before continuing on with his mother to his uncle's establishment on Curzon Street.

The servants gathered to receive their mistresses and quickly disposed of the small portmanteaus that held the personal necessaries which had been required the last few days. Chloe was excitedly investigating the rooms and stopped for a minute to test the sound of the pianoforte before checking out the master bedrooms on the second floor. She then climbed still farther to find her own room, which she immediately recognized because it was decorated in her favorite shade of blue. She flounced on the bed for a moment and then threw off her pelisse and went to the other side of the house to inspect Andrea's larger room, which was done in bolder colors—shades of red and beiges. She heard her sister coming and ran to the door to clasp her hands and swing her about.

"Andy, it is so exciting. I can't believe I am really here."

"My dear Chloe, I am sure the servants must think a whirlwind has arrived. You must give them a chance to become acquainted with your high spirits, or they will think you have run mad."

"Andy, you are such a tease. Do you like your room? Mama and I thought the colors would please you."

"Yes, darling, it is elegant. I particularly like the draperies and bedcovering and the lovely écritoire. I believe it is new."

"Probably from Jeffrey. I think Aunt Henrietta called on him for assistance."

"Then I shall have to thank him and make sure he will accept reimbursement."

"I doubt he will," Chloe said knowingly. "Now come see my room. Guess what color it is."

"I can't possibly."

With a happy laugh, Chloe dragged her sister across the hall and Andrea agreed that the decor was lovely, a perfect setting for a fairy princess.

Lady Jane came to join them to see if everything had been done satisfactorily and, being assured by her daughters that they were well pleased, suggested they call the maids to prepare baths for them so they might soothe the minor aches they had acquired from four days of travel.

During a late breakfast the next morning, the three ladies made their plans for the day.

"We have so many things to do," Andrea said with a gesture of uncertainty, "but I expect we had better start with the dressmakers, so we may have at least a few gowns ready in case we should receive visitors. I am hoping, though, that we can keep our presence relatively quiet for a while. Fortunately, we are a little beforehand and may beat the rush to all the shops. This business of assembling three complete wardrobes bids fair to be a major project, so we might as well get on with it if you are ready."

An hour later the ladies sent for Thomas and asked to be driven to the fashionable shops in the area marked by Oxford and Bond streets.

By four o'clock Andrea observed that her companions, having spent several hours examining the wares of the modistes and milliners, were definitely wearing down. She took pity on them, suggesting that they leave off for the day because they had enough to think over for the moment. They would try to decide that evening on which things they could safely commission immediately.

When they turned into Queen Anne's Gate, they noticed that an elegant curricle, with a young tiger on guard, had pulled up in front of their house. They soon recognized the crest and hurried inside to welcome their first visitor. Carson informed them, "The Earl of Stockwell has just arrived and said he would wait in the library."

The ladies' return had been heard on the next floor and a genial face peered at them over the banister of the curving stairway. "Hello, my loves. Have you been raising the expectations of our shopkeepers?"

Lady Jane answered, "Hello, Jeffrey, dear. Yes, we have and you can't imagine how accommodating they have been."

"Yes, I can. They are obviously anticipating a windfall."

He waited for them and kissed each on the cheek as they passed him, whispering mischievously to Andrea, "Hello, darling," for which he received a blighting look that in no way depressed him. He had long become accustomed to her efforts to dissuade him from his aspirations. He slipped his arm around Chloe's waist as they reentered the library and quizzed her, "So, my lovely cousin, you have come to dazzle the *ton*."

"Oh, Jeffrey," the girl answered with sparkling eyes, "don't be such a humbug. I am merely to be presented."

He smiled at her and turned to Andrea and said, "It's

marvelous to see you, my love. I have missed you dreadfully."

"Now *there's* a bag of moonshine," Andrea accused ungraciously, taking off her bonnet and pelisse and throwing them on a chair, "considering it's been months since we've been honored by your presence."

Jeffrey found that reproachful remark encouraging and jumped on it instantly. "So! You have missed me."

With an appreciative grin, Andrea replied unpromisingly, "Let us say rather that I have noticed your absence."

"Miserable girl! Nevertheless, I take heart and you know very well I would have come to Devon betimes if Andrew had not told me before Christmas that he was pushing for you to arrange Chloe's debut, so I have been waiting—impatiently, I might add."

"Such a silver tongue you have, my dear cousin. It quite devastates me."

"I wish that were true," he noted with a wry grin.

"Jeffrey," Lady Jane put forth, trying to distract him, "I must thank you for seeing to putting the house in order. Everything is excellently arranged."

"Which brings us to the matter of the écritoire," Andrea announced resolutely. "It is an exquisite piece and I should like to be sent a bill for it."

The Earl studied her determined face with unsympathetic amusement and told her curtly, "Andrea, don't be a goose. I have no intention of allowing you to pay. Can't you accept a gift graciously? I don't often succumb to temptation."

"Jeffrey, it is shockingly expensive and you cannot just expect me to condone such presumptions."

"The room needed another piece and it gave me great pleasure to find just the thing I thought you would like. You know that furnishings are one of my enthusiasms, and I found several things for my new townhouse when I was rummaging, so put a damper on it, my girl. I refuse to discuss it." He turned to Lady Jane. "My mother sends her love and will call on you in a day or two, but she hopes you will come for a family dinner Sunday next."

"That will be lovely, Jeffrey. We shall look forward to it."

"Good. I will look in on you before then, however, and am anticipating squiring you around. May I accompany you on some of your shopping forages?"

"No, Jeffrey," Andrea declared adamantly. "If today is any example, we are going to be extremely harried and we do not need another voice."

"I hope you realize what a stalwart swain you have, my love. A lesser man would find your unamiable manner quite depressing."

"Oh, Jeffrey, I *am* sorry," Andrea said contritely, realizing she had been unnecessarily uncivil. "Give us two weeks so we may not embarrass you with our dowdiness, and then we will accept your escort gladly."

"All right," he agreed. "I will see to your stables and two weeks from today we shall ride. Now I will be the gentleman and take my leave for you all look done up and are probably wishing me at Jericho."

While Chloe practiced that evening, Lady Jane and Andrea went over their notes to coordinate their selections and presently called their colleague to join them to give her opinion.

"Tomorrow we must take your new bonnet with us, Chloe, to match it up with material for a walking dress, and I am thinking the blue embroidered muslin we saw at Madame Claire's might be just the thing."

"Yes, and I have been thinking also, Andy, that the yellow silk dress with the green satin ribbons would be lovely for Mama once it were properly fitted."

"I agree with you," her sister approved, with an instant appreciation of Chloe's thoughtfulness.

"Oh, no," Lady Jane protested, "I shall not need anything so grand. I will not be attending the fashionable affairs."

"Of course you will," Andrea contradicted firmly, "Chloe's ball, if nothing else, and if you think we are going to see you play the part of fusty matron while we dress ourselves bang up to the nines, you are wide of the mark.

You are only thirty-six and look nothing like it, so do not imagine we will let you outshine us, but—forget about whether or not you need something and just concentrate on indulging your fancies. We are going to be shamefully extravagant and I for one intend to enjoy it. I think tomorrow we should order new riding habits, and I have my heart set on the elegant black velvet we saw on Bruton Place."

And so, Lady Jane let herself be drawn into the deliberations and admitted that she had always coveted an emerald-green riding dress, prompting the girls to declare that finding the very thing would be their first priority.

After a morning of canvassing some of the shops they had missed the day before, they settled down to serious business in the afternoon and began making selections and placing orders.

Chloe and Lady Jane, having similar tastes, found themselves very much in accord in the matter of colors and styles. Andrea did not interfere, merely giving her opinion when solicited and approving their choices, which were always tasteful, ladylike fashions in a succession of pastel colors. Andrea possessed more exotic tastes and felt she was now of an age to safely wear the more dramatic styles and colors she favored. She unhesitatingly ordered gowns in shades of red, orange, and amber and the dark, brilliant blues and greens. Her one concession to at least token demureness was a starkly simple ivory ballgown she thought would be more appropriate for Chloe's come-out.

In the evening once again the dedicated shoppers reviewed their accomplishments for the day and planned for the next. One such day followed another with the added ordeal of standing for fittings, and Chloe was reminded of her sister's warning about the tiresome and repetitious discomforts of shopping, but she did not complain because it was all new to her and she was fascinated by the proceedings.

Often Jeffrey and Jonathan stopped by and occasionally had dinner with them. The Marchioness arrived one early morning to discuss plans for Chloe's presentation ball, which she had scheduled for the last week in April, but the Wycliff ladies limited their visiting to the family dinner at Retford House. The Marquess and his wife welcomed the Devon clan with great warmth, mildly scolding them for their long delay and predicting they would come more often once they became acquainted with the varied attractions of London.

"Perhaps you are right, Uncle Edward," Andrea admitted fairly. "So far we have been having a famous time."

"Oh, yes," Chloe bubbled, "for it is the greatest fun to visit all the shops, though I own it is very confusing to have so much to choose from."

"You will learn to be selective, Chloe, my dear, and develop your own style," her aunt assured her, "and I must say you all look charming this evening. I am sure you will be the most fashionable ladies in town."

"Well, if we aren't, it won't be for not trying," Andrea remarked frankly.

They all laughed at her candor but the Marchioness chided lightly, "Andrea, I do hope you will try to control your whimsical nature and learn to dissemble just a little. You show a lamentable lack of reserve and sometimes say the most unseemly things."

"Oh, no, Mother," Jeffrey objected hastily with a devilish expression. "Do not try to repress her. Granted—she may set the *ton* on its ears, but what a lark it promises to be."

"Jeff! What a perfectly unfair presumption. I assure you I am quite capable of comporting myself properly in society," Andrea protested indignantly, "especially since I am to chaperon Chloe," she added, taking away some of the effectiveness of the first part of her speech.

Her aunt looked at her with some skepticism, remembering her other excursions into society. Andrea had not committed any damaging solecism, but one never knew what she might say to whom. More than once she had been politely described as "somewhat out of the common."

Chloe turned to her younger cousin. "Eddie, you promised to introduce me to some of your friends—especially young ladies—for I don't know anyone and I do not want to be a charge upon Andy all the time."

"Of course, Chloe. I have plans to do so. In fact, I had intended to ask if I might bring a young lady to meet you later in the week," the young man answered.

"A *special* young lady?" Chloe teased.

"Well, yes," her cousin admitted, reddening a little.

"Oh, Eddie, how exciting! Who is she?"

"Chloe, I must tell you," he said patiently with a sober air, "that I am known as Ned now. I hope you will try to remember. And the young lady is Miss Naomi Barrington. She is a daughter of Lord Thomas Barrington, who is a second son of the Earl of Clarkson. Her mother is a granddaughter of the Duke of Sidmouth."

As "Ned" was cataloguing the antecedents of his new romantic interest, Andrea gazed at him in amusement and glanced searchingly at the Marquess, realizing suddenly how like the father the son was becoming—a somewhat pompous but serious, worthy gentleman—and a little smile played at her mouth. She looked up to find Jeffrey watching her with a mischievous eye and had to turn her head to keep from laughing. How strange, she thought, that Jeffrey should be so different from the other members of his immediate family. He could almost have been a changeling were it not for the fact that he clearly favored his uncle in appearance and in personality—much more than Andrew did. She heard Chloe saying, "Well, Ned, I shall be pleased to meet Miss Barrington. Is she my age?"

"She is just eighteen and is to be presented this year also. Her home is in Norfolk and she will be arriving in town with her parents in a day or two. I am sure you will find her an amiable companion. I have told her you are a very good girl, and she need not scruple to be friends with you."

"Oh, Ed—Ned—thank you. It is very sweet of you to say so," Chloe remarked with a somewhat daunted and not too eager expression, being a little put down by her cousin's less than glowing description of her.

Jeffrey laughed and reassured her, "Don't let Ned's

manner unsettle you, love. Miss Barrington is really a very nice young lady and you will get on famously."

Chloe dimpled at him and said in obvious relief, as she had been having visions of being obliged to spend a lot of time with a prim sobersides, "Well, of course, Jeffrey."

At the end of the evening Jeffrey reminded Andrea that he would be bringing horses to them for approval and that he was holding them all to their promise to ride with him on Tuesday. "I have acquired some sweet goers for your use during the Season. Afterwards, I will add them to my stables, which I am just beginning to set up—and no objections, please," he commanded as he noticed Andrea's forbidding look. "Ned and I will come to escort you and bring Jonathan with us."

"Oh, but I do wish you would not worry about me," Lady Jane demurred. "I shall be perfectly content to remain at home."

"Nonsense, Ladyjane," Andrea said shortly. "You know very well that you adore riding, and we are certainly not going to allow you to play the part of a recluse."

"Of course not, Mama," Chloe concurred. "We should feel quite dispirited if you did not come."

Answering Andrea's silent appeal, Jeffrey added his persuasions, and after this successful campaign it was agreed that they would ride out at ten o'clock two days hence and then return to Queen Anne's Gate for a luncheon.

On the appointed day the two younger ladies had primed themselves for announcing their presence to the *ton* and their mother had resigned herself, so it was a sprightly group that rode along St. James's Park past Buckingham House and Green Park to the bridle paths at Hyde Park. The morning was brisk but sunny and the Park was unusually inhabited for so early in the year, though the party was able to enjoy a sedate gallop and the ladies found themselves very well pleased with their mounts. Jeffrey, being acquainted with their fine horsemanship, had chosen spirited horses that offered them at least a mild challenge. Occasionally, they stopped to be introduced to friends of one of the gentlemen and were obviously being catalogued for future reference.

When they were almost ready to leave, Jonathan reined in beside Andrea and said softly, "The Duke and Lady Carrington have just entered the lanes."

Andrea glanced up and was at the same time recognized. The gentleman pulled up a distance away and stared in surprise. With one of her eloquent expressions she regarded him squarely and then, letting her eyes stray to his companion before favoring him with a contemptuous look, she turned her horse slowly and deliberately so that her back was to him and calmly urged her companions to follow her out of the Park.

David sat almost in shock for a moment, having determinedly forgotten what a master of the consummate setdown she was. After leaving Devon he had resolved to block her out of his mind and had thrown himself back into his flirtations but, seeing her now, he was totally aware that the attempt had been in vain. He was furious at being caught out already and suddenly felt an acute distaste for his cool, beautiful companion, whose face rarely showed any emotion. He compared it to the dark-eyed expressive image that never left one in doubt as to her feelings.

Lady Carrington noticed his withdrawal and followed his eyes to the retreating group. She asked other riders who had stopped to greet them if that were the Earl of Stockwell who was just leaving.

"Yes, and he has stolen a march on all of us because he has a special relationship with the ladies in the party. They are his cousins and aunt from Devon," one young man replied regretfully.

"I see," the lady mused. She turned back to the Duke, who still seemed preoccupied, and said, "Isn't that the family you visited for a few days?"

"Yes," he answered curtly.

"Which one are you after?" she asked perceptively, if crudely.

"That is none of your affair, Marcia," he replied.

"Oh, I think it is, my dear. I know you must marry, but I do hope you choose wisely. A jealous wife could be such a nuisance."

The woman's presumption that he was hers to command angered David to the point of wanting to enlighten her forthwith, but he knew at once that Andrea had been right when she warned him he was not going to find it so easy to break off this affair.

As the group passed the newcomers, Chloe had recognized the Duke, but she refrained from commenting on it until they were all sitting down to lunch.

"Who was that lady with the Duke this morning?" she asked curiously.

"Lady Carrington," Jonathan answered simply.

"Is she one of his—?"

"Yes, Chloe, she is," Andrea announced abruptly.

"I thought she must be, the way you made us cut him."

Jeffrey looked at his cousins in surprise. "When did you meet Kensington?"

"He came to call on us in Devon after the holidays," Lady Jane replied.

"Why?" he asked suspiciously, turning to Andrea.

"Jeffrey, I will tell you," she said, "but I am trusting you and Ned to keep it under your hats." She raised her brows questioningly and received an affirmative nod from both gentlemen. She then reported, "He is hanging out for a wife under pressure from his grandmother and came to check out Chloe on Andrew's recommendation."

"My God! Are you serious? I hope you threw a spoke in the wheel. Chloe is no match for him."

"Jeffrey, please do not be so indelicate," Andrea admonished, adding with a reflective expression, "Perhaps he has retreated from his purpose since he obviously is connected with an ineligible lady, although I admit I thought, when he left us, he was determined to put it to the touch. However, let us not ruin our lovely day by dwelling on such a disagreeable subject."

They all willingly turned their minds to more pleasant matters, including current entertainments being offered by the theaters, and it was decided that Jeffrey and Jonathan would escort Chloe and Andrea to a play on Friday night.

CHAPTER SIX

While these discussions were taking place in Queen Anne's Gate, a private monologue was being enacted on Grosvenor Square. David had returned home immediately after dropping Lady Carrington off at her Park Lane residence, leaving a very outraged lady who was not at all pleased at having had their morning riding excursion cut short.

Her escort, however, found himself hardly able to hide his impatience to be rid of her, and he refused in a rather abrupt fashion to be coerced into any further commitments for the day. Now he was taking stock of his predicament, trying to decide just exactly what it was he wanted and how he was going to get it. The answer to the first part of this poser was not in doubt, for it was clear that he wanted Andrea and had from the first day he had met her; but the second half of the question presented a bit more of a problem and was not easily solved. He was definitely in her black books, as she had so clearly reaffirmed that morning. But he knew without a shadow of a doubt that he would never be a truly happy man if he could not have her for his wife. Certainly he would have to give up all his flirtatious diversions which, contrary to the general consensus, he would not look upon as any great hardship; he was actually a man of strong determination and self-control despite his reputation as a womanizer. As Andrea had so keenly informed Chloe, he merely took advantage of opportunities willingly offered.

With this fact clearly established in his mind, the Duke determined to make the break with Marcia Carrington immediately. He knew he would have to suffer virulent recriminations, but he resigned himself to taking his medicine and drove to her home to inform her of his decision.

As expected, Lady Carrington took violent exception to being dropped so abruptly. David stoically listened to her threats and accusations, thinking how different women could look when they were angry. Andrea, in one of her passionate tirades, could stir a man's blood; but this woman, with her cold, arrogant fury, merely bored him.

When he finally made his escape, he breathed a sigh of relief but thought ruefully, "So much for supposing I could slip through that one." She might calm down but he had no great hopes for it and suspected he had better be prepared for some malicious mischief-making.

He returned to his house and announced to the butler that he would be staying in that evening and would dine with his grandmother.

The Dowager Duchess was surprised to see him at the table and quizzed, "Are you taking a respite from your frolics?"

"In a way," he answered cryptically.

"What's that supposed to mean?" the Dowager demanded impatiently.

"I have decided to follow your direction."

"Whom have you chosen?" she asked instantly with an eager expression.

David had to laugh and teased, "What makes you think I have?"

"Well, haven't you?"

He still held off but eased into the subject. "I have never told you about my trip to Devon, have I?"

"You know you have not. Have you decided on young Chloe after all?"

"There were three ladies there, you know, ranging from ages seventeen to thirty-six."

"My God! Surely you have not chosen the mother!" the Duchess asked in shock.

"It would have been more seemly than to offer for a girl young enough to be my daughter so I was informed."

"David, if you don't stop equivocating, I will rap your fingers," the old lady said in exasperation.

He grinned and proceeded to tell her the whole of it, finishing, "When I saw Andrea today, everything became perfectly clear. She is the only woman I will ever marry."

"Well," his grandmother commented, reluctantly accepting his declaration, for it was obvious that he was serious, "from what you have said, it doesn't sound very promising. How do you propose to turn things around?"

"I don't know. Underhandedly, I expect," he admitted. "I don't think she would be receptive to a direct attack. I'm afraid I shall have to use Chloe."

"I hardly think that will be appreciated."

"It's one sure way to be favored with Andrea's company. She'd do anything to keep her sister out of my clutches," David said, grinning.

"When are you going to start this campaign?"

"Not for a week or so. I have to let my unencumbered state be remarked. Should you like my escort to any of your engagements?"

"So—I am to be a party to this charade."

"You were the instigator and I think I can fairly expect your cooperation. It would be providential if you should take a fancy to the Wycliffs on the basis of your affection for Andrew if for no other reason."

"I'm agreeable, my boy. You don't have to inveigle me. I am looking forward to an uncommonly interesting Season, besides wishing to see you settled, though it appears that to gain your end you may have to resort to an abduction."

"And so I will, if it comes to that!" he declared vehemently, causing his grandmother to experience a foreboding.

She informed him, ready to promote his case, "I am going to a musical soirée tomorrow night, and I would not be unhappy to attend the theater later in the week."

"All right. How about Friday?"

"That's excellent."

"And what time is the affair tomorrow night?"

"Eight o'clock."

"You have yourself an escort, my love," David said, as he rose from the table and offered his arm, leading her to the library, where they spent a quiet, companionable evening reading aloud some of Walter Scott's new work.

By the next afternoon it had become fairly well-known that the Duke had broken with Lady Carrington—not by that lady's admission, but the subculture of servants maintained a grapevine that spread news like wildfire so that many ladies heard of the break from their abigails and, in turn, circulated the rumor in their social circles.

In the evening the Duke's appearance with his grandmother sent speculative whispers around the room, but he blithely ignored the gossips and concentrated on making himself agreeable to the more conservative guests, particularly to the Marchioness of Retford, who was somehow drawn into a conversation about Chloe's musical talent. This led to other related subjects, and he soon perceived that the lady was inclined to promote a match between her son and Andrea, an undesirable aspiration David had suspected and categorically deplored.

The next day the Duke stopped by the Dandy Club and encountered the Earl, who was bargaining for some horses one of his friends wanted to sell. David asked conversationally if he had news from Andrew and grinned noncommittally when Jeffrey remarked meaningfully he had heard that his cousin had sent him on a wild goose chase to Devon. They made an arrangement to meet that evening for cards at Brook's, where David stayed late enough so it would be obvious he did not have another appointment.

Having learned that Andrea would be at the theater, he reminded his grandmother of their engagement, and they arrived at their box early so they might observe the rest of the gallery.

Very soon David saw the two couples enter a box on the other side, and he felt an immediate quickening of the pulses as he called the Duchess's attention to the party. In fact, all eyes were directed to the same point, for Andrea in bright red and Chloe in sapphire blue offered a glorious sight to behold.

The Dowager chuckled appreciatively. "They certainly know how to steal the limelight. Such a remarkable combination. But I can see why you chose as you did. She is magnificent—as beautiful as Andrew is handsome."

"If it were only that, I wouldn't be in such sad case. You will understand when you've met her," David said. And then he swore under his breath.

"What's wrong?" the Duchess questioned sharply.

"That shameless girl is wearing the earrings I sent her!"

"That displeases you?" his grandmother asked in a puzzled voice.

"She didn't have to wear them to dazzle some other man!" he answered darkly.

"I'm beginning to see what you mean," the Dowager remarked uneasily. "You're quite irrational where she's concerned."

"I know it," he said wryly. "I shall probably commit any number of follies before this is over, if my present sentiments are any indication. I am discovering that I have a very jealous nature and I find it insupportable that she should dress like that for someone else!"

At that moment, as though she could feel his eyes on her, Andrea turned to look in his direction. He smiled, bowed his head, and then sat back wondering how she would react this evening. There was a slight pause as she glanced at his companion and found herself locking eyes with an elegant bright-eyed little old lady. She was caught fairly and reluctantly acknowledged his greeting with a nod. She murmured something to the others in the box, unintentionally prompting Chloe to look immediately across the theater and smile broadly when the Duke saluted her. It was merely a friendly gesture on her part and she did not pay much mind after. She was so excited with her first night out that she found everything worthy of her attention and was thoroughly entertained the whole evening.

The Duchess scolded her grandson, "You ought to be

ashamed of yourself to think of playing a slippery game with that pretty little thing. She's a born innocent."

"It won't hurt her. Better me than some other less scrupulous bounder. Jonathan may have cause to thank me."

During intermission the Dowager expected him to present himself at the Earl's box but David declined, saying, "No, I will not approach her tonight and so demonstrate my sensibilities for I am sure she expects I will try to take advantage of her acknowledgment for which, by the way, I thank you, my love. She didn't dare cut me outright with you staring her down."

"Yes, I could see it took some self-discipline on her part," his grandmother agreed and they both laughed heartily and sat back to watch the final act, leaving a little before the end to avoid the crush.

The next day Ned brought his young lady for an introduction and Chloe was delighted to claim a new friend. Miss Naomi Barrington proved to be charming and sweet, if shy, and soon found herself very much a part of the little group that welcomed her without reservation. By the time the visit had come to an end she was received as one of them and was pleased to be included in many of their planned activities. In return, she invited Chloe and Andrea to tea the next week to meet some of her other friends and cousins.

So it was that Chloe was immediately accepted by the younger ladies, several of whom would also make their debut. Her lively personality and unspectacular loveliness were recognized as an asset to their undeclared purpose of calling attention to themselves, and she found herself much sought after so that she often had to be subtly reminded of her promise to devote some of her time and energy to her music.

A week passed during which it was brought to Andrea's notice by friends and family that the Duke of Kensington seemed to have abandoned his loose ways. His sudden uprightness could not go unremarked.

Andrea was not in doubt what this new posture portended and her nerves were on edge waiting for him to make his move. The suspense ended one day when the three returned to their house and found the Duke's calling card. The next morning, as they were preparing to leave, a message arrived with one of his servants who had been ordered to wait for an answer. The ladies were invited for a drive to Kew Gardens or to lunch at the Clarendon Hotel and an excursion to see some of London's attractions, for he was anticipating repaying them for their gracious hospitality.

"Oh, dear," Lady Jane lamented, "he makes it impossible to refuse. We can't say we are always busy."

"*I* could," Andrea said curtly, "but I know you could not be so uncivil, and I suppose he will contrive to make contact sooner or later anyway. What are your plans for the next few days, Chloe?"

"Well, so far, I have no engagements Friday."

"So soon? I hoped we might postpone it for a week or more."

"Andy!" Chloe gurgled, "he's not going to eat us."

"Don't be so sure. My intuition tells me he has some nefarious purpose," her sister advised with one of her glowering looks.

"I suppose we could put him off for a while," Lady Jane suggested. "Should we say next Tuesday?"

"All right. He will probably show up the next night at Almack's anyway when he discovers, and I feel sure he will, that Emily has sent vouchers for Chloe."

And so, Lady Jane composed an answer and asked Carson to hand it to the Duke's messenger, after which Andrea tried to ignore her presentiments of impending disaster and willed herself to enjoy the visit to the Paxton residence, where they were invited for lunch.

David had a strong desire to box her ears when he read the note. He decided he would leave town for a few days to attend the races since he was going to be forced to cool his heels for a week.

105

CHAPTER SEVEN

On Monday Lady Jane received a note from the Duke stating that he would call for them at eleven the next morning unless they should tell him differently. As the weather appeared favorable, he would tentatively plan to take them to the Royal Botanical Gardens.

Precisely on the hour he pulled up at Queen Anne's Gate with his barouche and in a very few minutes was helping three fashionable ladies into the carriage. He asked Andrea if she would care to ride with him on the box so the others might not be crowded and she agreed, knowing full well he would ask Chloe if she did not accept. On a lovely day, with a groom riding behind guarding a picnic basket provisioned from the Duke's kitchen, they began their excursion, passing through Chelsea and Kensington and crossing the Thames at Kew Bridge. The drive took less than an hour and the Duke's expert handling of the ribbons assured his passengers of a comfortable ride, which even Andrea enjoyed because David took care not to provoke her. All in all, he played the perfect host, giving them each equal time, engaging them in easy conversation, and, as a result, promoted his new image very effectively, although Andrea maintained her shield of skepticism.

By tacit agreement the others adapted themselves to Lady Jane's enthusiasms and Andrea, in justice, had to give the Duke credit for divining and abetting the girls' determination that their mother should come out of her cocoon. He walked by her side as they roamed leisurely over the grounds and helped her identify the profusion of herbs and flowers, shrubs and trees that gave Kew the reputation of being one of the foremost botanical gardens in the world. After a delicious lunch, they investigated the greenhouse and orangery, the Great Pagoda, and several classical temples that the great architect William Chambers had built in the last half of the previous century at the behest of the Princess Dowager, the Regent's grandmother.

The day passed quickly and finally Lady Jane came to a realization of the time. In trying to apologize for her absorption, she looked so guilty that they all laughed and assured her that they had not spent so enjoyable a day since they had come to town. And so, in total charity with one another, a condition that David found exceedingly auspicious, they returned to the carriage. When they were deposited at Queen Anne's Gate, all three ladies thanked their escort prettily and he promised another such excursion.

Before the Duke left them, he asked if they would be attending Almack's the next evening and Chloe responded eagerly, "Oh, yes, for you know that Lady Cowper is a friend of Andrea's and she has sent vouchers."

"I see. That explains some things," David remarked wryly, glancing at Andrea. "I must suppose you already have an escort?"

"Jeffrey and Jonathan are coming for us. Mama has not yet agreed to accompany us, but we are still hoping to persuade her."

He smiled and turned to Lady Jane. "Lady Wycliff, I believe you are up against formidable odds and, if your daughters should win their case, I am pleased to offer my services to bring you home early should you find the demands of the evening too overpowering."

"Why, thank you, Your Grace, that is very kind of you, but I really have no plans to attend. It will not be necessary for me to do so since both the Marchioness and her daughter will be there."

David, on cue from Andrea, did not pursue the matter and drove back to Grosvenor Square to announce to his grandmother his intention of accompanying her to Almack's the next evening.

In the manner of a clever strategist, he persuaded the Duchess to be early so he might claim his dances before they were all bespoken. As he had no doubt that the crush would be immediate, he stationed himself with an eye on the door and was the first to reach the party when they arrived.

He danced first with Chloe and then the quadrille with Andrea, neither of which exercise lent itself very well to conversation. He was impatient for his waltz so he might have Andrea all to himself.

When he finally was able to place his arm about her waist and swing her onto the floor, he was reaching a bursting point from having watched her give attention to all her other conquests, particularly to her cousin, who seemed much too familiar for David's peace of mind.

"You and your sister are huge successes and put all the other ladies in the shade," he told her. "I hope they will not resent your popularity."

"Oh, I doubt it," Andrea said with a laugh. "I am much too old for the lovely young things to worry about and Chloe is never disliked."

"I will agree with you on only half of that statement. No one could discount any woman as beautiful as you are."

She looked at him warily, wondering if he were going to press his suit, but merely said, "Thank you, but I was not fishing for a compliment."

"I know you were not," the Duke assured her, swinging her with an especially grand flourish that almost caught her off guard.

"Chloe has certainly blossomed spectacularly. She looks a far cry from the little schoolgirl I saw in Devon."

"Yes, she is gaining a great deal of confidence from being a leader among her new friends and her stylish clothes changed her appearance remarkably. I suppose it had to happen sooner or later but it does make me feel rather apprehensive."

"For her or yourself?"

"How perceptive of you," she admired. "For both, I suppose."

"It's about time you looked to your own interests," he noted abruptly. "It won't be long before she's no longer your responsibility. She will be betrothed before the year is out."

Andrea looked at him keenly, trying to divine his meaning. "You're not going to make mischief in that quarter, are you?"

David studied her closely for a moment, wanting to reassure her but feeling he must not give up his advantage. "It is within your power to prevent that, Andrea," he said softly. "The offer stands."

The sudden seriousness of his manner put her out of countenance for a few moments until she could recover with a hostile reproof. "That sounds very much like a threat."

"I'm sorry you take it like that. I was hoping you would look upon it as a profession," he told her regretfully.

Taking a deep breath, she admonished, "I hope you will not raise that subject again. I have told you my feelings already."

"So you did, but I did not think you knew me well enough to make a fair judgment—nor do you yet; however, that can be remedied."

As the dance was ending, he announced, "I have been ordered by my grandmother to bring you to meet her. That scamp of a brother of yours is quite a favorite with her."

Andrea laughed and commented, "He does rather have a way with the ladies."

David looked at her quizzingly. "And it amuses you?"

She seemed startled and then admitted, "I see. You think I am inconsistent and no doubt you are right, but, what it really amounts to is that one is inclined to countenance such foibles in an unmarried brother but not in a husband. However, I do not approve and often call him to book because, in spite of his resolution to remain a bachelor, I have hopes of his eventual realization of his responsibilities."

"He is young, Andrea, and has time yet. He will tire of his free-wheeling life, I'm sure. I am six years older and have only recently passed out of that stage," he remarked meaningfully.

At this additional oblique reference to his attachment, Andrea stopped short and asked hesitantly as an obvious thought struck her, "Your Grace, might I not meet the Duchess another time?"

"Are you afraid of what people will think?" he teased with a glint in his eye.

"Well!" she exclaimed heatedly, "you will have to admit that it is suggestive."

"Don't you imagine my grandmother will think it rather peculiar if we stop our progression now and turn our backs on her?"

"Couldn't you explain?" she begged.

"No," David answered uncooperatively.

"You abominable man!" Andrea accused vehemently with flashing eyes, once again displaying a lightening change of mood.

The Duke only grinned and, placing her hand on his arm, marched her firmly to his grandmother to perform the introductions.

Andrea made a small curtsy and murmured politely, still obviously reluctant, "I am pleased to meet you, Your Grace."

The Dowager cocked her head and commented dryly, "So—you two have been quarreling again. It would be more seemly if you could refrain from making a public display."

Not being accustomed to receiving such an unsubtle reprimand, Andrea raised her chin and almost came right back but quickly bit her tongue, much to the Duke's amusement. She acknowledged humbly, "You are right, of course, Your Grace, but I'm afraid I have never learned to dissemble."

"Well, I can't really deplore that as a fault, my dear," the Duchess assured her. "Now do sit down and talk with me for a while. I am fascinated by your appearance. I suppose you tire of being compared to your twin."

"Not really, Your Grace. In Devon we are no longer remarkable. Elsewhere we do not generally move in the same circles and people are not so aware of our resemblance when we are not together."

"David, why don't you go to procure glasses of lemonade for us?" the Duchess practically commanded.

When he returned with the refreshments a short time later, he was dismayed to discover the two ladies in a state of battle, for without actually mentioning names they had been discussing the merits and faults of one mythical gentleman and found themselves quite at odds regarding the chances of a leopard changing his spots.

"My God!" David exclaimed in amusement. "Talk about making a public display! You two look like a couple of bantams ready to strike. How did you manage to get to this point so quickly?"

The Duchess and Andrea looked at each other guiltily and then began to laugh. "Well, Your Grace, I fear we must declare a stalemate," Andrea observed. "It is obvious that we both are prejudiced but in opposite directions. Shall we call a truce?"

"For the moment, my dear," the old lady agreed affably. "However, I wish to make your further acquaintance and hope you will come to visit with me now and again."

"It will be my pleasure, Your Grace. I'm sure we can concentrate on other, less controversial subjects," Andrea replied, giving notice that she had no intention of renewing the debate.

At this point a young man came to claim her for the next dance and the Duke and his grandmother, having nothing further to interest them, left the assembly to return to Grosvenor Square.

In the carriage the Duchess approved David's choice. "But I am afraid she has a very unfavorable opinion of you," she said.

"Is *that* what you were arguing about?" David asked incredulously.

"More or less. I like her spirit, David, and I think she is just the woman you need."

"So do I," the Duke agreed fervently.

During the next week or so the Wycliff ladies, along with the Marchioness, were obliged to spend a good part of their time on completing preparations for Chloe's debut and standing for fittings for their gowns. Usually they were home by late afternoon to receive their callers, who were appearing with some steadiness. Quite often Ned came with Miss Barrington and cast approving eyes on the developing friendship between her and his cousin. Jeffrey usually looked in to advertise his special status and Jonathan presented himself occasionally to keep a watch on his aspiring rivals. The Duke also began to show up with regularity, but he took care not to antagonize Andrea with any display of partiality. As the news of the popularity of the late afternoon gatherings was circulated, a number of other young ladies and gentlemen found their way to Queen Anne's Gate around teatime as well so that there were seldom less than eight in attendance and often more.

One evening Lady Jane was persuaded to accompany Andrea and Chloe to a musical soirée at the Paxton residence, since Chloe was to be one of the performers. This occasion was unexpectedly remarkable because, purely by accident (as no one had been aware of a former acquaintance), Lady Jane was reunited with Lord Leslie Howell, an old childhood friend of hers who had lived near her father's estate and with whom she evidently felt completely at ease. This gentleman was about forty and had lost his wife two years before. He had three children, two boys and a girl, ranging in age from six to ten. He and Lady Jane became thoroughly engrossed in exchanging accounts of their past histories (somewhat edited on the lady's part) and expressed sincere sympathy for each other's bereavement. All this culminated with Lord Howell extending an invitation to the three ladies, along with Jonathan and Jeffrey, to a performance at the opera. Not surprisingly, this pleasant gentleman became a familiar figure at the afternoon assemblies and Lady Jane accepted his offered friendship without reserve, a development Andrea and Chloe were secretly disposed to regard with approval.

Finally the momentous evening arrived and Chloe was presented to an admiring congregation, looking so sweet and lovely in her flounced and embroidered white ball dress that there was very little adverse sentiment, for she was not a girl who excited feelings of envy. Andrea, on the other hand, with her more striking and sultry beauty, was recognized as serious competition, particularly by the older, more sophisticated ladies, and they were not unaware of the speculative glances of many of the gentlemen.

David also noticed the gravitating of uncommitted bachelors and philanderers in Andrea's direction but, having been subjected to an expressive discourse on her opinion of shallow relationships, he saw no cause for alarm. She was perfectly capable of keeping the Lotharios in their places. He had even dismissed Jeffrey as a significant rival because he had decided that the attachment was purely one-sided and that Andrea's obvious affection for her cousin was not of the degree or substance that could persuade her to matrimony.

And so the Duke relaxed and paid homage to the guest of honor, complimenting her on her grown-up appearance and predicting a successful Season for her.

Halfway through the evening, however, his serenity was seriously jarred when his amiable conversation with the Earl of Stockwell was interrupted by the latter gentleman's vehement expression. "Damn! What is he doing here?!"

The Duke turned his head just in time to see an obviously delighted Andrea holding out her hands in welcome to an elegant blond man who was just as obviously pleased to see her. Their greeting was observed with interest by the assembly but the two appeared unconcerned as they retired to a deserted corner to carry on an animated conversation.

David watched with misgivings as he recognized Lord Charles Loudon and realized he must be one of Andrea's serious suitors. Lord Charles was an extremely talented and impressive man who was highly regarded as a rising star in the diplomatic service. He had gained much distinction from his work during the recent peace negotiations. David remarked speculatively, "I thought he was assigned to St. Petersburg."

"So did I, but I should have known he would contrive to come to London once he knew Andrea would be in town," Jeffrey expounded ill-humoredly, revealing his respect for the competition as he advanced determinedly to break up the tête-à-tête.

David followed him and they converged on the pair just as Andrea was saying, "I am so glad you came, Charles. Correspondence is all very well, but it is much more gratifying to see one's friends."

"I agree with you, my dear, but you know how I feel about that," the gentleman replied meaningfully with a coaxing smile.

"Hello, Charles, what brings you to town—as if I didn't know," Jeffrey greeted him with less than his usual amiability.

Lord Loudon rose with Andrea as he replied with a grin, "Hello, Jeffrey. I have a temporary reprieve." He turned to the Duke, who was standing by with a formal manner, trying to disguise his disapproval of the familiarity between his love and her companion.

"So, David, you've returned from the wars. You must have been lucky, considering what I've heard of your early exploits before the Duke claimed your services."

"Don't remind me, Charles," David replied easily with a mild self-deprecative air. "I shudder to think of my youthful foolhardiness. Fortunately one is disposed to learn discretion with age. How do you find the Russian court?"

"Very elegant and very French—rather surprising considering the general backwardness of the country. What are your plans now?"

"Well, having unhappily succeeded to the title, I have had to revise my ambitions and have spent the last few months studying estate matters. I hope to have them in good order soon so that I can involve myself in supervising the acquisition of works of art for myself and others who have asked for my assistance."

"Yes, I have heard of your interest along that line. You should include a trip to Russia in your schedule. During her reign the Empress Catherine hoarded a fabulous collection of masterpieces. I was astounded at its magnificence."

Andrea had been listening intently but decided she had better break up this private conclave before she was completely ostracized for monopolizing the attentions of the three most eligible men in the room. "Come, gentlemen," she said reprovingly, "you can continue your conversation later, for we have a guest of honor this evening and you must all dance attendance." She linked her arm through Charles's to guide him toward a group of young people gathered around Chloe.

Lord Loudon did not miss the Duke's thinly disguised jealousy at Andrea's mark of preference and thought to himself, "So, another aspirant has entered the lists, who will bear watching." He had long since brushed off Jeffrey's chances and actually considered the Earl's persistent but light-handed courtship useful, since it in some measure protected Andrea from other eager candidates. He had always supposed that he was bound to be successful in his suit eventually, when Andrea's family responsibilities were lessened, and he was prepared to wait, knowing he found considerable favor in her eyes. But if Kensington were entering the ranks, he would have to take a more forceful line. He congratulated himself on his foresight for arranging this interlude in London.

Andrea was not unaware of the undercurrents of rivalry among the three men, and in order to avoid stirring the coals, devoted herself the rest of the evening to mingling with the other guests and keeping a watchful eye to see that everything went smoothly. No waltzes were played since many of the girls had not yet received permission from the patronesses at Almack's and could not disgrace themselves before these social leaders, several of whom were in attendance. Nevertheless, the ball was a huge success and Chloe had had her day.

Jonathan was standing with Andrea as the company began to thin out and he commented softly, "She was a perfect fairy princess and has certainly established herself in everyone's good graces. I believe she has grown up overnight."

"Yes, I am very proud of her but I have the most absurd idea that we should immediately whisk her back to Devon. I still have a nagging uneasiness," Andrea confessed apprehensively.

"With due cause, I expect," Jonathan said ruefully. "But I'm afraid we are going to have to see it through. I am glad we didn't deny her this pleasure."

Finally, the last guest left and the weary Wycliff ladies climbed into the family coach and were escorted to Queen Anne's Gate.

CHAPTER EIGHT

The next day no sound was heard from any of their bedchambers until noon, when Andrea decided to bestir herself and waken the others so they might be ready to receive callers who would be coming to congratulate Chloe.

All afternoon there was a steady stream of carriages coming and going, and Chloe was swamped with invitations from several interested gentlemen for rides in the Park, excursions to the library, and all the other entertainments the City had to offer. Several highly connected young ladies also proffered their friendship and made morning engagements with her. It appeared that the lovely Miss Wycliff was without reservation successfully launched into the *haut ton*.

Lord Loudon stopped by for a moment to claim Andrea for a drive in the Park the next afternoon, and Jeffrey demanded her company for a morning ride. She also commissioned Jonathan to escort her the second day so that they might chaperon Chloe and one of her admirers on an excursion to Chelsea. The Duke had been busy on his own behalf and, discovering that she was already fully engaged for the next two days, immediately spoke for the following afternoon, informing her he had made arrangements to take her to see the paintings he had told her about in Devon. She had admitted to a curiosity and could hardly refuse, so she accepted with as much grace as she could muster, considering that she wholly deplored his unprincipled artfulness.

Nevertheless, when the Duke arrived in his elegant curricle at the appointed hour, she realized she was looking forward to viewing the unusual collection, and she was even prepared to endeavor to keep a civil tongue in her head.

David was also in a conciliatory mood, being pleased to have Andrea all to himself, and told her contritely, "I must say I am certainly put in my place to find you so occupied that I must speak for your company so far in advance. I fear I owe you an apology."

Andrea looked at him suspiciously and said, "If you are referring to one of my more unadmirable moments, I beg you will not. I was never so mortified in my life as when I understood I let you goad me into that shocking display of conceit."

"We both said things that would have been better left unsaid. I have often wished we could begin again," David admitted, looking at her imploringly.

She had to turn away to keep from being swayed by his particularly appealing charm and presently asked in a reserved but cordial manner, "Are the paintings hung in a gallery, Your Grace?"

With a sigh of resignation, David answered, "No, they are being stored and protected. Some were in poor condition and are being cleaned. I am anxious to see them again myself and confess I regret the necessity of sending them back, though of course Wellington's strong sense of ethics compels him to return them to the new King of Spain. They were stolen from the Royal House."

When they arrived at their destination, David escorted her to the chamber where the paintings were being housed, and they were greeted by a caretaker who willingly showed them the treasures. Andrea was especially fascinated by the portraits, particularly the *Spanish Gentleman* by Velasquez.

She stood in front of it for some moments and then said half to herself, "My word, I have the strangest feeling. I almost imagine I am acquainted with the man. In fact, he could be a relative of mine," she added wonderingly.

"There is something in that," David replied. "I have met some of your Spanish connections, you know."

"No, I didn't. With Andrew?" she asked almost enviously.

"Yes, during one of our missions to the south of the peninsula," he replied, letting his mind dwell on how much pleasure it would give him to take her with him on his travels.

"I remember. Drew told me about that," she remarked softly.

They spent another hour or so studying the other paintings and Andrea was intrigued by the Duke's absorption. He seemed to understand what the masters had been trying to communicate with their unique talents and occasionally he would call her attention to some distinguishing mark of style or use of color and light.

"Do you paint, Your Grace?" Andrea asked curiously.

The Duke grinned at her sheepishly. "I have tried my hand at it, but I'm afraid I am the rankest amateur so I hope you will keep my secret."

"Of course," she agreed, returning his smile.

Quite in charity with one another, they returned to the carriage and David, scheming to prolong their outing, asked if he might treat her to a tea at the Clarendon Hotel.

Being pleasantly lulled by their agreeable companionship, Andrea accepted unhesitatingly and they refreshed themselves with tea and small pastries while exchanging comments about the collection and its ultimate disposal. Once or twice Andrea noticed that they were being remarked by other guests, but she ignored their curious stares even while reminding herself to avoid other public appearances with the Duke if she did not wish for notoriety.

When David returned her to her house, she gave him her hand and said gratefully, "Thank you, Your Grace. That was a memorable experience and I deeply appreciate your arranging for me to see the paintings."

"You're welcome, Andrea," the Duke responded warmly. "It was my pleasure. And, my dear, I do wish you could see your way to calling me David."

Summoning her reserves, Andrea withdrew the hand he still held and replied coolly, "I do not think under present circumstances it would be proper for me to do so, my lord Duke, anymore than it is proper for you to address me so—informally."

"I had hoped we had become friends but I see that you have not yet forgiven me," David remarked with a wry smile showing his regret. "So I suppose I must be patient. However, I refuse to bow so far to your sensibilities that I must think of you as Miss Wycliff. It is too much to ask. And—my dear—my grandmother wishes me to remind you of your promise to pay her a visit."

Andrea flashed her eyes at him for his deliberate familiarity but replied in a civil tone, "Of course. I shall send her a note immediately." She turned away to step into the house.

The day had not ended as well as it had begun and David realized he had, after all, rushed the fences. But he could not reconcile himself to being third or even fourth choice; he was impatient to elevate his standing.

For the next few days all his solicitations were politely refused and he was reduced to haunting the afternoon gatherings and showing himself at evening parties that were sure to include the Wycliffs. At these affairs he artfully divided his attentions impartially, and the interested observers were still uncertain which sister was actually the quarry. So far Lady Carrington had not unsheathed her claws, even though she had the opportunity to do so on two occasions. She had greeted the Duke with a scornful indifference, but he was not deceived into imagining that she regretted her outburst, and he took pains to disguise his preference.

David did manage to persuade Andrea to accompany him to an exhibition at the Royal Academy and introduced her to the aging and ailing Benjamin West. They wandered through the galleries and watched some of the students at work. In one room a lecture was being delivered by one of the academicians, but it was to be hoped that his application of his principles were more effective than his explanation of them. It was always a surprise to be confronted with the evidence that a master was not always a good teacher. In addition to the more illustrious names like Turner, Lawrence, and Constable, who regularly exhibited, there were also impressive entries by the landscape artists John Crome and John Martin, sculptor Joseph Nollegens, and the Scottish painter David Willkie. David was pleased that Andrea showed sincere interest in his favorite subject, and that she forgot for the moment her determined hostility toward him. However, just as before when they had seemed to be coming to a better understanding, he was once again relegated to a minor role and could not break her resolve not to be drawn into a closer friendship with him.

In exasperation he complained of this arbitrary behavior to his grandmother. "Every time I think I am making some headway she suddenly shows me a cold shoulder, even when I have been every bit the gentleman. I can't accept that she dislikes me so much when she seems to truly enjoy our outings and our conversations."

"Perhaps that's the trouble," the Duchess observed sagely.

"What do you mean?"

"Just that she does enjoy them and is afraid of becoming involved with you."

"Now that's an intriguing thought," the Duke mused with a speculative light in his eye. "You think she is running scared?"

"Possibly."

"Then I had better keep up the attack, though I shall have to make my own opportunities since it is obvious she means to keep me at bay. When is she next coming to visit you?"

"The day after tomorrow at eleven."

"Good. I'll contrive to drive her home."

Andrea harbored conflicting emotions about becoming friends with the Duchess since she was aware that the old lady meant to promote her grandson's cause, though she seemed to have tabled the issue for the moment. The truth was that the girl and the old woman had immediately accepted each other as kindred spirits and each thoroughly enjoyed their lively exchanges. It was not often that Andrea found someone with the wit and the firmness of mind to match her own, and she was naturally drawn to the Duchess, recognizing her as the strong mentor she had been denied in her early years.

As she came down the stairs after their visit, she was still smiling at the Duchess's acerbic observations about one of her contemporaries when she saw the Duke coming into the hall to meet her. "Well, it should be no surprise, after all," she told herself irritably. "He does live here."

"Hello, Andrea. I've been waiting for you."

"Why?" she asked ungraciously.

"To see you home."

"That won't be necessary. My coachman is to return for me as I directed."

"And so he did, but I sent him off because I mean to drive you myself."

"How dare you! To presume to order my servants is coming it too strong! I shall have to take Thomas to task!"

"That would hardly be fair. How should he know the arrangement would be unwelcome to you? You have accepted my escort before."

"Then I shall instruct him not to be misled again," Andrea declared heatedly. "I had some errands to run and I expected his attendance."

"Well, I place myself at your disposal," David offered, putting on his hat and gloves. "Where would you like to go first?"

"I—I will go home. I can shop another day," she replied hastily.

"My dear Andrea, I feel sure you have an unworthy disinclination to be seen with me. Are you afraid for your reputation? I wonder," he added whimsically, "if I would have a better response if I suggested clandestine meetings?"

In spite of herself Andrea had to laugh and then declared in vexation, "Oh, why will you not take a hint?!"

"Because, my love, taking such a hint as you are suggesting goes against the very depths of my feelings. It does not bear thinking of."

This provoking man certainly had a disturbing way of expressing himself, and Andrea was shocked to realize that she more than half wanted to believe him. As always, these wayward thoughts caused her to react contrarily. "I wish you will not speak to me in that manner. You show a lamentable lack of sensibility to pursue a subject you know is distasteful to me."

"My dear, I am beginning to think that your protests are just a little exaggerated," David remarked. "I wish you would stop fighting me and give me a chance to prove myself."

She shook her head stubbornly and then demanded angrily, "Where are we going?"

"For a ride in the Park."

"I have not said I wish to go for a drive with you. In fact, I definitely do *not* wish to. Take me home this instant!"

"If you don't stop having a tantrum, I shall likely lose my temper and we will have a couple of runaway animals on our hands. Do try to behave. I want to talk to you."

"This is outrageous! You cannot just go around abducting people."

The Duke laughed unsympathetically at her indignant expression and protested, "No, no, not that. At least not yet. I am not that desperate."

"Oh—you are impossible!" Andrea raged. "If you think this kind of presumption will raise your credit, you have windmills in your head."

"Being a gentleman did not produce better results so I am no worse off," David observed, unconcerned. "Now you may as well resign yourself to spending a few minutes in my company because I am determined you shall at least give me a hearing."

Realizing she had no choice in the matter, Andrea sat stiffly with her hands folded and stared straight ahead with a stony face.

Ignoring her uncompromising attitude David announced, "First of all, my dear, I find it extremely intolerable that you have this determination to regard me as some sort of libertine. I know you are wary of men and have reason for it. But you must not suppose that no man is capable of singleness of heart."

"I do not suppose so," she told him flatly.

"Andrea, I should insult you by supposing that you are so naive as to imagine that any of your other suitors are entirely blameless in this regard. I must presume that you are willing to grant them the benefit of a doubt. Why can you not accord me the same forebearance?"

"I believe the propensity is stronger in some men," she told him stiffly.

"I see. And you think I am one of them. Well, if in your mind you have some way connected passion and inconstancy, I can understand your hesitancy because I can assure you that, if you would look upon me with anything like the favor you show Charles or even Jeffrey, you would be my wife within the month. There is no way I would stand by patiently on the sidelines while you devoted yourself to your family. When did Loudon first propose to you?"

"That is none of your affair!" Andrea snapped testily and she turned her head away because she could not help but be stirred by his declarations.

"All right, love," David said gently. "I do not mean to tease you further, and I will not press you today. But I do beg you to think about it and ask yourself if you would be happy with a man who did not love you and appreciate you as much as I do."

Thinking this to be uncomfortably dangerous ground, Andrea declared primly, "This has been a most improper conversation and I do not want to hear more."

"Do not turn missish on me now. It is not as though we have not discussed these matters before in an even more candid fashion—at your instigation, I might add," David told her ungallantly.

She suppressed an angry retort and maintained a stubborn silence even as he handed her down from his curricle. For a moment she looked at him searchingly and then left him standing with a faint anticipation that he just might have persuaded her to give him a chance.

In her room Andrea slowly took off her bonnet, gloves, and light pelisse and curled up on the chaise to consider her erratic behavior where the Duke was concerned. She reluctantly admitted to herself that she was very much attracted to him and enjoyed his company. She had realized *that* even in Devon. But she was unnaturally beset with apprehensions about a man who had such a notorious reputation. Still, his intimation that her other suitors undoubtedly contrived opportunities to satisfy their desires could not be brushed off. The truth was that what they did mattered little to her. But the Duke was a different matter. She suspected that her problem was rooted in her having a jealous and possessive nature. She could never be as forbearing as Lady Jane. She had never understood how her stepmother had suffered her husband's infidelities so docilely. When Lady Jane had returned to Devon, she went on as before, accepting Lord Wycliff as her husband when he deigned to visit them, usually during the holidays, and putting from her mind his adulterous behavior when he was away. Even now the thought of her father's contemptible self-indulgence incensed Andrea. She would not be able to countenance such an inconstant relationship. She distrusted the Duke's inclination or even ability to change his ways. "But," she told herself, ignoring a warning voice from within, "you do not have to succumb to his blandishments. Why not handle him as you do Charles and Jeffrey? You have certainly had plenty of practice." Having persuaded herself to the point she wished to reach, she decided she would relax her disapproving attitude and treat him in a more natural way.

And so, for the next several days Andrea was seen in the company of four gentlemen, occasionally with more than one of them, when there was some group activity, and though the Duke still favored Lady Jane and Chloe also, his special attentions to Andrea were of such a degree that it was fairly well concluded that he had chosen her to be his Duchess.

This interesting development was widely remarked at the fashionable affairs. The gentlemen exchanged amused comments that the Duke of Kensington obviously relished a challenge. The ladies were not as good-humored about the matter and were less than charmed by the New Beauty, who was monopolizing the attentions of the three most eligible men in London.

Lady Carrington was particularly ill-disposed because she had never accepted the fact of her dismissal. She decided to take steps to disrupt the Duke's pursuit of Andrea and to this end she presented herself early one morning at Queen Anne's Gate to request a private interview with Miss Wycliff.

When Andrea was informed of her presence, she had an immediate impulse to refuse to see her, but knowing she would just be postponing the ordeal, she decided she might as well get it over with in the privacy of her own home.

Not being one to wait for an offensive, she swept purposefully into the parlor and asked in an obviously inhospitable tone, "Good morning, Lady Carrington. To what do I owe this honor?"

Being confronted with an unexpectedly aggressive adversary, the visitor was obliged to marshal her forces and replied abruptly, "Good morning, Miss Wycliff. I thought it was time we had a talk."

"I wasn't aware we had a common interest," Andrea remarked innocently.

"Come now," the lady said shortly, irritated by the girl's insolent manner. "We will not beat about the bush. I merely mean to do you a good turn and to warn you about putting too much faith in the Duke's constancy and honorable intentions."

"My dear lady," Andrea said with raised brows, "you can't tell me anything I don't know about men of the Duke's stamp. And if you feel inclined to go more deeply into the matter, I must tell you that I consider myself quite capable of handling my own affairs and do not take kindly to unsolicited advice."

Lady Carrington had already realized that she would not be dealing with the missish provincial she had visualized, but this girl's provoking self-assurance was more than she had bargained for. She concluded she might as well give up any attempt to intimidate her and tried a more conciliatory approach. "I somehow overlooked the obvious connection, but I knew your father well."

"I am not surprised," Andrea remarked caustically.

"My dear girl, you do have a sharp tongue," the lady accused, looking at her through narrowed eyes, "and lack a certain discretion."

"So I have been told," Andrea agreed. "But it would appear that I am not alone for I expect you did not come here to be discreet."

"All right, since we are to be frank," the Countess acknowledged, dropping all pretense, "I thought it might be of some interest to you to know that I do not mean to release the Duke so easily. I was willing to stay in the background while he went about the business of finding a wife, but I expected him to choose a pretty little widgeon."

Andrea laughed irrepressibly and blurted out, "No wonder you are out of humor. By no manner or means could I fit that classification. Tell me, Lady Carrington, did you come here to ask me to step out of the picture?" she asked undiplomatically.

"It could be put that way," the discountenanced lady admitted reluctantly.

"My word! How diverting! I had no idea a lady of your *consequenc*e would consider me serious competition. It makes me feel quite set up with myself," Andrea crowed insensibly. "But," she added, forestalling an angry retort, "you have nothing to worry about where I am concerned, because I have no intention of marrying the Duke."

This declaration was received with a look of skepticism and the Countess observed knowingly, "So—you are playing hard to get. No wonder he is in pursuit. It is always so with him, a sort of game, to go after what seems unattainable or what somebody else has. He loses interest once he has won. Even I was taken in and, in spite of your bold posture, I think I can lay claim to being more worldly than you."

"I am sure you are right," Andrea agreed readily. "But, on the other hand, I am not taken in, which was a rather interesting expression on your part, when one considers it, and could lend itself to several intriguing interpretations."

This calculated provocation earned her a thoroughly malevolent look but Lady Carrington recognized her error and did not mean to compound it. She rose to leave, voicing a parting shot. "I hope you are sincere in your resolution, Miss Wycliff. The Duke will never be satisfied with one woman, but I mean to keep my place."

Andrea just looked at her uninvited guest noncommittally. Standing by the door, she said as the lady passed, "Good day, Lady Carrington. I do hope you will not feel the temptation to repeat this act of benevolence. I am often not at home."

Not being able to counter this last insult, the Countess entered her carriage in a testy mood with the uncomfortable feeling that she had come off the worse in the contest.

Had she but known how successful she had been in her purpose, however, she would have been in transports, for as soon as she drove away, Andrea hurried to her room to change her gown and told her maid to call for the carriage. In less than half an hour she was deposited at Grosvenor Square and was ushered to the Duchess's sitting room.

"Andrea, my dear, I did not expect you today and certainly not so early," the Dowager remarked pleasantly. Noticing the girl's agitation, she added, "Whatever is the matter?"

"Is the Duke home?" Andrea inquired bluntly, as she paced the room.

"Why, I believe so," the Duchess said slowly, wondering what had brought on this state of barely controlled fury. "Do you wish me to send for him?"

"Yes, because I should like to speak my piece just once," the girl replied tersely. She flung herself into a chair and began to tap her foot impatiently.

The Duchess rang for her maid and asked her to request the Duke to attend her and Miss Wycliff.

He came immediately and greeted them cheerfully. "Good morning, ladies. This is an unexpected pleasure." He stopped short as he noticed his grandmother's warning look.

"Andrea, is something wrong?" he asked, puzzled by his beloved's forbiddingly cold expression.

She rose and drew herself up to stand before him as she announced, "My lord Duke, I have come to tell you that I will not in the future welcome your attentions or spend any time in your company. I thought it best to tell you so privately so there need not be a public demonstration."

"Great heaven!" he exclaimed, taken aback by this sudden repudiation. "What maggot have you got in your head now? Have you been listening to more defamatory accusations?" he demanded.

"Defamatory denotes false, does it not?" she retorted pungently.

"You might at least tell me what brought on this instant rejection," he suggested, ignoring the gibe.

"I have just this past hour been visited by Lady Carrington."

He stared at her incredulously. "My God! I can't believe she actually had the nerve! What the devil did she want?"

"She is displeased that I am not a 'pretty little widgeon,'" Andrea replied sarcastically, eliciting a snort of laughter from the Duchess, who was immediately awarded a quelling look.

"Andrea," David said gently, trying to calm her, for she was clearly at the boiling point, "whatever you are is none of her concern, I promise you. She has no claim on me whatsoever."

"She thinks otherwise, my lord Duke," Andrea told him sharply.

"She couldn't," David protested. "I made my position perfectly clear."

"Did you? Did you say to her 'My lady, we are finished'?" the girl persisted.

"No, I did not," he answered truthfully. "I had hoped to avoid a scene and tried to ease out of it, which was an entirely wasted effort because it developed into a nasty turnup and ended with her threatening that she would not forgive or forget and would make me pay. So I say again that she knew."

"Well, she obviously has had second thoughts, and I do not wish to be subjected to any more objectionable contact with her," Andrea stated coldly, not in the least mollified.

"Andrea, you did not let her bully you," David admonished with a frown.

"Are you serious?" the furious girl asked. "How could you suppose *I* would countenance such a likelihood. She set my back up, a most unfortunate circumstance considering that I am heedlessly intemperate when I become angry. No, my lord Duke, I was discourteous and insulting, and I turned the knife and, in general, comported myself in such a way as to make an enemy for life!" And with this outburst, she turned a darkly accusing look on him.

"Dear God! You are the most reckless little imp I have ever encountered," David said disapprovingly, trying to hide his amusement.

"Reckless!" she exclaimed in outrage. "You are one to

talk. You were warned about the vindictiveness of that woman and you blundered on anyway."

"Andrea, you must believe me. I have had nothing to do with her or any other woman since you came to town."

She put up her chin. "It would have been more deserving of notice if you could have predated that—condition."

"Is *that* what has been bothering you?" he asked in sudden understanding. "You rejected me pretty ruthlessly, you remember, and when I left Devon, I was angry and blue-deviled. I tried to convince myself that I would conquer my passion for you, and yes, I got involved recklessly. But the minute I saw you again I knew I had been deceiving myself. I beg you will not let that malicious woman prejudice you against me."

"Your Grace," Andrea explained, with an exaggerated patience, "you do not understand my reservations. After one of our conversations I decided I was perhaps unfair in my judgment and I was prepared to accept your friendship. I have since come to regret it. Even if my other friends are not 'blameless,' at least I have never been approached and warned off by their mistresses. It is not a position I wish to find myself in again, so you may consider my forbearance at an end," she stated resolutely, starting to move to the door.

"If you cut me, she will think she has accomplished her purpose," the Duke expostulated angrily.

"I do not care what she thinks. I just do not propose getting into anymore cat fights with her," Andrea said coldly.

"Andrea, are you going to call craven? If you wanted to, you could cut her to pieces."

"So I could, my lord Duke—if I wanted to," she replied expressively with a shrug of her shoulders.

David winced at her barbed remark and warned her, "I will not accept this, you know."

"You will have to. I have no intention of becoming involved with a man who can play such a fool. It's a matter of trust and respect."

"Do you consider that you have not given me a chance to prove myself? You are making a case out of past history."

"Not all that much past, Your Grace. And I am inclined to concur with the Countess's estimation of your character."

"All right," David said in exasperation. "You may as well tell me what she said so I will know what I have to contend with."

Andrea was about to refuse but then looked him in the eye and recounted, "She said you always wanted what you thought you couldn't have and then lost interest when you got it. As a parting shot, she reminded me that you would never be satisfied with one woman and that she meant to keep her place."

"She doesn't have a place!" he almost shouted. "You must know that. How can you blind yourself to the love I have for you that directs my every move?"

Once again Andrea forced herself to turn from the devil's temptations and addressed the Duchess politely. "Your Grace, I know that you sought me out at your grandson's instigation, but I feel we have become good friends on our own volition and I have enjoyed our conversations; however, unless you can assure me that the Duke will not approach me in this house, I shall feel constrained to discontinue my visits, although I should be pleased to welcome you in my home."

"Andrea," the Dowager said soothingly, "do not be foolish. If you insist, I shall order David to closet himself when you come, but I beg you will not desert me because of your breach with him."

"Of course not," the girl replied with obvious relief. She bent to kiss the older lady's cheek and then, without looking at the Duke, walked toward the door.

The mercilously harassed gentleman was by now hardly able to suppress his frustration and anger at this most inauspicious development. He declared passionately, "Andrea, if you persist in this unreasonable posture, I shall likely do something we will both regret."

Never being able to countenance a threat, Andrea turned an equally challenging eye on the object of her wrath and warned, "I hope not, my lord Duke. I will not be responsible for my actions if you try me too far." With this last word, she walked out of the room and closed the door behind her.

David sank into a chair and put his hand to his brow, groaning, "My God! What a muddle!" He began pounding the arm of the chair with one fist, repeating, "Damn, damn, damn." He looked up to see his grandmother watching him with interest and asked ungraciously, "And just what is your estimation of that little scene?"

The Duchess answered slowly. "I'm not sure, though it appears that her antagonism is rooted in the fact that you came back here to pursue Marcia Carrington after you left Devon."

"Yes, that does seem to be the crux of the matter," he agreed ruefully. "But what did she expect? She cut me down as if I were the merest sapling, and I convinced myself that I could not be so irrevocably committed after only four days acquaintance."

"Well, it would certainly have been wiser on your part to have waited to find out for sure," the Dowager commented unsympathetically.

"Do not tell me what I should have done," her grandson cut at her, venting his ill-temper. "The question is, what can I do now?"

"Not what you are contemplating, I beg," the Duchess admonished perceptively.

"I know of no other way, and I cannot give up the offensive. She is liable to accept Loudon, and then I will really take leave of my senses."

"David, can't you give her a day or two to reconsider?"

"No. She is determined and I have a great deal of respect for her powers of resolution. She is a stubborn little devil."

And so, with a desperate, ill-judged determination the Duke began to address himself to a plan of action that was destined to be a collision course.

CHAPTER NINE

When Andrea returned home, she went directly to her room to try to puzzle out just how it was that she always managed to make such a sad botch of her squabbles with the Duke. Since she had left Grosvenor Square, she had been having qualms about her harebrained actions. It certainly would have been more prudent to effect a gradual retreat, but she had been so angry with him for having been the underlying cause of her unpleasant interview with Lady Carrington that she could not resist her impulse to fly out at him. Why could she not learn to control her ungovernable temper! Now she had set his hackles up again and she knew he was going to strike back where it would disturb her most, just as he had done before. He would not scruple to use her credulous sister as a cat's paw. Jonathan would be furious with her. But what was she supposed to do—accept the Duke to keep him away from Chloe? She wondered if she might hope for any assistance from the Duchess. Very likely not. It was a result of *her* importunities that he should marry which had brought them all to this sorry pass. "Well," Andrea thought, "there is nothing for it now but that I shall just have to play it out." This pessimistic resolution gave her little consolation because she knew in one of her prescient flashes that there would be the devil to pay before it was over.

Society was diverted the next few days with speculations about the Duke's sudden change of direction. He attached himself to the coterie of Chloe's admirers and was never far from her side. He managed to cut out some of the younger men and was often seen driving her in the afternoons in the Park, riding with her in the mornings, or escorting her to the theater in the evenings. It was true that Andrea was usually with them but obviously in the role of chaperon with some other gentleman. She was finding the situation extremely upsetting and was unnaturally edgy with her family and friends.

Jonathan, losing some of his forbearance, viewed the proceedings with a jaundiced eye. He thought how beneficial it would be if he could just knock a couple of heads together. He had no doubts about the eventual outcome of this extremely unorthodox courtship, but with the Duke and Andrea always at loggerheads with one another, there was bound to be any number of calamitous difficulties along the way. It seemed that he and Chloe were going to be caught in the middle.

One day Andrea was engaged to spend the afternoon with her friend, Lady Emily Cowper. After they had talked for a while, Emily broached a subject that she had been suppressing with some effort.

"Andrea, whatever happened between you and Kensington? I thought you might make a match of it."

Andrea looked at her friend noncommittally. "Why should you think so?"

"Well, my dear, it was obvious that he had serious intentions."

"Even if he had, that doesn't make it a sure thing, you know," Andrea commented caustically.

"You refused him!" came an astonished exclamation.

"Emily, I beg you will not jump to conclusions. And you sound surprised at such a possibility. Considering you were the one who apprised me of his promiscuous proclivities, I wonder you should think I would have done otherwise if it had been put to me."

"Oh, dear. Now I know what he meant."

"What are you talking about?"

"Well, he recently told me I had done him a bad turn but he wouldn't explain."

Andrea did not offer any comment and her friend tried to make amends. "I did not mean to imply that he was a profligate, because he is not."

"Emily, if you have an odd notion that you must now right some wrong, you may save your breath. I do not wish to be connected with him."

"There is a case of being too prudish, you know," Emily hinted.

"I realize that a certain laxity is accepted by society," Andrea acknowledged unwillingly, knowing she was on sensitive territory, "but I could not live like that, Emily—I just could not. Now please let us not talk about it anymore." She stood up and said, "I must go because Jonathan and I are accompanying Chloe and the Duke to the opera this evening. I will see you at Almack's on Wednesday."

"Certainly. I would not miss the show. You have created quite a stir, and I understand the betting books at White's are full of all sorts of wagers on which sister gets the Duke and when."

"Oh!" Andrea exclaimed angrily. "That's positively mortifying! It's too bad those fine gentlemen are so birdbrained that they can't think of something more constructive to occupy their time. I must tell you that I take exception to your making so light of it."

Still feeling a sense of outrage as she dressed for the evening, Andrea had an almost unconquerable desire to pack up and head for Devon. But she was unwilling to disrupt the lovely intimacy developing between Lady Jane and Lord Howell. She was frightened by her increasing animosity toward the Duke. It was beginning to color her every action, and she often wished, when she was in one of her furies, that she could clap her hands and make him disappear into thin air. These almost daily contacts, which were forced on her since she was determined to keep a vigilant eye, were driving her to distraction and he knew it. She could not enjoy her other friends and would only accept their invitations when Chloe was safely occupied with someone besides the Duke. Both Jeffrey and

Lord Loudon were finding this state of affairs extremely exasperating, and though Andrea had told them of her disapproval of the Duke's attention, they were—as it was intended by one wily strategist—successfully thwarted in their efforts to improve their positions.

Andrea slipped on her red silk gown, hoping that it would brighten her mood. She fingered the gold gypsy earrings which she knew were a striking accessory with this dress, but she would not give the Duke the satisfaction of knowing how much she liked them. Instead, she chose to wear only a diamond pendant. Thinking she was late, she went downstairs directly and found the Duke and Jonathan waiting in the parlor.

David turned to gaze at her admiringly and observed, "Andrea, you are especially stunning in that dress. I thought so the first time you wore it and then," he added quizzically, "I particularly liked the gypsy earrings with it."

She looked at him sharply because she could not recall having worn the gown in his presence and felt confused and suspicious by his suddenly intimate manner. She was saved from answering by Chloe's entrance.

The Duke quickly moved to dance attendance on the young girl with a lavish compliment on her appearance, noting that he and Jonathan were certainly lucky to be favored by two such lovely ladies.

Chloe laughed delightedly and then said to her sister, "Oh, Andy, I do think you look beautiful in that dress, but you should be wearing the Duke's earrings."

"I am glad to be seconded, my dear Chloe," David agreed quickly. "I have already made such an observation, but I must think they do not please her."

"Of course they do. She likes them excessively," Chloe protested artlessly.

"Then," the Duke remarked almost wistfully, with a cast-down expression that made Andrea want to throw something, "I have to assume she holds the giver in such dislike that she does not wish to gratify him."

This patent petition for sympathy persuaded the tender-hearted Chloe to cast a reproachful look at her sister, and she put her hand on the Duke's arm as if to make up for Andrea's slight, saying soothingly, "You must not take Andy's prejudices too seriously, Your Grace. She sometimes can be uncharitable." With a toss of her head, she allowed the Duke to escort her to the waiting carriage.

Andrea looked apologetically at Jonathan and moaned unhappily, "Everything I do seems to be wrong. I am beginning to feel doomed."

"You're up against a devilish determined antagonist, my dear. He never misses a chance to nettle you. What do you suppose would be his approach if you stopped playing the protectress and pretended indifference?" Jonathan queried softly before handing her into the Duke's chaise.

Andrea did not answer but she thought about the speculation and wondered if she dared take a chance that he would not actually commit himself. It would be worth considering and during the evening she gave only half her attention to the stage as she pondered the question and finally came to the conclusion that she should call his bluff.

David had positioned himself to the side and back of the others, so that he might covertly keep Andrea in his line of vision. He soon noticed her air of abstraction and suspected that she was hatching some new difficulty for him, a prospect he did not particularly welcome. He had been hoping she would see the absurdity of their maneuverings, at least recognize that she had overreacted, and agree to reestablish their relationship on a friendly footing. This little charade was becoming an intolerable bore for, while Chloe was a lovely, sweet girl, she was not the Duke's choice, and he found himself nearly overcome by impatience, especially at times like this evening when he wanted Andrea so desperately. He decided it might be best for him to leave town for a few days before he lost his resolution to pressure her into a more reasonable posture. There was a painting that was being offered for sale by a Berkshire family, and he had been intending to examine it for possible addition to his collection. He would take time out to do so now.

He informed the others of these plans over a late supper at one of the fashionable hotels. When he noticed Andrea's evident relief that they would be denied his presence, he experienced an intense irritation that almost made him change his mind. Chloe did not seem the least perturbed that he was leaving, and Jonathan would certainly not miss him—all of which caused David to fall into an unnatural state of the blue-devils. It was not exactly inspiriting to be so obviously dispensable.

With a considerably less than happy frame of mind the Duke left two mornings later on his excursion, which he planned to make in only three days. It would be something of a push, but he intended to drive most of the way himself. He was looking forward to making a good run on the first and last stages with his new greys, since it seemed to be the only source of pleasure he might expect for the moment.

With the Duke's departure, Andrea's other suitors took immediate advantage of his absence and claimed her for themselves morning, afternoon, and evening. With the two determined rivals she exercised her horse, rode in elegant carriages, and attended a supper party and a diplomatic reception. Jeffrey arranged for an elegant, intimate picnic at Richmond with Lady Jane and Lord Howell, Chloe and Jonathan, and Ned and Naomi. Lord Loudon prevailed upon her to accompany him on an overnight visit to his Essex estate to look in on his mother, who was not well enough to come to town. Andrea hesitated before accepting because she did not want to give Charles false encouragement. She knew that such a journey would lead to speculation even though she, of course, would be accompanied by her maid. But she decided he knew very well where he stood and would not make presumptions. It would be a refreshing diversion. She did have qualms about leaving the day the Duke was to return, but she reminded herself that she had determined to disguise her concern and to give him a freer hand with Chloe. Her sister was completely engaged the following day anyway, as Jonathan was to escort her to Almack's in the evening, and she had arranged to spend the afternoon with a group of young ladies who gathered every so often to rehash all the interesting happenings at the dozens of parties, all of which would have been impossible for any one person to attend. Andrea considered these little gossips a harmless enough amusement and felt reasonably reassured that Chloe would not be adversely influenced for the next day or two. And so, on the day the Duke was racing back from Berkshire, Andrea was traveling leisurely to Essex.

CHAPTER TEN

David returned home late in the evening and decided to stay in to recover himself. The long drive had taken more time than expected because of unfavorable weather conditions. It had rained most of the way and some of the roads were slippery and treacherous. He felt unnaturally exhausted from the strain of controlling his horses and left a note for his grandmother, who was out indulging her passion for cards, that he was making an early night of it and would see her the next morning.

He slept until almost ten o'clock and woke in a much brighter frame of mind. With renewed determination he primed himself for another assault on Andrea's defenses. These past three days he had contemplated the results of his campaign thus far and realized he was really making no progress, that his strategy left much to be desired. The only advantage he had gained by courting Chloe was that he did keep Andrea occupied. But that sort of unsatisfactory contact could go on indefinitely, and he suspected she meant to leave town very shortly. The Season would begin to slow down in a few weeks and she would have fulfilled her promise to Chloe.

Somehow he was going to have to bring the issue to a head. He hoped he would not have to resort to drastic measures. It never once occurred to him that he would not gain his objective. Such an unfavorable outcome was not worthy of consideration, and he was not beyond imagining that this fantasy of abducting her, which often occupied his mind, might very well become a reality if all else failed.

He went down to breakfast and was shortly joined by his grandmother, who had risen earlier than usual to apprise him of what he no doubt would view as a particularly insidious development. She decided to let him finish his hearty meal before she ruined his day and made light conversation. "How was your trip?"

"Exhausting—and unprofitable."

"You didn't like the painting?"

"It had been advertized as a Hals but it didn't measure up to his usual standard, and I am inclined to doubt its authenticity. I was not enough interested to take the chance."

"I suppose the weather was miserable as it has been here."

"Yes. This promises to be one of our famous rainy stretches, I'm afraid. Now," he said, sitting back in his chair with a cup of coffee between his hands, "tell me what has been happening here."

"Well," the Duchess began hesitantly, "Andrea was promised to me this morning, but I received a note early yesterday telling me she could not keep the appointment and would see me later in the week."

David eyed his grandmother suspiciously and ventured, "I have an uncomfortable feeling that you are reluctant to tell me something, my dear. What new problem do I have to contend with?"

"David, do put down your coffee because you are not going to like this and I am afraid you will react violently."

He did as she asked and leaned forward, asking uneasily, "What is it?"

"I saw Lady Jane at the party last night and elicited the information that Andrea has accompanied Lord Loudon to his Essex estate for a few days."

"What?" David exploded. "My God! I should have known better than to take off and leave a clear field for those two damnably persistent suitors. I suppose Jeffrey has been making hay, also, though he must certainly have his nose put out of joint by this escapade. Did she go alone?"

"Yes, I believe so."

"That miserable girl!" David raged as he got up to pace back and forth. "Does she want to be compromised? Proper ladies do not travel alone with a man to his country home."

"David, I'm sure she had her maid with her, and it was only a few hours' journey. They went to visit his mother, who is not very well."

"How long are they staying?"

"Lady Jane expects them to return possibly tomorrow but more likely the next day. Do you suppose," the Dowager asked tentatively, "that this means Andrea will accept Loudon?"

The Duke turned a thoroughly incredulous look on his grandmother and said, "She would never do so!"

"David, it's about time you faced up to reality. If she stands firm, you might *have* to accept your rejection," the old lady admonished unpromisingly.

"Never! I tell you, never! She belongs to me and I will have her one way or another!" With this passionate declaration the Duke turned to stalk out of the room but was called back sharply.

"David, do not go off in a huff. I must remind you about the reception the Queen is giving tomorrow in honor of Princess Charlotte's wedding."

"Oh, no," the Duke groaned. "Do you really want to subject yourself to that ordeal?"

"No, and, if I were not a Duchess and you were not a Duke, we might be able to cry off, but I'm afraid our absence would be remarked. We are obligated by our positions."

With a sigh of resignation, David surrendered. "All right, but I hear that hundreds have been invited, far more than Buckingham House can accommodate. We shall have to wait for hours and will be lucky to get out alive."

"I expect you are right, but we will go early and I shall count on your protection," the Duchess agreed unconcernedly.

David grinned amiably and came back to kiss her cheek.

"One would think that at your age you would be content to slow down a little. Are you going to chase about like this until your last day?" he asked quizzingly.

"I hope so," the old lady replied with a lively eye.

They both laughed and then the Duchess cautioned, "You are not going to do anything rash, are you?"

"No," the Duke replied. "At least not today. I'll put in an appearance at Almack's this evening to see if I can discover what brought on this sudden excursion. Do you plan to attend?"

"Are you taking Chloe?"

"No, I shall let Jonathan have the honor. I can bring you home at a reasonable hour."

"All right, then. I will rest a little this afternoon to prepare myself for tomorrow."

The Duke decided to look in on the action at White's and was dismayed and deeply disturbed by the public denunciation of George Brummell by one of his creditors. The unpleasant scene did nothing to improve David's temper and, not waiting to discover the further developments, he returned home to spend some time with his secretary, going over the accounts and reports from his properties.

Meanwhile, at a beautiful classical mansion nestled in a parklike setting near the town of Chelmsford, Andrea was feeling very uncomfortable. From the moment she and Charles had arrived at his mother's home, she had found herself unexpectedly daunted by Lady Loudon's somewhat less than enthusiastic reception. The frail, seriously ill lady greeted her graciously, but Andrea soon became aware that she was being regarded with a faint air of reproach. It did not take much imagination on her part to divine the cause of this silent reproval, for she had just had a bit of a turnup with her cousin Charlotte, who had come to London for the Season from her husband's estate in Gloucestershire, on what she suspected was a similar grievance. Charlotte had waylaid her one afternoon at Retford House and took her to account for refusing to accept Jeffrey's proposal.

"Really, Andrea, I do think it frightfully insensible that you keep Jeffrey dangling at your shoestrings," she had charged bluntly.

"Charlotte, you know that is not the case," Andrea had retorted indignantly. "He knows very well that I have no intention of ever marrying him. Besides the fact that it is obvious we would not suit on such terms, there is the further obstacle in that I do not approve of marriage between first cousins."

"I don't think he is all that convinced that you will hold to that position. He won't be until you marry someone else. Why don't you?" her cousin asked almost petulantly. "You are twenty-six, after all, and are not without prospects."

"Charlotte," Andrea replied, trying not to laugh at this plain-spoken attempt to get her out of the way, "I refuse to accept someone else just to prove to Jeffrey that I won't have him."

"He has told me, you know, that he will not marry anyone but you," the older lady admitted reluctantly.

"I suspect that might be just as well," Andrea observed unsympathetically. "He really would not make good husband material. He is very much like my father and he uses this supposed passion for me in the same way that Father used his marriage to Ladyjane—to protect him against any compromising involvement. He poses as a victim of unrequited love and shamelessly accepts comfort from other conveniently sympathetic ladies."

"Andrea!" the proper matron admonished with a shocked expression. "If that is the case, it is a perfectly unacceptable state of affairs. He is the elder son and should make some push to continue the line."

"There are other heirs, Charlotte, and he does not feel pressured. Besides, Ned is obviously anxious to start his nursery and I fully expect Jeffrey to prove to be a perfectly unexceptionable bachelor uncle."

The conversation had ended on this unsatisfactory note, at least as far as one lady was concerned, and now Andrea felt sure that, at an opportune moment, she was going to be faced with another such interview. As anticipated, Lady Loudon seized her chance when Charles rode out to look over the estate with the steward.

Lady Loudon was not above playing on Andrea's sympathy and, after a jockeying sort of exchange, she eased into the subject with the confidence, "You know, my dear, my doctor is no longer trying to deceive me, and I know that my time is short. I have come to accept it, albeit reluctantly, and it has become my dearest wish to see Charles happily settled before I go."

"Oh," Andrea thought indignantly, "that is a perfectly infamous trick. How dare Charles let me be subjected to such a mortification!" She did not for one minute suppose that he had prompted his mother to advance this patently emotional appeal, but he surely must have been aware of her sentiments and might have anticipated such an attack. Andrea really felt quite put out with him especially since she had come to realize these last few days that the faint idea she had once had that she might marry him eventually was no longer even a glimmer, and she had meant to somehow convey to him before they returned to town that he should not continue to hope that she would reconsider in his favor. It was not that she had come to like or admire him any less, for he was a charming gentleman who had an interesting career before him and would be an attentive, thoughtful husband. Even so, Andrea felt, there was some ingredient lacking in their relationship that would render their marriage less than satisfactory—at least for her. The strange thing, Andrea mused, was that one of the main problems seemed to be that he thought too well of her, and she admitted to herself it would be contrary to her nature and too much of a strain to try to live up to the exactions of the role of paragon. He was always considerate, agreeable, and sensitive to her moods and wishes to the point of his solicitude being oppressive. Never once did she feel really needed, challenged, or free to indulge her capriciousness, which was a vital facet of her many-sided, sometimes, volatile, personality. The truth of the matter became evident during the days that they had spent almost entirely together, for she discovered herself often bored and restless in his company and knew she would never be content as his wife. She did not stop to analyze how it was that this had suddenly become clear, but it was almost with a sense of delivery that she confidently came to the indisputable conclusion that she would never marry Charles. However, because she knew that she had selfishly accepted his friendly devotion even though she realized he still had aspirations, it was with a vague feeling of guilt that Andrea tried to explain her position to his mother.

"My lady, I understand why you are telling me this and I wish I could personally ease your mind, but I must make my sentiments known to you so that you will not expect what cannot be. Charles and I have been good friends for many years, and I have a special fondness for him, but it is not of the kind that would dictate marriage."

"But, Andrea," an angry lady objected, "Charles has never considered anyone else because he always has expected you would marry him when you have settled your family. After all these years you cannot disappoint him! It is unthinkable!"

"Lady Loudon, I am sorry he has not transferred his affections to some other lady but, perhaps, if I can make him finally realize we have no future together except as friends, he will look about for a woman more worthy to be his wife. I am not, you know. He has put me on a pedestal and blinds himself to my faults. I'm afraid he would soon be disenchanted with me, were I so imprudent as to accept his proposal."

"Well! I must say you have certainly deceived Charles and I am thoroughly at odds with you for your deplorable lack of sensibility. You have treated him most shabbily, and I hope you will have the goodness to remove yourself from consideration unequivocally," the Countess expostulated with an air of outrage.

By this time Andrea had begun to imagine herself as some sort of adventuress and she was experiencing a depressing self-reproach. She could not even sustain her indignant humor at being so relentlessly badgered by her hostess, so she merely hung her head and promised meekly, "Of course, Lady Loudon. I will speak to him frankly and tell him it would be best if we did not see each other. Now, I think, if you will excuse me, I will walk for a while in the gardens."

"Very well, Andrea, but I wish you to know that it would please me exceedingly if you would follow the alternate course."

"Thank you, my lady," a subdued young woman replied with a regretful sigh, "but I just can't do it."

As she wandered slowly through the garden paths, admiring the profusion of flowers which were glorying in their first bloom, Andrea wondered once again how it had happened that her life had suddenly become so complicated. If only she had remained in Devon, things would have been so simple. She was inclined to disagree with Jonathan that Chloe should not have been denied the excitement of being presented. She had not yet caused Andrea any serious anxiety, but her obvious gullibility where the Duke was concerned was making her sister extremely nervous. "It is time to go home," Andrea decided. "Lord Howell will just have to find some way of continuing his courtship. I will suggest inviting him and his children for a stay in Devon."

While these plans for escaping were being so unilaterally devised at a country setting in Essex, back in London, Chloe—as ill luck would have it—was being led into an unpropitious delusion, notwithstanding Andrea's presumptions that her immediate planned activities offered no pitfalls.

A group of romantically minded young ladies were exchanging confidences and advancing opinions and suggestions on each other's conquests or pursuits. They had unanimously agreed that Chloe's situation presented the most interesting speculations, and they became extravagantly caught up in establishing her as the Season's heroine.

"Dear Chloe," gushed one dashing brunette, "you are so fortunate to have engaged the Duke's affections."

"Oh, but, Harriet, I do not think he has any serious intentions," Chloe objected. "You must know that he is a great friend of my brother and is being especially attentive to his family."

"Well, what a little goose you are! It is obvious to everyone that he has decided to marry and I have heard gossip from some of mother's friends that he has given up all his *chères amies* since you came to town."

Chloe blushed at this indelicate revelation but demurred, "As to that, you know, he first seemed to be interested in Andrea and only became more partial to me after she put him off."

"I think perhaps you did not realize what he was about," Miss Carolyn Milton advised knowingly. "Did you not say your sister had taken him in dislike before you ever left Devon?"

"Yes, she did," Chloe admitted hesitantly.

"Well, that explains it! He was trying to earn her good graces so she would not object to his courting you!"

"Oh, dear, surely not," Chloe protested again, for she was not at all happy with the turn of this conversation.

"Chloe," chided another young lady in disgust, "I do believe you must be the veriest greenhead. How can you not see what is in front of your face?!"

"Yes!" chimed in the others.

Miss Milton added dramatically, "And just think of the chance you have to play the heroine. To woo a man from his vices must be a particularly admirable design. It is like one of the romantic novels where the beautiful, innocent, young maiden leads a gentleman steeped in profligacy back to the path of righteousness."

This expression of eloquence earned applause from the

rest of the girls, who elaborated the theme until Chloe herself was almost convinced she was destined to be an instrument of salvation.

That evening at Almack's she became more fully aware of the Duke's attentions and read them in an entirely different, more personal way than she had been used to. Later, in her bed, she lay awake for several hours thinking about the afternoon's conversations. Could her friends be right? How could she be sure? It was true that the Duke had singled her out. What would she say if he proposed? She liked him very much and found it hard to imagine him a philanderer or worse. But it must be so, for everyone talked about how he had changed. Was it really because of her? She did not think she loved him, though she enjoyed his company. He treated her like a grown-up and it was very pleasant. Perhaps she *was* deceived by the romances she had read and that this feeling of harmony was as much as one should expect. She knew that Andrea did not approve of the Duke, but she did not think it fair to suppose he was beyond redemption. And then, remembering that Andrew had brought her to his friend's attention and thinking that he wished for the connection, she reluctantly reached the conclusion that, though she did not truly love the Duke, she would sacrifice her total happiness before the fact of his reformation for her sake.

Andrea did not have the same sentiments for self-sacrifice—at least in that particular area—and determined to come to an understanding with Charles that very evening. He had noticed the coolness between her and his mother and brought up the matter himself when they were alone.

"Andrea, has my mother been plaguing you?"

She gave him a rueful smile and replied, "A little."

"I'm sorry. I hope you don't think I encouraged her to do so. In fact, I asked her not to, but I'm afraid she is not very biddable."

"No, Charles, I understand, and I have to sympathize with her not only because of her unfortunate illness but because I feel I am deserving of some blame for not being more firm in my refusals. I am very fond of you and shall always cherish you as one of my dearest friends, but I cannot reconcile myself to a situation that would bring no real happiness to either of us and, because you have not truly accepted this decision, I have told your mother I would break off our friendship and try to convince you to choose another for your wife."

Charles moved to sit beside her and took her hands in his. "Andrea, my mother and I have been very close, especially since my father died, but I know her for a meddler, and I have never allowed her to deter me from what is important to me. I have loved you very deeply and sincerely, and I am convinced I always shall. It is true I had hoped you would marry me one day, but I shall not beleaguer you because I do not want to lose you completely. If you will not be my wife, I must accept only your friendship but nothing less, I beg you. We shall continue just as we have been these last few years. Do I have your promise?"

"I should like it that way, Charles," Andrea acknowledged gratefully, "but I did promise Lady Loudon."

"I will talk to her," he reassured her. "If you wish, we will go back to town tomorrow, since I put no great store by my mother's discretion."

"But, Charles, I do not want you to cut your visit short. She so jealously treasures these days with you."

"I plan to make the journey often now that I have talked to the doctor and he does not give her much time. I have noticed a definite decline since I was here three weeks ago, so I am thankful that I am close at hand rather than at the court in St. Petersburg. If we go back tomorrow, I can reorganize my work schedule to spend more time here."

"I am sorry, Charles, truly I am, to be a cause of some unhappiness for her. Would it make it any easier if I pretended to accept you?" Andrea asked humbly.

He smiled ruefully and told her, "I am sorely tempted to take you up on that, my love, but I'm afraid my mother is no fool and would call our bluff and insist we be married immediately. It would only complicate matters further. Do not tease yourself. If she did not have that to worry her, it would likely be something else, because her situation and condition contribute much to her inclination to lash out in some way about some real or imagined grievance."

Tears welled up in Andrea's eyes and she murmured sadly, "How awful for her. And she is really not so very old. It is quite depressing."

Charles put his arms around her and agreed, "Yes, so it is, my dear, but she has been ill a long time, you know, often with much pain, so, when the end does come, it may be a great release for her."

"Well, there is that," Andrea allowed, "but not much of a comfort, after all."

Because of the more clearly defined understanding between herself and Charles, Andrea felt better able to make allowances for his mother's irascibility and treated the older woman with indulgent consideration in a pleasantly natural manner. She confessed herself in total agreement with all the praises sung in behalf of the favorite son and the Countess soon concluded that such obvious mutual affection must surely lead them to the altar sooner or later. She began to speak as though it were an accomplished fact. Andrea said nothing further to disabuse her of the notion, thinking it a perfectly harmless deception, so that by the time she and Charles left for London the next afternoon they were all on very good terms.

During the long carriage ride both parties were less talkative than on their earlier journey—Andrea because she was affected by the melancholy atmosphere and Charles because he had suffered more of a disappointment than he had acknowledged. He suspected Andrea did not truly understand the reason for her sudden realization that she would not marry him, but he was afraid he did, and he silently berated himself for his unimaginative, protracted courtship. If he had been somewhat more aggressive years ago, things might have worked out very differently, but it was too late now. He would just have to sit back and wait for developments. "I would hardly have earned high marks for my diplomacy in this business," he thought as he cursed himself for "a damned fool."

They arrived at Queen Anne's Gate in the late afternoon and parted amicably, with Andrea promising to accompany him to a play and a reception before he returned to Essex. She found the usual group gathered for tea and stopped to chat with them for a few minutes before going to her room to change from her traveling clothes. She noted the Duke's absence but did not remark on it and refused Jonathan's invitation to accompany him, Chloe, Lady Jane, and Lord Howell to the theater that evening, saying that she felt a little tired and a peaceful night at home appealed to her.

Andrea had promised to spend the next morning with Katherine Hanley, and Jonathan found them together when he stopped by to speak to his mother before leaving for an appointment. "Good morning, ladies. How are you feeling today, Andrea? You looked a bit done-up yesterday."

"I'm all right, except I would like to go home."

"Any particular reason?" he asked with a speculative eye.

"Well, after certain recent vexing conversations, I am beginning to feel like a femme fatale," she answered dismally. "Maybe I should consider entering a convent."

The other two laughed at her woeful expression, and Mrs. Hanley remarked dryly, "That seems a little drastic, my dear. I think just going home would suffice."

Andrea gave her friend a wry smile and Jonathan asked, "Did Lady Loudon plead Charles's case?"

"Yes, and before that, Charlotte ripped up at me about Jeffrey."

"Poor Andrea," Jonathan sympathized with a grin. "What some women wouldn't do to have your fatal attraction for men."

"Well, *I'd* like to know how to get rid of it," the unappreciative girl complained acerbically.

"No way, I'm afraid. You're a natural enchantress. You'll just have to learn to live with it."

"That's a perfectly worthless observation," she accused resentfully. "Tell me, my friend, just how did you manage to escape my charms?"

"You're not my type, dear Andrea. I prefer a peaceful life," Jonathan answered dampeningly.

The ladies burst out laughing at this candid admission and Andrea said, "Thank God!—I *do* want to go home, Jonathan. Something dreadful is going to happen. I just *know* it is!"

"Another of your premonitions?" the gentleman asked quizzingly.

"Yes, and you know I'm usually right."

"Well, I'm ready to leave anytime. Can you persuade Chloe and Lady Jane?"

"I don't know. I'll sound them out today."

When Andrea returned to Queen Anne's Gate, she found both her mother and sister home between morning and afternoon engagements. She suggested they have an intimate lunch with just the three of them, since they had had had very little occasion to do so recently, what with one or the other of them always chasing about.

Lady Jane asked her about her trip and how she found Lady Loudon.

"Very ill, I'm afraid. She is not expected to live much longer and the depressing atmosphere was quite unnerving, especially since she had taken it into her head that she wanted to see Charles married before she died and called me on the carpet for keeping him out of circulation."

"Oh, dear, how uncomfortable for you," Lady Jane remarked sympathetically. "I can't believe Charles would have permitted it."

"As he said, he doesn't have much control over her, particularly now. Anyway, bringing it out into the open again gave me the opportunity to make my position clear to him, and he does understand now that I do not mean to marry him."

"Oh, Andy! Truly not?" Chloe exclaimed incredulously.

158

"He is such a lovely gentleman. I thought you might."

"So it seems to have appeared to others also," Andrea acknowledged ruefully. "I fear I have been at fault in allowing this misunderstanding to persist. My loves, I hope you will forgive me for what I am about to suggest, but the truth of the matter is that I am weary of London and all the frivolities, and I wondered if you would be willing to leave for Devon soon."

She noted with a detached amusement the expressions of dismay on the two very similar faces before her and felt guilty for presuming to interfere with their pleasures.

Lady Jane was the first to recover and apologized. "I am sorry to seem so surprised, Andrea, dear, but it is the middle of the Season and I had expected we were staying through."

"I know it seems unusual, Ladyjane, but we have been here for more than two months and we have enjoyed a gay social whirl but I have had enough and I long for the lovely peacefulness of Devon. I thought we might ask some of our friends to go with us—perhaps Ned and Naomi—and I think it would be famous if Lord Howell would come to us with his children."

"Oh, I don't know," said Lady Jane, coloring a little. "I don't think that would do at all."

"Why not? It's a marvelous place for children."

"Well, yes, but it just seems so forward."

"Nonsense. I'm sure he would be immensely pleased." Andrea turned to her sister and coaxed teasingly, "You haven't said anything, Chloe, darling. Are you ready to come to cuffs with me?"

The young girl had been stunned at first, but it had come on her while her mother and sister were talking that it might be a way out of her predicament. Perhaps she might escape before the Duke offered for her, an increasingly undesirable possibility that had been causing her a great deal of anxiety. She smiled sweetly and answered easily, "No, Andy, I'm not. I was just thinking. I wouldn't mind, really. I know you did not want to come in the first place, and I appreciate your arranging everything to please me. I have been enjoying myself excessively, but I know what it is all about now, and I shouldn't think I would look forward to such a bustling life on a regular basis. It is much too energy-consuming and leaves no time for onself."

Once again Andrea felt such a rush of love for her lovely, unaffected sister that she gave her a fierce hug. "Chloe, you are a darling to put up with such a bear of a sister. You make me feel quite selfish."

"Andy, don't be a goose. When would you like to leave? I *should* like to go to the concert next week," she hinted wistfully, for she had especially enjoyed the musical entertainments and had learned a good deal from watching other accomplished performers.

"Of course, love. Let's see—this is already May seventeenth. Perhaps we could plan our departure for May twenty-eighth. Most all of the grand affairs will be over by then anyway. Jonathan said today he was ready to leave anytime and would escort us. We will go home and prepare for our guests and have a lovely summer in Devon. Perhaps Andrew can get leave to spend some time with us. Is that all right with you, Ladyjane?" Andrea asked diffidently as she realized she and Chloe had been having a two-way conversation.

"Yes, dear. That is quite agreeable, but I do not think it would be at all proper to invite Lord Howell. I hope you will not go contrary to my wishes on this."

"Well, my dearest mama, I do think you are being very missish about the matter, but I have enough confidence in your beau's ingenuity to believe he will find a way to get himself invited, so I will not interfere."

"Andrea! Really! You presume too much," objected an unusually flustered lady. "Leslie and I have had a very agreeable companionship these last few weeks, but it certainly has not gone beyond friendship, nor should I wish it to. I beg you will not make a piece of work of it." And, with this attempt at self-deception, for it certainly did not deceive her daughters, she rose, saying she had some notes to write. She left two impiously amused young women congratulating themselves that their connivance to persuade their mother to reenter society had produced such admirable results.

Andrea went to inform the staff of their tentative plans for departure, and remembering her resolve to call the Duke's bluff, told Chloe she had another engagement that afternoon. She thought it would be perfectly proper for her to drive alone with him, since they would merely be riding in an open carriage in Hyde Park with a multitude of people around.

At this first evidence of Andrea's new approach David, who had been wracking his brain for some more effective strategy, realized he was already circumvented. He was even more frustrated when the next few days followed the same pattern, and he did not even get a glimpse of her. She had refused to accompany him and Chloe on any of their engagements, delegating the chaperon duties to others when it seemed desirable and attending most affairs with Charles and Jeffrey.

The Duke was beginning to experience a feeling of panic, especially after Chloe unwittingly let fall that they would be leaving for Devon shortly. He had not seen Andrea for more than a week by the time he claimed her for a waltz at Almack's on Wednesday. He felt so pleasantly bemused to be holding her in his arms that at first he could think of nothing to say. Presently he remarked, "Chloe tells me you are leaving for Devon Monday. Aren't you rushing it a little?"

"Maybe," she admitted dreamily, lulled by the movement of the dance and an uncommonly comfortable feeling. "But I have tired of the city and Chloe and Ladyjane are indulging me in my whim."

"Don't you think it is rather callous for three such popular ladies to decamp so beforehand, leaving behind a string of languishing beaus?"

"I know of only one who would actually languish, and I am hoping he will come up to scratch before we leave. In fact, he has asked for a private interview tomorrow."

"Loudon?" he asked angrily as he tightened his arm

around her waist, which for some strange reason made her feel quite lightheaded, a condition she conveniently attributed to the warmth of the room. "It is none of your affair, my lord Duke, but since I am so happily in accord with his aspirations, I shall tell you that my visitor will be Lord Howell. I suspect he wishes to have my opinion of the depth of Ladyjane's feelings and inquire if it would be too soon to press his suit."

She felt him relax as he swung her about the room and he grinned boyishly as he observed, "Yes, he is obviously moonstruck, and it would be an excellent match. What are you going to advise?"

"Well, I'm hoping to contrive some way of inviting him and his children for a stay in Devon. Ladyjane will not be able to resist, I'm sure, and in fact, if she would only admit it to herself, would be very happy to accept him now. However, I don't think she is ready yet and I shall suggest he hold off for a bit longer."

The waltz was almost over and David realized he had not yet served himself. He moved quickly to the attack and said lightly, "I have missed you this past week. I have not had to keep my wits sharp and am fearful of getting out of practice. Will you please stop avoiding me? We have not been to the Academy for weeks. Shall we go tomorrow or any other day you are free?"

Now, if Andrea had only followed her inclination to accept this most tempting invitation and encourage what she knew deep in her own mind to be a prelude for renewing his courtship which, had she been a less stubborn girl, she might have admitted was not an exactly intolerable prospect, she would have saved herself and everyone else a great deal of misery. But she still could not conquer her prejudices and so she replied off-handedly, "Oh, really, that is very thoughtful of you, Your Grace, but I'm afraid I am totally engaged the next few days, and there are several obligations and business matters to conclude before we leave town."

They had been walking off the floor, and before he could try to persuade her or protest her complete rejection, she was appropriated for the next dance by one of the younger gallants. The Duke was furious, but knowing that he would not be able to isolate her again that evening without creating some sort of scene, he decided that his present temper did not lend itself very well to a creditable performance of all the social amenities required of a gentleman. Rather than make himself miserable watching Andrea with her other admirers, he left the assembly to closet himself in his library with a bottle of brandy as he tried to formulate a scheme for preventing her from escaping him.

He absolutely must not allow her to leave town. He could think of only one action that could accomplish his purpose and, nefarious though it was, it at least offered enough of a provocation to cause her to discard this new pose of indifference.

The next morning he reviewed his conclusions and, on reflection, saw no reason to suspend his intention, even feeling an unholy satisfaction that he had envisioned a sure way of upsetting Andrea's complacence. Still in a black mood, he decided that she had goaded him beyond what it was reasonable to expect any man to endure. She would learn that he was not one of her amiable suitors, content to worship at her feet.

Letting his anger and frustration cloud his better judgment, he presented himself at Queen Anne's Gate for his afternoon appointment with Chloe. As had become the custom, they were allowed to proceed unaccompanied, an act of studied omission that added fuel to the Duke's resentment and pushed him into persuading himself that he was taking the only course left open to him.

He drove slowly through the park, acknowledging the usual greetings and observing the rituals, but soon he turned onto a less crowded lane, where it appeared they might not be interrupted for a time. He here initiated his offensive. "Chloe, my dear, I am finding it very difficult to accept the fact that you will be leaving town in a few days. I hope you have enjoyed our companionship as much as I have."

These words brought an immediate feeling of inevitability to the impressionable young girl, and she found part of herself withdrawing, leaving only a submissive alter ego to speak for her.

In a hollow, almost defeated tone that was a marked contrast to her usual animated manner, she replied dutifully, "Oh, but, of course, Your Grace. You have been most kind and have made my visit to London particularly pleasurable."

"I am glad, Chloe. You are a lovely, sweet young lady and," he added resolutely as he made the plunge, "I should like to ask you to consider accepting my hand in marriage."

The girl sat staring at her folded hands in her lap and remained silent for a moment. She had enjoyed the Duke's company because it had been great fun to be squired about by such an exceptional gentleman in her very first Season. Even an unpretentious girl like Chloe could not help but feel flattered and a little set up with herself. But she knew that she did not love him, and she could not believe he truly loved her. He had never even kissed her —not that she had really wished him to, but it did seem that he should have at least tried. Still, he *was* proposing. And why should he do so if he didn't want to marry her? She felt confused and was having trouble bringing herself up to the mark, in spite of her noble-minded resolution.

She heard his voice telling her, "I realize, naturally, that you must discuss this with your sister and your mother, so I will not press you for an answer today. I will call on you tomorrow, and you may then tell me what you have decided."

This proposal had the opposite effect to what David had hoped. Chloe suddenly knew that if she did as he suggested, she would likely lose her resolve. It was not all that strong now and she doubted she could withstand Andrea's protests and admonitions. She would have to announce an accomplished fact. With a feeling of having been driven into a corner, she sighed deeply and asked quietly, "Your Grace, Andrea told me before we came to town that you had visited us in Devon because you had decided to marry and that Andrew suggested you give thought as to whether or not I might suit. Is that true?"

David felt a sudden apprehension but answered cautiously, "Yes, my dear, it is."

"I see. Well, then, it will not be necessary to consult with my mother and sister, for I must tell you that Andrea would be violently opposed and I am persuaded my mother would be unhappy, also. But, since Andrew is my guardian and must approve or he would not have sent you, I am free to make my own decision." She paused for a moment, placing a terrible strain on David's composure. He suddenly realized things were not going as planned. The world seemed to end as he heard her say, "I shall be honored to accept, my lord Duke."

The turmoil in David's mind communicated itself to the horses and he had to concentrate on bringing them together as he raged at himself, "My God! My God! How could this be happening! The girl must be befuddled. She's not in love with me and doesn't want to marry me. She was supposed to tell Andrea I had offered so that that miserable girl would realize she had underestimated my resources. How could I have guessed Chloe would accept me outright! Does she want so much to be a Duchess? I wouldn't have thought that would be important to her. No—but what else? Andrew—that's it—because Andrew approves. Good Lord, I overlooked that aspect completely. Now I *am* in the basket. How does one take back a proposal?" He had to say something. After all, it was not the girl's fault, and he cursed himself for the blackest scoundrel to have used this poor innocent for his own purposes after he had promised his grandmother he would not hurt her. He turned to her and said gently, "Chloe, of course I am very pleased, but I think it would be best if you talked with your sister and your mother. I should not wish to alienate you from them and cause you any distress."

"Oh, no, Your Grace, it would not be like that. You see, we love each other very deeply and, while they will not be pleased with my marriage to you, it will not alter their feelings for me."

Being thoroughly confounded by this artless confidence, the Duke resigned himself to playing out the game and said, "Very well, then. If you are sure, I shall take you home, and you can tell your family. I will come tomorrow morning with a betrothal ring unless you send me a message to the contrary."

"I will expect you, Your Grace," Chloe acquiesced calmly.

At her home he handed her out of the carriage and brought her hand to his lips as he smiled kindly. "Good luck, my dear. I hope you do not have too much difficulty."

"Thank you, Your Grace. It will be all right in time," Chloe answered softly and turned to go into the house. A very subdued gentleman, smarting under well-deserved self-recriminations, made his way rather aimlessly to Grosvenor Square.

CHAPTER ELEVEN

In the morning Andrea had had a very successful conference with Lord Howell and assured him that she was confident he would not be disappointed in his hopes. But she suggested that he not move too quickly and gave him an abridged version of Lady Jane's first marriage so that he might understand that her standoffishness had nothing to do with him personally.

"Thank you for telling me, Andrea," the gentleman acknowledged appreciatively. "It does rather explain her withdrawal if I become too particular. I shall know better now how to proceed."

"I think it might hurry things a little if she met your children. I had hoped there was some way I could contrive to invite you and them for a visit to Devon, but Ladyjane has rebelled at the suggestion. Do you think you might inveigle an invitation?"

"Not likely, but I could invite all of you to my estate in Sussex. It would be more appropriate."

"Now there's a thought," Andrea exclaimed approvingly. "My lord, I leave the stratagems to you. For what it is worth, I am happy to tell you that both Chloe and I are on your side."

"I find that very propitious," a pleased gentleman admitted with a twinkling eye. "Now, perhaps, you will tell your mother I am looking forward to our morning ride."

Later in the day, after her sister had left with the Duke, Andrea went to the City for her appointment with Mr. Barnstable, so she was not home when Chloe approached Lady Jane to make her announcement.

It must be admitted that the girl found it a happy circumstance that her mother was alone, because she felt better able to deal with her than with Andrea. Nevertheless, it was with some hesitation that she entered Lady Jane's sitting room and, without any introduction, told her almost apologetically, in a subdued voice, "Mama, the Duke has asked me to marry him and I have accepted."

Falling back against her chair, Lady Jane stared at her daughter incredulously. It was some moments before she could speak. "Chloe, I am sure I misunderstood—"

"No, Mama, it is as I said."

"But, Chloe," her mother protested distractedly, "surely the Duke would have spoken to me first. It is most improper for him to approach you without permission, and even if he did, you ought to have come to discuss it with me. You are only seventeen!"

"I know, Mama, but Andrew approved and he is my guardian, you know," Chloe reminded her gently.

Lady Jane put her hands to her head and moaned, "Oh, dear! Oh, dear! I don't understand. I wish we had never come to town! Andrea was right—"

Having felt peculiarly lightheaded since she left the Duke, Chloe was very little moved by her mother's distress. She merely said, "Mama, please do not take on so. It is not such a terrible thing, and though I know it is not what you wanted for me, you will become accustomed." She leaned over to kiss her cheek and then begged to be excused, so she might go to her room to write to Andrew.

Lady Jane became more agitated as she thought about the dreadful consequences. By the time Andrea returned, she was hardly able to contain herself. She opened her door as she heard Andrea coming up the stairs and the girl immediately noticed her pale face and bewildered expression.

"Ladyjane, whatever is the matter?" she asked apprehensively. "You look as though you've seen a ghost."

"Andrea! The most unsettling thing—I can't comprehend it. My nerves are completely overset. Whatever are we to do?"

168

"My dear, do get yourself in hand and tell me what happened," Andrea said soothingly, leading her back into the room.

The elder lady sank into a chair and announced abruptly, "The Duke proposed and Chloe accepted."

The enormity of this revelation caused Andrea to react as if she had been struck. She grasped the back of a chair, feeling suddenly faint. Breathing heavily, she objected vehemently. "No! Not without any warning—surely she would have come to us. I would have sworn she was not truly interested. How could she have been so compliant?"

"Because of Andrew. She reminded me he was her guardian and that he approved," Lady Jane advised despondently.

"Dear God! What have I done?" Andrea exclaimed in self-reproach. "I didn't think he would go so far. It is all my fault."

"Andrea, how can you blame yourself? You have tried to prevent it, but there was really no chance once he decided to commit himself."

Andrea's guilty conscience would not permit her to absolve herself, and she wondered how Lady Jane would feel about it if she knew all the circumstances. She hesitated to reveal the skirmishes leading to this disaster because she had not yet convinced herself that the decision was incontrovertible. She still had a strong suspicion that something was not quite right—not only in the Duke's proposal but also in Chloe's acceptance. It had to be a discomfiting situation for both of them and yet by some ill-judged act of folly they had managed to get themselves in this muddle. She wondered if she could bring herself to tell her sister of the Duke's two-faced behavior but reluctantly decided that it would be a cruel thing to do, at least before she had discovered just what Chloe's feelings were and what had prompted her to land herself in this bramble. She wished Jonathan were here, but he had gone to Oxford for a couple of days and wouldn't return until the next evening.

Lady Jane had begun to cry. Even though she could not

help but like the Duke, she knew this would prove to be an unsatisfactory marriage. Chloe, it seemed, would follow in her own footsteps and would never know true happiness. Andrea put her arms around her. "Don't worry, darling. I shall never permit it to happen. But before I decide what to do, I had better see Chloe. I am completely dismayed because I cannot imagine why she acted in this harebrained manner, Andrew or no Andrew. It just doesn't make sense."

She went up the stairs and knocked at her sister's door.

"Andy? Come in," Chloe called as if she had been waiting for her. She rose from her little writing desk to ask a bit warily, "Has Mama told you?"

"Yes, darling," Andrea answered calmly. "Could we talk about it?"

"Oh, Andy," the girl declared thankfully as she threw her arms around her sister and began to cry softly, "I am so glad you have not come to rip up at me, for I made sure you were going to be terribly angry."

"And so I am, love, but mostly I am confused and I want to try to understand," Andrea said comfortingly, thinking with a feeling of relief that this spontaneous fit of the vapors certainly did not speak too strongly for a happy frame of mind. She immediately fell into her normal role of devoted sister.

"Now, come, what is there to cry about? Do you wish to change your mind? It is not too late, you know."

Slowly Chloe drew away, wiped her eyes, and tried to smile brilliantly, a pose which came off a little forced as she protested gaily, "Oh, no, of course not. It is settled and I am to be a duchess."

Andrea recognized the attempt at bravado and proceeded cautiously. "I had no idea you were taking the Duke seriously, my love. When did you decide you wanted to be a duchess?"

"Andy!" her sister exclaimed with a hurt expression. "It is not like that and I—I decided last week that I should accept if he offered."

"Why?"

Chloe was somewhat daunted by this uncompromising question, but she rallied, "Because—because I wished to."

"Is it because you think Andrew approves?"

"Well, you said yourself that it was his idea but—that is not the main reason."

"What is, then?" Andrea coaxed. "Did the Duke pressure you?"

"No! I told you! I *wish* to marry him," the harried girl declared stubbornly. She turned away to straighten up the papers on her desk.

Andrea realized that she would get no further for the moment. Chloe had obviously made up her mind she would not be swayed. There was some unknown factor involved here which she had failed to uncover but, whatever it was, it had nothing to do with Chloe's being in love with the Duke. She was not in love and couldn't even bring herself to say so.

"All right, Chloe," Andrea surrendered. "I wish you would confide in me, but if you are determined to play the martyr or whatever role it is you envision for yourself, we shall just have to hope that in time you will be relieved of your delusions." With these harsh words Andrea left the room to report the unsatisfactory results of the interview to Lady Jane, leaving Chloe in a depressed mood, staring dully in the mirror and lamenting, "Oh, *why* did he have to choose *me*?"

"I don't know, Ladyjane," Andrea remarked in frustration. "There is something in this I do not understand, but it seems she is resolved to go through with it."

"I would not have thought it, but perhaps she is in love with him," Lady Jane ventured doubtfully.

"No," Andrea demurred reflectively, "she doesn't even imagine she is. She merely keeps repeating that she *wishes* to marry the Duke."

"Whatever has possessed her?"

"It's a puzzle to me, but it doesn't signify," Andrea reassured her mother confidently. "I promise you I will scotch this affair one way or another. That abominable, unprincipled, arrogant, spiteful, thoroughly depraved devil will never marry Chloe. I'll see him dead first!"

"Andrea!" Lady Jane admonished in horror as she observed the increasingly vengeful expression on the girl's face. "My dear, you must not frighten me with these ravings. It's enough that I have Chloe to worry about."

"Sorry, my love. You know I have an ungovernable tongue when I am angry. I daresay I may not have to resort to violence. I do wish Jonathan were here to consult with us. Surely there must be some way we can prevent an announcement." She brushed her hand across her eyes and then said thoughtfully, "Let me change for dinner and, perhaps, when we talk to Chloe again, things will become clearer." With these faintly encouraging words, which in no way reflected her private convictions, she left her stepmother and went to her own room.

If there were overlapping moods of consternation, unhappiness, and self-reproach at Queen Anne's Gate, these emotions were more than equalled at Grosvenor Square.

The Duke had returned home in a despondent mood and retired to the library, where he sprawled dejectedly in the large leather armchair. His air of melancholy was remarked by the butler and reported through channels to the Duchess. Having been so purposefully alerted, she decided she had best find out what new scrape he had gotten himself into and went downstairs to find him sitting slumped forward with his head in his hands.

"Good God! What brought you to this state?" she exclaimed with her usual forthright approach.

Her grandson looked at her glumly and motioned her to sit down before he spoke. "Your Grace, you see before you the vilest, most infamous, accursed, miserable wretch alive."

Undismayed at what seemed to be rather excessive self-disparagement, the Duchess remarked dispassionately, "Has Andrea been raking you over the coals again?"

This bit of drollery brought a weak smile to his lips and

he answered ruefully, "Not yet. But she will, and I am almost looking forward to it, because I deserve everything she will lay at my door and more."

"David," his grandmother said impatiently, "stop playing the dog in the manger and tell me what you have done."

He took a deep breath and confessed gloomily, "I have gotten myself engaged to Chloe."

"My God!" the Dowager groaned as she stared in disbelief. "Have you gone mad?"

"I have been asking myself the same question."

"Just how did you manage to commit such an idiocy?"

"For me it was easy," the Duke answered bitterly.

The Duchess had to restrain herself from boxing his ears, for she was no believer in letting oneself be defeated by any circumstance, no matter how overpowering, and she held no sympathetic sentiments for this posture of unprofitable self-condemnation. "David, do bring yourself out of the doldrums long enough to tell me how this came about."

Her grandson confessed he had grievously misjudged the matter and he described the interview. "How was I to know that the little widgeon would accept me on the spot?!"

Shaking her head in disbelief, the Duchess said, "I don't understand why she did. I am persuaded she doesn't in the least wish to marry you."

"She doesn't. But I was such a chowderhead as to forget Andrew's part in this business."

"Well, you have told me how you got yourself into the briar patch, but have you figured out how you're going to get out of it?"

"I'm not beyond hoping Andrea will come to my rescue," the Duke answered with a wry face.

"And if she can't?"

"I suppose I shall have to play out the game."

"You will not actually marry the child! I absolutely forbid it! It would be the most dastardly act imaginable, considering how you feel about Andrea."

"My dear grandmother, please do not let your lively imagination run away with you. I know I have played the knave in this business but I am not totally lost to shame, nor am I mad. I have no intention of marrying her. If worst comes to worst, I shall just have to keep postponing the actual event until she comes to her senses. Since there isn't one person in favor of this connection, I have no fear of being pressured to set a date, so my immediate problem is not getting out of it but having to deal with Andrea."

"What of Jonathan Hanley?"

"If he continues to play the role he has been playing these many weeks, Jonathan will likely just stand back and let us dig holes for ourselves," David muttered with considerable resentment.

The Duchess laughed and began to feel less anxious about the situation, though she had to admit the worst was yet to come. "I suppose you will be wanting the Newbury betrothal ring."

"Certainly not!" the Duke denied forcefully, causing his grandmother to raise her eyebrows.

"I shall never give that ring to any woman but Andrea. Is there another that will serve? If not, I'll make an early visit to a jeweler tomorrow to find something appropriate."

"That omission will certainly cause some comment," the Dowager warned.

"If the subject should arise, I will accuse you of tenacity," the Duke teased wickedly.

"Indeed you will not!" the Duchess bridled indignantly. "But I suppose you could dodge the issue by claiming it needs to be reset or that it is safely housed in Dorset. I imagine we can find a substitute. Come to my room and we will go through my jewelry case."

With a resigned sigh David followed his grandmother, even though he still cherished a hope that he would somehow be delivered from the sorry plight to which he had so mindlessly brought himself.

Dinner at the Wycliff residence was a strained affair. Chloe maintained an unusual silence, as if she were steeling herself against some sort of attack, while Lady Jane seemed to have delegated the leadership of the inquisition to Andrea and merely parrotted her step-daughter's probings and comments. Andrea made a determined attempt to suppress her desire to unequivocally forbid any further contact between her sister and the Duke, which really was beyond her authority and would likely be challenged. Instead, she resolutely kept her temper and gently urged Chloe to be sure she was aware of the importance of the step she was taking. Wanting to bring Jonathan into it some way or another, she suggested that she postpone the final commitment until she had had the benefit of his advice.

Not completely understanding what it imported, Chloe began having perplexing reservations about her decision whenever Jonathan entered her thoughts, which had been happening with some frequency. She dared not wait to consult him lest she be deterred from her purpose. Instead, she informed her mother and sister that the Duke would be coming to bring her a ring the next morning and would then send an announcement to the *Gazette*. With this note of finality, she excused herself and went to play some of her more melancholy pieces on the pianoforte.

Lady Jane and Andrea looked at each other in bewilderment, neither able to accept that this dreaded blow had actually fallen. They were frustrated at having made no progress or impression and, moreover, had elicited very little in the way of an explanation, merely being advised again and again that Chloe *wished* to marry the Duke.

Andrea informed Lady Jane that the distressing infelicity of the situation had quite unnerved her, and she thought she would retire to her room to put cold compresses on her head while she tried to devise some counteraction that would scotch the Duke's fell designs.

Once in her room, however, Andrea found that she could not relax, being completely confused by the conflicting emotions that beset her: disbelief, disappointment, despondency, and something suspiciously akin to jealousy.

Since all of these sentiments would not bear close examination, she once again took refuge in her anger and in very short order had worked herself into a fury, imagining all sorts of horrible fates for the despicable Duke. She even conceived a fantastic notion of disguising herself as a gentleman, so she might go to Manton's Shooting Gallery to engage in target practice.

Finally exhausted, she fell into a deep sleep and did not waken until almost eight o'clock the next morning. With the new day she found herself free of most of the disquieting emotions that had plagued her the night before, and in the remaining pose of cold anger, she determined to confront the Duke to advise him of the total unacceptability of his nefarious intentions.

She dressed carefully, choosing one of her older, subdued, less stylish gowns, and groomed her hair in a severe fashion, pulling it back into a heavy knot. Satisfied with the resulting image, which projected a certain implacability, she stopped to have a few words with her stepmother before going down to breakfast.

Lady Jane had not yet risen, but she called for Andrea to come in, hoping to hear she had miraculously solved their dilemma.

"No, my love, I'm afraid I have not been at all inspired, beyond threatening the Duke with dire consequences, and I can't quite see meeting with any success by such a milk-and-water attack. Do you suppose there is any chance that Chloe might have come to her senses?"

"Oh, I hope so," Lady Jane said doubtfully. "I can't think what Jonathan is going to say when he gets back this evening." She moaned and put her hands to her head. "I am feeling miserably queasy this morning and I don't know how I am going to get through the day."

"Well, I am not in fine feather myself, when it comes to that," Andrea admitted, "but we must pull ourselves together for, if this farce is to be continued, we will both have our roles to play and you must show yourself as an outraged Mama."

With a sudden resolve, Lady Jane got out of bed and

vowed staunchly, "And so I will! I hope I am not such a poor creature that I cannot voice my disapproval of the Duke's ungentlemanlike conduct in approaching Chloe without my permission. I shall certainly call him to book for dealing me such a slight."

"Bravo, my love," Andrea approved with a smile. "We shall marshal our forces and try to rout the enemy, for I will have some graphic words for him myself."

In spite of the abnormal relations between the three ladies, they met as usual for breakfast and Andrea and Lady Jane were so struck by Chloe's unnaturally sober, almost apologetic demeanor that they could not bring themselves to badger her. They reserved their fire for the Duke.

The villian of this piece was at the same moment lingering over his coffee, hoping against hope that a messenger would bring him a release. By half-past ten he realized time had run out and he reluctantly drove his curricle through the rain, which had almost become a permanent condition since early spring and today seemed especially fitting, as the heavy gray skies reflected his dampened spirits.

David had decided to first seek an audience with Lady Jane, for he knew she had to be deeply offended by his precipitate action, and he wished he could explain or at least ease her mind, since he had no desire to cause her any further unhappiness. In fact, he had spent the better part of the night chastising himself for having shown so little sensibility toward such a vulnerable, gentle lady. It was bad enough that he had misled Chloe, but she had more well-grounded reserves than her mother and would come about unharmed if he handled the affair with subtlety. He waited uncomfortably while the butler announced his arrival, wondering with a conscience-smitten air of resignation what maledictions Andrea would have invented to bring down on his head.

After a hurried conference with her stepdaughter, Lady Jane went to receive the Duke. When she entered the drawing room, David was immediately reminded of

Andrea's pithy comment that he would more properly have offered for the mother than the daughter. It was the height of absurdity to imagine this petite, youthful-looking lady as his mother-in-law.

"Good morning, Your Grace," Lady Jane greeted with noncommittal simplicity, waiting for him to initiate their conversation.

"Good morning, Lady Wycliff. It is good of you to receive me so graciously when I know you must be wanting to give me a rare trimming," the Duke submitted with a guise of self-approach. "I have asked for this interview to apologize for my exceedingly blameworthy behavior. I cannot offer any excuses other than that I did not intend for this to happen in this way, and I most humbly ask your forgiveness."

Confronted with such a forthright admission of guilt and contrition, Lady Jane was at a loss to know how to proceed, but she remembered Andrea's admonition not to be deceived by the devil's oily tongue. She summoned enough resolution to scold, "You are right that I am deeply disturbed by this most dismaying development, Your Grace. I feel sure that you must have known Chloe's affections were already engaged, though she has not yet realized it, and I thought better of you than to imagine you would stoop to taking advantage of her susceptibility to the circumstances of your being her brother's friend, to say nothing of your having the impropriety of speaking to her without consulting me."

"My God," David groaned to himself. "This is going to be worse than I expected. I never dreamed this meek little lady could be so fierce, and it certainly speaks wonders for the concept of a mother's protective instincts, although I expect she has been well-primed by one eloquent little witch." He took a deep breath and acknowledged sincerely, "Believe me, my lady, I count myself well-deserving of any and all approaches you can heap on me, and if you feel that Chloe wishes to retract, she need only say so and I will not contest her decision."

Lady Jane looked nonplused at this unexpected capitulation but soon recovered and rang for the butler to send for Chloe and Andrea. She felt in need of new guidance, now that the Duke had shown himself so penitent and accommodating.

The two girls appeared shortly, with Andrea following Chloe into the room and remaining a little apart near the door. David looked at her apprehensively and was so affected by the anguished expression in her eyes that he had an almost uncontrollable impulse to get down on his knees to beg her forgiveness. It was with a shock that she read his message. She closed her eyes and leaned against the door, unable to believe the unmistakable evidence that he still wanted her and yet was engaged to her sister. If she had needed any grounds to convince her that she must save Chloe from the clutches of so unprincipled a man, he had certainly provided it in that telling instant.

David had managed to get control of himself and was saying to Chloe in a gentle voice, "My dear, I have been speaking with your mother as I should have done before and we are agreed that, should you wish to change your mind, I will not press my advantage."

For a moment Chloe had an illusion of a weight being lifted, but when she raised her eyes and saw the Duke looking at her with such a kind expression, she experienced an immediate feeling of guilt as she thought how terribly nobly he was behaving. Not having the heart to disappoint him, she replied softly, "No, Your Grace, I have no wish to refuse you and indeed will be greatly honored to be your wife."

This very charming little speech was met by an incredulous silence. There was not a person in the room who did not wish to shake the girl to remove the cobwebs from her head, but they were all so fascinated by her quiet but firm determination that they were at a total loss to decide on the next move.

Finally, coming to the conclusion that, short of an outright confession, there was no way out of it at the moment, the Duke stepped forward to take her hand and said chivalrously, "All right, then, Chloe, if you are sure, I am pleased to give you this ring which is one of the family jewels." He slipped a very elegant sapphire surrounded by diamonds on her finger and then brought her hand to his lips.

"Thank you, my lord Duke. It is lovely," Chloe responded, blushing prettily, even as she wished she had not been defeated by a call to martyrdom.

Andrea had remained silent during these dealings, being overcome by a sense of unreality, but she now remarked coldly, "Your Grace, before you leave, I should like a private word with you."

This request brought an immediate protest from her sister, who admonished heatedly, "Andy, I beg you will not try to interfere because I will not have you rip up at the Duke."

The prospect of being protected by this sweet child was too much for David and he burst out laughing. "My dear Chloe, it is quite elevating to find myself with a charming champion, but I am used to fighting my own battles. I have known that I would be faced with a true test when Andrea should let fly. However, I have steeled myself, and I would prefer to get it over with, so you need not scruple to leave us. Go now with your mother and I will come back this afternoon to take you for a drive."

Lady Jane secretly applauded this proposal and was thankful to be spared the next few minutes, for Andrea had been unnaturally quiet and Lady Jane would lay no odds on how much longer her stepdaughter would be able to suppress her denunciations. She urged Chloe to pay heed to the Duke and took her by the hand to lead her out of the room, judiciously closing the door behind them.

The two antagonists eyed each other challengingly and Andrea spoke first, saying with heavy sarcasm, "Is that how you mean to treat her, Your Grace?—'Run along now with your Mama like a good girl and I will give you a treat later.' Rather fitting, though, when one thinks about it."

Taken by surprise by the unexpected line of this opening thrust, David could offer no rebuttal and stood waiting in sufferance for the next volley.

It was not long in coming. Andrea noted succinctly, "I must say your timing was well calculated. If Jonathan had not been so conveniently out of the way, you might not have had such an easy time of it."

As this circumstance had in no way had any bearing on his actions, the Duke was goaded to object to the injustice of her assumption and denied emphatically, "I was not aware that he was out of town. You know very well that this scrambling proposal was precipitated by the fact of your imminent departure for Devon."

Refusing to examine what was left unsaid in this declaration, Andrea observed regretfully, "I suppose I must blame myself to some extent for this wretched business, having foolishly misjudged you again because, in fact," she continued, taking a quivering breath and looking at him with an accusing face, "I—I did not think you would actually do it."

The revealing disappointment in her voice and the hurt in her eyes were more than David could bear. Taking a step toward her, he pleaded, "Andrea, do not look at me like that. You know I—"

Perceiving the danger in allowing him to continue, Andrea put up her hand and said sharply, "Your Grace, I beg you will not compound your ignominy with any shameful indiscretions and," she added bitingly, "when—when it comes to looking at people, you had best censure yourself because your present expression borders on the obscene, considering you are engaged to my sister."

Realizing that the battle had just begun and that he would have to weather considerable punishment before he could hope for any reversal in her attitude, the Duke checked himself and asked humbly, "Andrea, do you think we might sit down? I am finding these exchanges much more exhausting than I had anticipated."

"Of course, Your Grace," Andrea said agreeably, not wanting to rout her quarry prematurely. She had not done with him by a long chalk.

"And I might bring to your attention that all this formality is somewhat misplaced now that we are to be closely connected," the gentleman suggested. "Could you use my name?"

"Well, I will have to admit I *would* like to call you something else because everytime I have to say Your *Grace* I feel positively nauseated," Andrea acknowledged pungently.

The Duke had a hard time suppressing his amusement as he thought, "Now *that* is more like it." Aloud he prompted, "Could you settle for David?"

"Do you have another name?" Andrea asked hesitantly.

"Don't you like David?"

"Yes, I do. It actually is one of my favorite names and much too charming for you!"

"I see," he commented meekly, not taking offense. "Well, then, how about Stephen?"

"Stephen?!" she exclaimed, staring uncomfortably.

"Another of your favorites?" he quizzed, thoroughly enjoying himself. "I'm afraid John is the last choice."

"John," she said weakly, looking completely defeated.

"That, too?" the Duke sympathized, shaking his head. "It seems we are at a standstill."

Becoming angry with herself for having been tripped up by her capriciousness, Andrea drew herself up and snapped at him, "Do be quiet! I will call you David since that is your name. Now—David—I don't know what maggot Chloe has gotten into her head (an admission that prompted the Duke to say to himself, "I don't either, love, but I was wishing you would find out") but I mean to find out, and when I do, I am sure I will be able to talk some sense into her. In the meantime, take care that you do not hurt or humiliate her and make sure your paramours do not bare their fangs."

This taunt pierced the Duke's resolution to give her her head. "Andrea," he warned, "I am prepared to take a good measure of abuse from you, but when you go off on that tangent, you are out of line and well you know it."

With a look of skepticism she retorted caustically, "I must say that for someone who has just committed the basest flimflammery, you are remarkably self-righteous and," she added belligerently, "being well aware of the magnitude of your deceit, if I were a man, I would call you out." Suddenly caught up with this tempting idea, she looked at him with a speculative eye and ventured hopefully, "I don't suppose you would accept a challenge, would you?"

"Andrea, for God's sake, don't be ridiculous," David remonstrated with an involuntary grin.

"You need not be so derisive, my lord Duke," Andrea advised, taking immediate offense. "If you have at anytime been impressed with Drew's marksmanship, it might interest you to know that I have always been able to outshoot him."

David had an almost uncontrollable impulse to burst out laughing and crush her against him, but he restrained himself and merely informed her depressingly, "Whether you can or not is of no consequence, you little fire-eater, because you are going to have to bury this fantasy. You have obviously been reading too many gothic novels."

"Not too many—just enough," she instructed calmly. "They can be very informative in matters of this kind, you know. I will tell you how it might be," she offered as she fixed her gaze on a blank space across the room and began speaking in a slow, conjectural voice, "I shall be dressed all in black and appear as a shadow in the dark of night. Suddenly, there will be a flash of light and the sharp report of a pistol. You will feel a searing pain and then . . . no more. No more." She looked at him sorrowfully with tears running down her face and murmured, "What a pity."

It was the first time David had been treated to one of her dramatic posturings, and he stared in disbelief at this utterly incredible performance. She never ceased to amaze him, and he wondered if he would ever completely understand her. He was about to take her in his arms to comfort her and brush the tears from her cheeks when she suddenly changed her expression and turned to eye him expectantly.

"My God, Andrea," he spouted in complete confusion. "Your damnably unsettling unpredictability is enough to send a man to Bedlam."

"Or to his Maker," she promised darkly.

"I wish you would stop playing the humbug," he said in exasperation. "This conversation has gone beyond the amusing."

"It was never intended to be amusing," Andrea informed him softly. "Tell me, David, if you had a lovely young sister whom you loved more than life itself and she was being hoodwinked by an out-and-out bounder, what would you do?"

"This situation hardly fits that description," he demurred.

"It's how I see it."

"Well then, I suggest you reexamine the facts and ask yourself how it is that we have all arrived at this impasse."

"Do not think to blame *me* for your foolhardiness," Andrea protested indignantly. "*I* do not lose my direction in a fit of pique every time I do not get my way."

"That's a cock-and-bull story if ever I heard one!" the Duke charged. And then, deciding that they had best cease hostilities lest he end up throttling her, he said, "As we are reduced to cutting at each other, there seems to be very little purpose to discussing this further. I hope you can at least contrive some guise of civility when we are in company so that we do not set tongues wagging."

"I will make a supreme effort," she submitted with heavy exaggeration.

David bowed mockingly and left her to ponder the results of their duel. Andrea was brought to the depressing conclusion that it had been an exercise of total futility since neither side had gained the slightest advantage. With a deep sigh she decided she had best call on Katherine Hanley so that Jonathan might be apprised of this revolting situation the moment he arrived home.

CHAPTER TWELVE

At Grosvenor Square the Dowager Duchess was impatiently awaiting her grandson's return. She had canceled her appointments for the morning feeling she could find no better entertainment than in her own sitting room. She was not disappointed and listened avidly to the Duke's tale of woe, showing a less than sympathetic face, especially when he reported his verbal contest with Andrea, succumbing to outright laughter when he mentioned the matter of having to refuse a challenge.

"David, that is the most outrageous girl but I adore her. I hope you realize that if you do take her on, you have your work cut out for you for the rest of your life."

"I know, my dear, and it's not *if* but *when*," David acknowledged with a devilish grin.

"How can you be so sure?" the old lady asked skeptically.

"Because today I made the most unexpected discovery —that the little vixen is in love with me."

The Duchess looked at him incredulously and remarked drily, "Well, if you have gathered that from the pitched battle you've just described, I am afraid I must presume you have become queer in the attic."

"It wasn't what she said, love, it was how she looked. She couldn't hide her hurt and her disappointment. I desperately wanted to take her in my arms and confess the whole, but I knew she would never forgive me if I disillusioned Chloe so heartlessly. So I am forced to play this game for a little while. Let us hope my 'betrothed' has second thoughts before too long."

"Did you send the announcement?"

"Yes, I felt I had to and I have been cursing myself ever since, not only because it is a total hum, but because of the insult to Andrea," David responded irritably.

"Well, if you are right and can keep from committing some other untoward folly until this blows over, perhaps you may win out, after all."

"Don't worry, my faithless Grandmother. I have had so much practice at being a pattern saint, I am beginning to think I have a natural inclination for the role," the Duke assured her with a wry face.

This astonishing pronouncement sent the Dowager into a fit of laughter, causing her grandson to counterfeit an offended look as he chided, "You must give me credit, you know. I have been behaving with the utmost propriety."

"Maybe, but I know just how long *that* will last," the Duchess observed brashly.

"So do I, my love, so do I," the Duke allowed, grinning roguishly as he stooped to kiss her cheek.

The matter was not being treated so lightly in another part of town. Andrea had driven to Curzon Street to inform Katherine Hanley of the unhappy state of affairs, and they were both considering the subject with the utmost seriousness. Mrs. Hanley tried to refrain from deploring Chloe's part in the imbroglio, although she privately thought her son and Andrea were inclined to be overindulgent. She suspected the girl was not as fragile in spirit as they imagined and would be better served if they did not always humor her in her flights of fancy. Instead, she confined her animadversions to the Duke, thus fueling Andrea's anger, and, between them, they blackened his character with the greatest enjoyment and a total lack of reservation. Their biggest concern, of course, was Jonathan's reaction.

"He will be upset I don't doubt," Andrea said matter-of-factly, "but we spoke of this possibility before we came to town and we were both agreed that such an arrangement could not be countenanced. I am persuaded that he will take some action to prevent the actual event but," she added darkly with an ominous expression, "even if he doesn't, I certainly will!"

Her friend looked at her warily and admonished, "Andrea, I hope you will behave with discretion."

"I shall try, but it is not going to be easy because I have the most exquisitely fiendish visions of putting a bullet through that unscrupulous blackguard," responded a most uncommonly bloodthirsty young lady.

With this incredibly indiscreet assertion, Andrea left Katherine Hanley in a highly anxious state and this lady remained at home impatiently waiting for her unsuspecting son. She began to have serious apprehensions about the girl's freakish turn of mind.

By the time Jonathan arrived at his uncle's house that evening, his mother was somewhat the worse for wear, having had several hours to bring herself to distraction, a most unusual emotional state for a woman of her normally equable temperament.

With considerable surprise Jonathan found himself pounced upon and unceremoniously pulled into her room when he stopped to see her before changing out of his riding clothes.

"Good Lord! What has happened?" he exclaimed in amazement, struck by her unnaturally harassed appearance.

"Jonathan, this has been the most trying day. I have always prided myself on my composure, but it seems there are limits to which even I may be pushed."

With an amused look of exasperation the young man suggested, "Will you please order your thoughts and answer my question?"

"Well, for a start, overnight Chloe has become engaged to the Duke!" his mother announced dramatically.

"My God!" Jonathan groaned, sinking into a chair. "How the devil did that come about?"

"It seems that you and Andrea underestimated him when you decided to stop dogging his heels whenever he was with Chloe. He proposed yesterday afternoon when they were driving unchaperoned in the Park."

"Damn! I shall have to take the blame for that. It was at my suggestion that we changed tactics but not for one moment did I think there would be any danger. It was so obvious that he meant to have Andrea."

"Getting engaged to her sister is a remarkably roundabout way to bring that to pass," Mrs. Hanley observed drily, regaining her equanimity now that she had a confidant.

"Yes, I give you that," Jonathan said musingly. "I confess I find this development incredible, however. There must have been some misconception because, while he used this trump card as an underlying threat, he never meant to play it. Still, it appears he has and that Chloe thought he was serious. But why did she accept?"

"Because she thought Andrew wished it," his mother informed him, "although Andrea believes there is more to it than that."

"Lord! What a muddle!"

"Yes, you might say that, but I must tell you that it promises to be a lot worse."

"Why?"

"Because Andrea is on the warpath."

"I'll bet she is!" Jonathan said, grinning. "Kensington is going to pay dearly for this fool's trick."

"Let's hope it's not with his life or at least an arm or a leg," the worried lady remarked anxiously.

"What do you mean by that?"

"I mean, my dear boy, that she is threatening to shoot him."

Jonathan looked at his mother in disbelief and then went off into peals of laughter.

Mrs. Hanley viewed this reaction dubiously and she remonstrated, "I do not think you would be so unimpressed if you had seen the look on her face."

"Mother, surely you cannot envision Andrea as an assassin?" Jonathan said chidingly.

"Well, when you put it that way, it does seem a little

farfetched," the lady allowed. "But I must say this whole affair is proving extremely nervewracking. It's no wonder I am become fuddlebrained. What are you going to do?"

"Tomorrow morning I will first call on the ladies and then I'll have a chat with the Duke."

Her son's unruffled, matter-of-fact response caused Mrs. Hanley to observe him closely. She asked in a puzzled voice, "Jonathan, aren't you disturbed about all this?"

The young man turned a serious face on his mother and replied soberly, "Yes, my dear, of course I am. To use one of Andrea's more vivid expressions, I could wring her neck for being so stubborn and unreasonable. As for Kensington, I hold him at fault for his damnable impatience and lack of finesse; and," he added wistfully, "I *could* wish that Chloe had been more discerning and not so susceptible, though I suppose I must assume some blame for her falling into error. I have been so used to waiting for her to grow up that I failed to see she already has."

"Well, Jonathan, I have not said anything, but it has seemed to me that you have misjudged the girl's emotional capabilities. It is true that she is an innocent and seems young but, I think, only in comparison to Andrea. She is a great deal more mature than other girls her age, in spite of her romantic fantasies, which I suspect led her down this path. You should have made more of a push to assure that they were directed toward you."

"Yes, I see that now," the young man admitted ruefully, "and I shall have to pay the price for being so behindhand." With a deep sigh he left his mother to retire to his room, where he gave considerable thought as to how he might best circumvent this inauspicious development.

The next morning Jonathan was admitted to the Wycliff residence just as Andrea was descending the staircase. With a fervent "Thank God" she motioned him to the parlor and closed the door after them.

"I must say you look properly knocked up," an ungallant gentleman remarked undiplomatically.

"I didn't sleep well last night," Andrea admitted with a

downcast expression as she sank into a chair. "Jonathan, I am so confused and frustrated I don't know which way to turn. I hope you will able to make some sense out of it."

"It seems there has been a deal of miscalculation by all parties. I suspect Kensington is every bit as much flummoxed as we are."

"He *did* propose, Jonathan," Andrea told him dully.

"Not with any thought of being accepted, I imagine. I feel sure his intent was merely to wage a battle of nerves."

Andrea looked at her friend noncommittally and warned, "I'm afraid you are going to find Chloe quite adamant, for she has closed her mind to reason and will only say that she *wishes* to marry the Duke."

"Well, she has got some maggoty notion in that funny little head, so I suppose we are just going to have to practice forbearance until we can discover what it is."

"I might have known you would take a passive approach," Andrea said witheringly.

"One hotspur is more than enough, my dear girl," Jonathan declared pointedly. "*And* I beg you to stop making murderous threats. It is very unsettling to the sensibilities of more delicately minded females."

Andrea gave him a wry smile but only asked, "Do you have any constructive ideas at all?"

"I shall plant seeds of doubt. My mother thinks we have been guilty of poor judgment in not recognizing that Chloe is no longer a child."

"I expect she is right and, after all, she *will* be eighteen in less than three months. I shall go tell her you're here and you may start your campaign. I am glad you are to take over. If I hear her tell me what she *wishes* one more time, I think I shall go mad," Andrea avowed passionately.

She went to Chloe's room and informed her sister that Jonathan was waiting downstairs to see her, watching closely for any sign that would betray her. She was gracelessly pleased at the perturbed expression that immediately showed on the girl's face.

Chloe rose and began to move about nervously. "Andy, do you think Jonathan is going to scold me?"

"Certainly not!" Andrea replied sharply and was perversely irritated at her sister's obvious air of relief, which incited her to add provokingly, "He loves you too deeply to wish to cause you any distress."

Had she not been in an uncommonly uncharitable mood, Andrea would have been overcome with guilt on seeing the almost horrified look on Chloe's face, but she had convinced herself that her sister was going to have to learn to face facts. Still, she had a feeling that Jonathan would not thank her for that abrupt disclosure, and she decided she had best make her exit before her sister insisted on an explanation.

After Andrea's revelation it was some minutes before Chloe could compose herself enough to go downstairs. She entered the parlor hesitantly, suddenly uncomfortably shy before Jonathan.

He noticed her discomfiture and unwittingly found himself apologizing. "I'm sorry, Chloe."

She looked at him in bewilderment and asked in a faltering voice, "What do you mean?"

"It's a little hard to explain now. But I have been something less than mindful, and so we must all suffer for it," Jonathan replied gently.

The girl was looking so miserable that he took pity on her and held her hands, saying tenderly, "Don't worry, love. It will be all right. And whenever you wish to talk about it, I should like to try to understand."

Close to tears, Chloe could not trust herself to answer but merely nodded and kept her head down when he bent to kiss her cheek. "I have an appointment so I will not stay now," he said. "Don't let Andrea upset you too much."

He left a very distraught young lady. Now that everything had suddenly become perfectly clear in her own mind, Chloe was appalled at her situation. She fled to her room to have a good cry.

Jonathan went directly to Grosvenor Square and was ushered into the library to await the Duke. David appeared immediately and the two men stood facing each other for a moment in silent appraisal. Finally Jonathan remarked caustically, "You let yourself become a little carried away, didn't you?"

This laconic observation had the effect of stirring the Duke's temper and he demanded testily, "Do you get a special pleasure out of standing back and watching the rest of us make fools of ourselves?"

"If I do, it seems I am well-served for my arrogance," Jonathan answered ruefully. This rejoinder elicited no further comment from the Duke, so he continued, "Chloe has been singularly uncommunicative about the affair, so I might ask you for the true story of how you managed to contrive this contretemps."

A responsive flicker showed in David's eyes but he only offered, "Let us just say that she did not ask *me* to marry *her*."

"I see—so now you are belatedly going to play the gentleman," Jonathan mocked with deliberation.

This calculated provocation put considerable strain on the Duke's determination to keep control of himself. He cursed inwardly for having placed himself in such a position that he must be obliged to permit this self-assured younger man, who was at least five years his junior, to lecture him like a schoolmaster.

Jonathan pursued, "If it would make any difference to you, I will tell you that I am aware of your previous offers to Andrea and, for that matter, of your continued aspirations."

David grinned in appreciation and noted candidly, "I thought you might be. Did she tell you?"

"Yes—only after some prompting, however."

"Do I detect a certain approval?" the Duke asked interestedly.

"Well, I had thought you might be the one man with enough resolve and desire to surmount the obstacles, but now I am not so sure, being less than impressed with your strategy," Jonathan answered drily.

Ignoring the taunt, David declared, "I couldn't let her leave town."

192

"Why not? Devon is not the end of the earth, you know. A more astute man might have persuaded Andrew to come home and invite him to the country. Or he could have foisted himself on me," Jonathan pointed out reasonably.

David looked at him with respect and confessed, "I can see that I have been amiss in not having taken advantage of your superior counsel before now. Normally I am not so harebrained, but my mental faculties have been greatly impaired ever since I met up with that abominable girl."

Jonathan laughed outright at this admission and suggested, "I hope you have devised some scheme for setting things to rights in short order. However, I suppose we will have to let things ride for the moment until Chloe confides in me, which I am sure she will do eventually." He rose to leave and added significantly, "Under the circumstances I will not be so buffleheaded as to make a piece of work of this, but I warn you, do not presume to take any liberties with Chloe or I *will* call you out."

Not taking offense and being in sympathy with a frustrated lover, David grinned and assured, "Don't worry. I think it can be said that we understand each other very well."

In spite of a decided lack of enthusiasm by all parties, the next few days the betrothed couple, their family, and friends were obliged to try to convey a convincing impression of happiness, or at least benign acceptance, and to bear with the vexing consequences of the Duke's regrettable indiscretion.

Once Andrea was given an unwitting clue to the mystery when she overheard a group of Chloe's friends rhapsodizing over the engagement, but the implication was too vague and she could not properly puzzle it out. She was becoming extremely resentful and depressed at having to continually respond to expressions of surprise and at having to determinedly ignore the speculative looks cast in her direction by those who had expected quite a different announcement. She was thankful that the social affairs were beginning to taper off and that the crowd was thinning out. Many of the *haut ton* were preparing to leave London for the coastal resorts or their country homes.

Afflicted with a severe case of the blue-devils, Andrea found herself wishing to visit with the Duchess for the first time since the proposal had been made and accepted ten days before. She sent word that she would call at eleven o'clock if it was convenient.

Andrea lacked her usual animation and the Dowager had a hard time preventing herself from letting the cat out of the bag. David was going to have to make a clean breast of it. The girl was working herself into a decline, and there was no reason she should be put through such misery just to preserve the sensibilities of her misguided sister. The Duchess avoided the sensitive subject and drew her into ordinary conversation.

While they were talking, Andrea noticed a copy of *Glenarvon* lying on the table. She asked if her friend had read it yet and received an affirmative answer spiced with a biting opinion of the character of the author. "Never have I seen such a glaring example of deliberate scandal-mongering. I'm afraid the Lambs pushed Caroline too far when they persuaded William to file for separation. They underestimated her instability and her revengeful nature."

Andrea was silent for a moment and then speculated, "It does give one pause."

The Duchess looked at her questioningly. "What do you mean?"

"Oh, just that, considering the terrible torments that some people must bear, one's own situation is not so very bad, after all."

"Andrea," the Duchess scolded crossly, "I beg you to pull yourself out of the dismals. I am finding your long face extremely depressing this morning."

The girl started at this curt reprimand and then apologized with an abashed face, "I'm sorry, Your Grace. It's just that this business between Chloe and the Duke has been preying on my mind. Besides, the miserable weather is enough to dampen anyone's spirits. I have the most fervent wish to escape to Devon and so retire from the world."

"For God's sake, girl," the Dowager exploded, "where is your mettle? I never thought I would see the day when you would act like a die-away ninny."

Andrea had to laugh and noted, "You see? I knew I should come to you. I do have these moods, you know. They don't usually last this long, however." Preparing to leave, she announced, "I think I shall go browse through the shops and buy myself something really elegant and extravagant to put me in a lighter frame of mind."

"An excellent idea, my dear," the Duchess approved with a smile. "I shall give you a commission to perform for me while you are about it. I need some white gloves and a new lace cap."

CHAPTER THIRTEEN

Having witnessed Andrea's arrival, David remained at home to receive a report from his grandmother and went to her room on being informed that Miss Wycliff had departed.

"Good afternoon, Your Grace," he greeted brightly. "May I have the pleasure of your company for lunch?"

"In a few moments. I want to talk to you first."

"Did you hearten my love?" he asked with a slow smile.

"So you have noticed how unhappy she is," the old lady remarked with an air of reproach.

"Yes, and I promise you that I am not going to continue this farce much longer. I am finding it exceedingly unsatisfactory."

"Good. That's what I wanted to hear," the Dowager approved. She told him about the conversations with Andrea, describing the girl's uncommonly depressed mood, and they both laughed at her purely feminine remedy for a case of the doldrums.

"Well, I can see I am going to have to fling a cat among the pigeons," the Duke observed whimsically.

"Have to WHAT!" the Duchess exclaimed in surprise.

Her grandson looked at her wickedly and instructed, "You know that an admirable cure for low spirits is a good fight. She is always at her best when she's angry."

The Duchess shook her head and admonished, "David, sometimes I doubt you know what you are about! You have the most unique way of conducting a courtship. If you ever pull this off, it will be something wonderful."

The Duke admitted ruefully, "It isn't exactly the way I

would prefer to carry on, you know, but this affair has been a comedy of errors from the beginning and setting up her bristles is the only way I can get her to talk to me. She persists in showing me an uncompromising cold shoulder."

"Well, I wish you would get on with it. I should like to return to Dorset, but I don't want to miss the next chapter," the Duchess declared impatiently.

"All right, love. I'll see what I can do," the Duke promised with a laugh.

That evening all principal actors of the ensuing drama, their friends and relatives, along with many other fashionables, were in attendance at Retford House for a musical soirée. Chloe had been asked to be one of the performers, and when she went to take her place at the pianoforte, David seized his chance and quickly moved to the chair next to Andrea. She glanced at him stonily and then pointedly turned her back to speak to Lady Jane.

The Duke experienced a strong desire to turn her over his knee and had no trouble at all getting himself in the proper frame of mind for offering provocation.

"You are not exactly following your resolution to show a civil face," he murmured close to her ear.

"I find it beyond my capacity," Andrea informed him curtly, moving away.

"Unworthy, my dear. You are eminently capable of doing anything you set your mind to."

"You will please not speak to me while Chloe is playing," the girl admonished primly.

"But I wish to have a talk with you, and now that I have you captive, I must take advantage unless, of course, you will agree to a tête-à-tête later," the gentleman persisted.

"All right!" Andrea fairly hissed.

"I will call for you tomorrow morning and we will visit the Academy," the Duke advised, fully prepared to make the most of the opportunity.

But Andrea would have none of that and depressed his

ambitions firmly. "No! I shall merely grant you an interview. Now do be quiet."

"Very well," he agreed resignedly. "Half a loaf is better than none." And he settled himself comfortably to enjoy the music.

As usual, Jonathan, being familiar with Chloe's repertoire, offered to turn pages for her. They presented an elegant picture, both blond, dressed in complimentary shades of blue, and situated under a glittering chandelier against a background of red velvet draperies. David whispered admiringly, "They *do* make a charming couple, do they not?"

This calculated prick had the desired effect and he could feel Andrea's animosity as she accused vehemently, "You odious man!"—an invective David blithely ignored as he stretched his legs lazily and leaned back with closed eyes in perfect imitation of a man completely entranced with the performance.

When Chloe had struck the last chord and was graciously acknowledging the compliments of the company, Andrea rose and put as much distance as possible between herself and her tormentor. The Duke caught his grandmother's eye and winked conspiratorily. She joined him and commented drily, "I see you have stirred the coals."

"Yes, my love, very effectively. I shall finish the job tomorrow." Then, as befitted a devoted fiancé, he escorted Chloe to the refreshment tables.

At ten the next morning the Duke presented himself at Queen Anne's Gate and informed the butler that he had come for his private audience with Miss Wycliff. He was shown to the parlor and left to cool his heels for a good half hour, a deliberate affront, he understood, as Andrea was usually punctual for her appointments. He put this discourtesy on his mental list of offenses for which he meant to exact payment in the not so far future. However, this particular incivility served him well since it offered him a perfect excuse for calling her on the carpet.

She finally entered and, leaving the door open, came to stand with one hand resting on the back of the chair, giving notice by her demeanor that she did not intend this to be an extended interview.

The Duke looked at her quizzically and, with deliberation, crossed the room to close the door. He returned to stand before her and attacked immediately. "I asked to speak with you particularly because I have not been at all happy with the way you have been conducting yourself."

Andrea could not believe her ears and stared at him as if he were some sort of viper. The gall of the man! To take it upon himself to criticize her behavior was outside of enough and she asked menacingly, "By what right do you presume to instruct me?"

"By right of being a prospective member of your family," he answered promptly. "In view of the fact that we are to be so closely connected, I think it only reasonable to expect you to force yourself to an accommodation with the inevitable."

"I believe," Andrea retorted frigidly, "that you are generally reported to have excellent understanding, but in this case, you seem to be extremely slow of comprehension. I have told you without mincing the matter that we are *not* to be closely connected."

"Oh, but we are, my dear," the Duke insisted maddeningly, "truly we are, and I wish you would try to reconcile yourself to the certainty."

"My lord Duke," Andrea said wearily, "it seems we can never come to any agreement and only vex ourselves with battling to a standstill. I see no point to continuing this conversation."

"I am not at all vexed," David announced pleasantly. "In fact, I always find our exchanges exceedingly stimulating."

Andrea awarded him with a baleful look and advised. "Obviously we have totally divergent views on the matter, but I give you notice that I am incontrovertibly resolved that you shall not gain your end."

"And I, my dear Andrea, am equally adamant that I shall. And so, it will be extremely interesting to see which of us shall prevail." With this last aggravation he bade her good day and walked to join some of his friends at White's on St. James's Street, feeling monstrously pleased with himself, especially since he had spoken truly every word, never once having mentioned Chloe's name.

He had certainly accomplished the intended purpose of dispelling Andrea's dispirited mood, for the girl was in a fury and indulged herself with imagining all sorts of harassments that would disturb that insufferable man's complacency. She finally settled on a plan of action and determined to implicate Jeffrey in a course bent on intimidation. He was coming to drive her that afternoon and she would cozen him into abetting her designs.

Anxious to get on with her plan, she became impatient for the Earl's arrival but, in order not to rouse his suspicions of her motives, she forced herself to engage in small talk until they were riding in the Park. She then led up to the business she had in mind.

"You know, Jeffrey, I have had my fill of London and am becoming deucedly bored."

"My dear girl, what a remarkable way you have of puffing up a man's ego!" the Earl commented in pretended outrage.

She giggled appreciatively and chided, "Don't be a gudgeon. You know what I mean."

He grinned and agreed, "Yes, I do, and I have been hoping you would say it is time we went to Devon. I have been looking forward to it. When do you think we can leave?"

"Soon," Andrea replied agreeably.

"There is a complication, however—the matter of Chloe's wedding," her cousin suggested. "Any idea when that will be?"

"Never!" Andrea declared fiercely. "You should know I will not permit that to happen."

"Well, I wouldn't have thought so, but it does seem to be rather a settled thing."

"Jeffrey, I beg you will not dwell on that unpleasant subject," Andrea said irritably. "Instead, I wish you will put your mind to devising some unusual entertainment for me. I am tired of shopping and parties and excursions and other such namby-pamby occupations."

"Well, we can't very well race our horses or our carriages as we do in Devon. Do you have anything in mind?"

"Oh, I don't know. If I were a man, we could go to Manton's for a shooting contest," she suggested whimsically, masking her true designs.

Jeffrey burst out laughing and said, "If that's the kind of thing you are itching for, I can probably arrange something. We'll get up a party, find a target area a little out of town, and I'll take you on."

"I hope you can offer better competition than that," she derided scornfully.

"You are a perfectly shameless girl," the Earl accused amiably, "but I know you for my better, so I will invite the best marksmen in town to join us."

"Uh—Jeffrey, I suppose, in the interests of propriety, you had better include some ladies."

"Of course, love. We will make a picnic of it."

"All right. But just don't include the Duke," Andrea directed caustically. "I should like to enjoy myself."

He raised an eyebrow and noted, "We couldn't very well invite Chloe then."

"That's probably best. She can't stand the sound of gunshots anyway."

"How about the day after tomorrow? I'll come for you at ten o'clock."

"Excellent," Andrea agreed smugly, sighing with satisfaction at having so easily accomplished her purpose.

The next day the challenged gentlemen, who were happy to have been presented with a most unusual proposition, addressed themselves to the problem of devising a suitable target and drawing up the rules of the contest. One gallant gentleman suggested giving the lady a handicap, but his host quickly overruled such condescension, not only because it was totally unnecessary, but because

Andrea would be insulted and likely give them a sharp set-down for their pains.

At the appointed time the Earl called for his cousin and they proceeded in his curricle to a prearranged starting point at Marylebone fields, where they were joined by four other carriages, each conveying a lady and a gentleman. The party set out immediately, turning north toward Hampstead Heath, where the exhibition was to take place.

Ned and Naomi were included in the excursion, for this proper young man, on discovering the unconventional activity that was scheduled and knowing that it was beyond his power to dissuade his brother and his cousin from one of their capricious starts, decided to accompany them in the hopes of lending a semblance of respectability to the affair. He may have been influenced in this decision by his impression that he was rather a good marksman himself and was thus irresistibly tempted to participate in the competition.

They arrived shortly at a lovely spot where the ladies might settle themselves under some trees only a short distance from the scene of the contest. With a lot of good-natured bantering and a hurried placing of any number of involved wagers between all the gentlemen, the five men and Andrea took their places to fire at several strategically placed targets.

At first Andrea's accuracy was not particularly praiseworthy and she exclaimed in vexation, "My word! I am certainly become rusty and, in consideration of my lack of opportunity to shoot these past many weeks, I beg you will allow me to practice for a few minutes, else you will not have much of a contest."

The gentlemen gallantly granted her request and Jeffrey reloaded her pistols as she took aim and fired repeatedly. At last she decided she had regained a fair measure of her proficiency and consented to take on the first challenger.

Charles Newbury, one of the Duke's cousins and his heir, stepped forth to claim first chance by right of his being the acknowledged master of the group.

The match proved to be fairly equal, but after several attempts Andrea found herself bested, although she felt she had given a good account of herself. "I bow to your superiority for the moment, Mr. Newbury, but I ask for a rematch after I have competed with the other gentlemen," she begged, confident that she could do better.

"Of course, Miss Wycliff. Wasn't quite fair, after all—should have given you more time. Know I'm the best shot here. 'Pologize."

"That's all right, sir," Andrea assured him pleasantly. "Now I know what I have to contend with. You are a formidable opponent."

The other gentlemen took their turns eagerly and were all duly chagrined at being outshot by this slip of a girl. Andrea's marksmanship had improved steadily and, by the time she was ready to take on Charles Newbury again, she was in top form. After several maneuvers by the gentlemen to increase the difficulty of the contest, since the two competitors had reached a stalemate, it was obvious that Andrea was not to be beaten. She was good-humoredly hailed as the winner by all contestants and adjudged the most remarkable marksman they had ever seen.

"Thank you, gentlemen. I don't know when I have enjoyed myself more. You have been most gallant, but I think we must now pardon ourselves to the ladies and turn our attention to their entertainment. I am sure they have long since come to the point of wishing me at Jericho."

With good humor the young women protested at this pronouncement. As one wide-eyed innocent admitted, "We, of course, knew why we had come and I, for one, am lost in amazement that you have learned to be so skilled in such an unusual pastime."

"I'm afraid I have a very unfeminine competitive spirit, Miss Johnson. When I was growing up far away in Devon, I was used to spending most of my time with my brother and his friends," Andrea acknowledged with a sheepish smile.

"Well, I must say I am glad the competition has ended,"

Naomi admitted with a shudder. "I never realized how unnerving the sound of a pistol can be."

Andrea said humbly, "I do apologize, Naomi. I am a miserable wretch for having subjected all of you to such a peacocky demonstration, and I am most grateful you have shown such forbearance."

Having set herself to rights with this pretty speech, she proposed that they unpack the picnic baskets. This suggestion was greeted with enthusiasm and the rest of the afternoon passed pleasantly as the elegant ladies and gentlemen relaxed and engaged in light flirtations. Finally they reluctantly made ready to return to town. Andrea was inordinately pleased with the day's work, for she had every confidence that reports of this escapade would quickly reach the ears of the evilhearted villain for whose benefit it had been staged.

Her presumption was proved correct as several of the young men, after depositing their charges at their respective homes, arranged to meet at White's for a rehash of the day's activity and a settling up of their wagers.

Both the Duke and Jonathan had arrived earlier and were just preparing to leave when the card room was invaded by a noisy group, evidently in high gig, taunting each other good-naturedly about being so thoroughly laid by the heels.

Charles Newbury spied his cousin and approached him in a friendly manner, for there was actually no ill-feeling between the two men since David did not share his grandmother's antipathy. The only thing that could be held against the young man and his younger brothers was that they were a bit wanting in the upper reaches, and this failing was enough to put off the sharp-witted Duchess, who had a horror of the Dukedom falling into unworthy hands.

"Hello, David. Thought you might be out of town. Should have been with us today—great fun." And then, with a suggestion of raillery, he advised facetiously, "Shouldn't cross swords with your fiancée's sister if I were you—dangerous woman, that."

This remark immediately aroused tremors of suspicion in David's mind and he asked sharply, "What the deuce are you talking about?"

"Had a shooting contest up at Hampstead—Stockwell arranged it. Miss Wycliff challenged us all—Stockwell, Wycliff, Barnes, Clarkson, and myself. Outshot every one of us. Most amazing thing—deadest eye and steadiest hand I ever saw. Remarkable girl. Looking forward to another contest. Promised us a rematch."

"The devil she did!" the Duke exploded angrily. "May I inquire if she was the only female present?"

Being suddenly aware of his cousin's ominous expression, Charles replied hastily, "No—no—of course not. Not so dotty as that. Made a picnic out of it—ladies, too."

"Well, thank God for that," the Duke said, somewhat relieved. "Even so," he reprimanded with scowl, "it is not exactly *comme il faut* to involve a lady in such a business, even if she is agreeable."

"Don't see that. Didn't arrange it anyway—Stockwell did. Nothing improper—great fun," the young man repeated stubbornly.

The Duke just stared balefully at his heir, who hastily beat a retreat and joined his friends, wondering what the devil had put his formidable cousin in such a temper.

Throughout this exchange Jonathan had been sitting back with a look of unholy amusement on his face and he did not make any attempt to disguise it when the Duke turned to him with a glaring expression. They locked eyes for a moment and then David relaxed, admitting with a wry grin, "I meant to aggravate her a little to bring her out of the doldrums, but I must have pushed her too far. However, she has really overplayed her hand this time and is going to have to be checked before she becomes fodder for the tattlemongers. How could she be so lost to propriety as to conceive such a scheme!"

"I expect she's decided to wage her own battle of nerves," Jonathan replied. "At least," he added reflectively with a mock-serious expression, "I hope that's all it is."

David did not appreciate this exercise in levity and declared resolutely, "Well, it's time this charade is played out. I wonder, my good fellow, if I might persuade you to accompany me to Grosvenor Square. We have some matters to discuss."

Jonathan stood and bowed. "At your service, Your Grace."

The Duke threw him a scornful look and said caustically, "Don't pretend to play the toad-eater with me. You're not at all suited for the role," and then led the way outside where he called for a hackney. They were soon comfortably settled in the library, and David demanded rhetorically, "Whatever possessed Stockwell to fall in with her crackbrained notion?"

"Don't expect Jeffrey to draw bridle on her. He's a shocking scapegrace, and they have fallen into disfavor more than once with their escapades."

This bit of information only exacerbated the Duke's resentment and fed his jealousy besides.

Jonathan recognized the danger signs and tried to mitigate his error by adding, "Don't fly into the boughs. This is the first time in years I have known her to be so foolhardy. You seem to have that effect on each other. She actually has been much more reserved with Jeffrey since he proclaimed himself a serious suitor."

The Duke regarded his guest speculatively and said, "Chloe is going to have to be undeceived, you know."

Jonathan looked at him noncommittally and waited for him to continue.

David refilled their glasses and then turned to spout in an exasperated voice, "For God's sake, man, you have every bit as much reason to set things straight as I have. One of us will have to tell her. I will unless you prefer to do it yourself. You understand her better and will know which would be best. I shall follow your direction."

"Perhaps," Jonathan said tentatively, "if you will inform me just exactly how you managed to create this situation, I might know better how to proceed."

The Duke sat down and explained how he unwittingly

became an engaged man. "I realized it was a scurrilous trick to pull, but I never once expected to be accepted, and I still can't figure it out. I didn't realize Andrew's good opinion carried so much weight with her. It just didn't enter into my calculations."

"Andrea thinks that's not the whole story."

"It is as far as I am concerned."

"Well," Jonathan stated firmly, "I'll take on the commission. Just give me a day or two. I've had the feeling lately that Chloe was almost ready to make a clean breast of it. I'll just offer her a little encouragement."

"Don't delay too long," the Duke cautioned. "My patience is wearing thin and that disgraceful little demon is about to have her wings clipped."

"That's a brave posture, my friend, but rather untenable, I'm afraid," Jonathan warned as he rose to leave. The two clasped hands in recognition of their perfect understanding and David said, "I have an engagement to escort Chloe this evening, but I will send a note begging off and ask her to accept you as my deputy."

Jonathan merely bowed in mock-servility and, refusing the Duke's offer of a carriage, walked hurriedly to Curzon Street.

CHAPTER FOURTEEN

When Chloe received the Duke's note, her mumpish mood lightened considerably. She no longer suffered from any delusions, a transitory condition Andrea had defined perfectly, and she tardily realized, without any qualifications, what a terrible mistake she had made. It was becoming increasingly difficult to pretend and she desperately wanted to cry off but was in a quandary as to how she should go about it. Broken engagements always created a certain sensation and became a matter for speculation, and she did not want to embarrass the Duke or anyone close to her.

Until a few weeks ago she would not have hesitated to discuss it with Andrea, but their usually warm, uncomplicated relationship had become perceptibly strained, a dismaying situation that caused Chloe great unhappiness. She had known that Andrea would not approve of her arbitrary show of independence, especially since she had carefully and earnestly warned her about putting faith in the Duke, but Chloe had truly believed that she was so securely placed in her family's affections they would not put her from them for any reason. It seemed she had sorely misjudged her status. The unwelcome thought so depressed her that unbidden tears came to her eyes, which she vainly tried to excuse by unfairly accusing her hapless maid of having pulled her hair.

Her mother did not appear to be as disturbed about the awkward business as Andrea did. She was so deeply preoccupied with her own surprising situation—for Lord

Howell had announced his serious intentions and was in full pursuit—that Chloe hated to distract her. Only Jonathan—dear Jonathan—stood ready and waiting to help her. She would have called on him before now but her new awareness of their subtly changed relationship had an inhibiting effect on her willingness to discuss her predicament.

She had dismissed her maid and was staring unseeingly into her mirror when suddenly she sat upright and, squaring her shoulders, scolded her image with a resolute expression. "Well, Chloe, it's about time you faced up to your accountability. You have let your success in the *ton* turn your head and have shown yourself to be the perfect ninnyhammer. Not only did you foolishly deceive yourself into thinking you had been chosen to play the long-suffering heroine, a totally fallacious presumption, as it happens, since it is glaringly obvious that the Duke is no more in love with you than you are with him, but you have carelessly dishonored your true love by awarding him second place before society." Having completely and succinctly clarified the matter with this self-reproachful monologue, she felt a surge of indignation that Jonathan had suffered such an insult at her hands, and she determined to set things in order immediately. With this admirable resolution she felt immeasurably relieved and happier than she had been in weeks.

A gloriously radiant Chloe came eagerly down the stairs to stand before a surprised Jonathan, who was instantly bemused by the expression of love so openly bestowed on him. He took her hands in his and said softly, "Chloe, my love, you look enchanting, and I must count myself the luckiest gentleman to have your company tonight."

"Thank you, Jonathan," the girl acknowledged, awarding him with a sweet, affectionate smile, thus making every effort to acquaint him with her newly resolved sentiments. "I am in excellent spirits because I have come to a decision, and I am impatient to talk to you about it."

"Are you, love? How strange that you should say so because this very day I made up my mind that it was time we all stopped working at cross purposes. I meant to ask you to hear me out."

"Oh, Jonathan, truly?"

"Yes, darling, but why don't we put off our confidences until tomorrow, for I have the greatest desire to escort a princess to the ball this evening. I will come in the morning and we can have a private talk. All right?"

"Yes, please, only I want to tell you first," she stated firmly.

Jonathan smiled and, placing a light wrap around her shoulders, led her to the waiting carriage.

The party was one of the last grand affairs scheduled for the Season and it proved to be a tremendous crush, but Jonathan and Chloe remained close all evening, dancing every waltz and going down to supper together. He was aware that they were being remarked upon by some of the guests, and he warned Chloe that he was very much afraid they were creating material for the tattlemongers.

She was not the least disturbed and with a mischievous twinkle reminded him that he, after all, was acting as the Duke's deputy and certainly was being no more favored than would have been that gentleman's right under present circumstances.

"My dear, what a perfectly reasonable argument, one that fits in very well with my inclination," Jonathan approved.

The evening had been a delight for both of them, and it was very late when they returned to Queen Anne's Gate. Jonathan took both Chloe's hands in his as they stood at the door. "I will come at noon tomorrow. Will that be too early?"

"Oh, no! I shall be up long before that," the girl demurred, sounding almost disappointed.

"Very well, then—eleven. Try not to be impatient," he teased.

"Well," Chloe said doubtfully, "that will not be easy because I am just bursting to tell you how it was that I got myself in such a hobble."

"I know you are, darling, and I want very much to hear

about it so I shall hurry back tomorrow—but *not* before eleven," Jonathan acknowledged with a laugh. He bent to kiss her lightly on the lips. "Good night, love."

Not to be outdone, Chloe threw her arms around his neck and hugged him fiercely, declaring, "Jonathan, I am *so* happy."

"As to that, my dear, so am I," the gentleman admitted and, giving her a little shove, ordered, "Now off with you, miss. I'll return to continue this very interesting conversation in just a few hours."

With a giggle the young lady did as she was told and disappeared into the house.

The next morning Jonathan came downstairs a little before ten to find his mother and his aunt still at the breakfast table.

"Good morning, ladies. It's a beautiful day, isn't it?"

Both women looked at their young relative suspiciously. The gray, wet skies could not, by any stretch of the imagination, confirm this optimistic observation.

His mother quizzed, "I must suppose your affairs are progressing favorably since you are in such high feather."

"Right, as usual, my dear. This is the day of reckoning, and I expect to have some momentous news for you this afternoon."

"Jonathan, whatever are you talking about?" his aunt inquired in a puzzled voice.

"I'll tell you later, Aunt Clarissa," Jonathan promised and concentrated on doing justice to the various dishes being brought to tempt him.

At five minutes to eleven he presented himself at Queen Anne's Gate and was ushered to the first floor drawing room, where he found Chloe waiting for him.

She jumped up immediately and, taking his hand, led him to a chair near where she had strategically placed a footstool. When they were both comfortably settled, she began immediately, "Jonathan, I am not going to marry the Duke."

"Really? I must say I am unconscionably glad to hear that," he declared with a twinkle in his eye.

Chloe looked at him forbiddingly and shook his hand. "Jonathan, do not laugh at me when I am trying to be perfectly serious."

"Sorry, love," he apologized as he turned her hand and kissed her palm. "When did you come to that conclusion?"

"Well, I knew all along that I didn't really want to, but a few days ago I decided I wouldn't. You see, it was all so silly in the first place. I just forgot Andrea's warning that the fantasies in all those romantic novels really had no relation to real life," and she told him with an embarrassed but determined manner about the fateful afternoon when she let herself be seduced into imagining herself an angel of redemption.

Jonathan heard her out with difficulty, repressing the urgent desire to laugh at her artless confession and envelop her in his arms.

When she finished and looked at him with soft apologetic eyes, he leaned over to take her face between his hands and said tenderly, "Darling, are you telling me that you meant to sacrifice yourself because you thought it was your duty to persuade the Duke to follow the path of righteousness?"

She lowered her eyes and nodded and then suddenly found herself locked in a fierce embrace by a delighted, laughing young man, who declared fervently, "Chloe, darling, you are the sweetest, most adorable little monkey and I love you to distraction. I am sorry I waited so long to tell you, but I thought you were too young."

With as much indignation as she could muster under the inhibiting circumstance of being crushed against a gentleman's breast, she proclaimed, "I am *not* too young!"

"No, I have come to realize that very acutely these past few weeks. I meant to propose when we returned to Devon because I thought there were too many distractions here and I wanted you all to myself."

"I am not distracted anymore," she hinted mischievously.

"Aren't you? I am—dreadfully," Jonathan teased as he buried his face in her hair.

She giggled but did not mean to be put off and pursued, "Well, yes, but I mean—"

Jonathan leaned back and, placing his fingers on her lips, whispered softly, "Chloe, my dearest love, will you marry me?"

"Oh, yes, darling, you know it's what I wish above all things," came an ingenuous reply, which prompted an amorous young man to take advantage of his interesting new position. He kissed her long and passionately until she was breathless. Presently she pushed a little away to look at him in awe and exclaimed with starry eyes, "Oh, my! I didn't know you felt like that!"

"Well, I do, darling, and all this noble bearing has been very hard on me."

She laughed appreciatively and agreed, "I should think so. I can't wait to tell Andrea. She will be so happy and—and perhaps won't be so distant with me anymore."

"I can explain that, love, but first tell me when you decided not to sacrifice yourself, after all."

"Well, I had accepted in the first place, you know, because I had been led to believe the Duke had fallen in love with me, but I soon discovered that wasn't true. He never acted the least bit loverlike and treated me like—well, a young sister. I came to understand that, if a man wanted you to know that he was in love with you, you would know it," she said, smiling ecstatically, "and so I felt I no longer had to pretend, especially when I had finally realized where my true happiness lay. But, Jonathan, I don't understand at all why he offered for me."

"I will tell you the whole story. Can we expect to be private for a while? Where are Andrea and Lady Jane?"

"Oh, they went shopping today and will not be back for hours."

"Good," he said, as he lifted her up and settled her on his lap, meeting with not the slightest objection.

"Now, it started several months ago back in Devon," he began, and he proceeded to give her a detailed account of the Duke's unorthodox courtship of Andrea.

"I can't believe it," Chloe said with a dazed expression. "How could all this have been happening before my very eyes and I not have the slightest notion?"

"That is one of the drawbacks of the fast pace of a London Season, my love. Everyone is always rushing about so caught up in personal concerns that it becomes difficult to get below the surface of how things seem, particularly when a very deep young lady wishes to keep her affairs private."

"*You* were not so insensible if you know all this," Chloe suggested admiringly.

"I had a special interest in keeping an eye on things, love. I had no intention of letting you be spirited away from me."

"You didn't?" a contented young lady said wonderingly. Then she asked with a little pout, "But why didn't you do something when I became engaged to the Duke?"

"Because, darling," Jonathan replied, kissing her nose, "there wasn't a chance in the world that you would ever marry him as he and I both knew. I did warn him to keep his hands off you or I would call him out," he was pleased to confess.

"Really?" she asked, laughing happily. "But there was no need to do so because he had not the least desire to make love to me."

"I didn't intend to take any chances, although I expect an even stronger deterrent for him was that he knew he would have to deal with Andrea."

"I am so relieved that I know the reason for Andy's coolness. It must have been very difficult for her to keep all this to herself, although I must say she should be called to account because I should never have been so gullible if she had not been so close-mouthed."

"Yes, and it has been preying on her conscience so that she has been actually threatening the Duke with violence," Jonathan admitted, deciding to tell her the rest of it.

"Jonathan! What do you mean?"

"She decided that I was not showing enough concern

and Kensington kept taunting her, so yesterday she inveigled Jeffrey into helping her make a point." He went on to repeat Charles Newbury's story.

"Oh, dear! That shocking girl! Is that why she cried off last night? I'm surprised we didn't hear about it, though, because it is just the sort of thing that intrigues the gossips."

"It probably didn't have time to make the rounds, but I must confess I was too high up in the clouds to have noticed anything unusual," he murmured as he nuzzled her ear.

"I suppose that accounts for it," Chloe agreed with a radiant face, willingly cooperating with his renewed amorous demonstrations.

Presently she said, still puzzled, "But, darling, if Andy knows that you would never have allowed me to marry the Duke, why is she so anxious and belligerent?"

"I suspect it all falls under the heading of her being involved in a heavily disguised lover's quarrel."

"Jonathan, are you saying that Andy is in love with the Duke?" Chloe demanded incredulously.

"Yes, my sweet, she is most certainly. She didn't want to be because she has a deep-rooted fear he might emulate your father. She has been fighting like the very devil, which is why she has been so unnaturally edgy."

"Do you think the Duke is like my father?"

"No, Chloe, I don't. He has committed his share of indiscretions, which naturally causes Andrea to be suspicious of his capacity for fidelity, but I am confident that he would not deceive her. He is so deeply in love with her that he has almost taken leave of his senses. In fact, he has reached the limit of his patience, and I am telling you all this partly at his request."

"I do think he could be gentlemanly enough to tell me himself," Chloe remarked huffily.

"He offered to, love, but I told him I would rather do it because I thought you were ready to confide in me anyway."

"Oh," she said meekly.

Jonathan grinned broadly and suggested, "Why don't we send a note to inquire if David will receive us, and while we are waiting for an answer, you can play for me. I feel marvelously in the mood for some romantic music."

"All right," she agreed and moved to the pianoforte while Jonathan wrote a note which he handed to the footman, requesting that he take it to Grosvenor Square and wait for a reply.

Within the hour the messenger had returned and Jonathan informed Chloe, "The Duke is home and is looking forward to enjoying our company."

Chloe jumped up and stated determinedly, "I *hope* he is because I have been thinking and I mean to give him a trimming, for not only did he encourage me to make a Jack Pudding of myself but he has played Andrea the meanest trick by announcing his engagement to me. No wonder she is so put out."

"She doesn't blame you, darling. Kensington is her target. Now go get your bonnet and we will get you unengaged."

"I already am and, in fact, I never really was," she answered somewhat vaguely and went upstairs to refresh her toilette which, after certain recent activities, was perceptibly in need of repair.

When they arrived at Grosvenor Square, they were ushered to the main drawing room, where the Duke and his grandmother were waiting for them. Chloe was a little disconcerted because she had expected they would have a private audience, but she made a small curtsy and greeted pleasantly, "Good afternoon, Your Grace."

The Duchess had not missed the quickly disguised expression of annoyance and she smiled impishly. "Good afternoon, my dear. I hope you will permit me to sit in on this conference, for I admit to being a nosy old woman and am all ears to hear the latest episode in this extremely entertaining drama."

"Oh," Chloe said uncertainly. "Then you know all about —everything?" she asked cautiously.

"I believe so, at least from David's standpoint. I shall be most interested to hear yours."

"Yes. Well, I came to explain, but first I wish to set things straight." So stating, she walked purposely to stand before her ex-fiancé and handed him his ring, saying primly, "My Lord Duke, we have both made a dreadful mistake and I wish to cry off from our engagement."

David smiled at her understandingly and acknowledged, "So we have, Chloe, but I hope we can remain friends. I should very much like you to keep the ring to wear on another finger."

"No!" she refused curtly. "I don't want to and I wish I never had," once again using less than perfect diction.

Her abrupt reply surprised David and he said apologetically, "I see you are very angry with me, as you have every right to be, and I can only tell you how sorry I am."

"And so you should be," she agreed with a reproachful look. "But I am not so much angry with you as I am with myself. I shall tell you how I came to make such a hash of it, because I know now that you did not mean for me to accept you." She lowered her eyes and blushed but began hesitantly, "It is—it is very embarrassing to have to admit I was so foolish, but you see—" and she explained how she was betrayed by her false illusions. When she finished, David put his hand under her chin and raised her face to look at him. "Chloe, you are the sweetest lady I have ever known, and I can understand why you have such fierce protectors. Please believe me when I say that, if I could choose anyone in the world, there would be no one I would rather have for my—little sister."

This deliberate brass-faced innuendo promptly relieved the awkwardness of the situation and Chloe laughed. "Oh, David, you are the drollest man and I shall like you very well for a brother, even though I find the prospect rather incredible. Jonathan says that you mean to have Andrea and that she will give in eventually."

"Yes, Chloe, he is perfectly right, and I must say that our quiet friend could have kept us out of this muddle if he had said a little more a little sooner," complained the

Duke, casting an accusing eye in Jonathan's direction.

"Well! I hope you don't mean to hold Jonathan to account for our blunders," an indignant Chloe protested, "and I understand very well why he did not interfere, especially after he had satisfied himself that it would not go any further. He is not such a coxcomb as to presume to order all our lives, particularly when we, none of us, had shown any signs that we could be persuaded to behave in a reasonable manner."

This forcefully delivered speech was received with some amusement, especially by the Dowager, who had been finding it hard not to laugh ever since Chloe had made her unaffected confession.

The Duke smiled also but demurred, "I must beg to differ with you, my dear Chloe. I am of the firm opinion that your Jonathan is very much the coxcomb for, in spite of the several points in my favor—my position, my wealth, my not exactly repulsive countenance, and my reasonably agreeable personality—he was not the least bit worried. He knew that, when it was all said and done, you would have no hesitation in choosing him over me."

To this immodest argument Chloe replied scathingly, "Just because he knows his own worth does *not* make him a coxcomb!"

The Duke was visibly taken back by this stinging setdown, and he looked quizzically at Jonathan who, with a smug grin, merely shrugged his shoulders and rolled his eyes upward. He was finding Chloe's uncompromising determination to show her partiality extremely gratifying.

The Duchess was laughing heartily and she crowed, "So, my dear boy, you are hoist on your own petard. Let that be a lesson to you not to so shamelessly plume yourself."

Not having meant it the way it had sounded, Chloe turned a sheepish face toward Jonathan, who assured her with a twinkle in his eyes, "It's all right, love. We know you are prejudiced and did not intend to be insulting." He put out his hand and she went over to sit beside him on the couch.

The other two regarded them indulgently, and David remarked pointedly, "Now that we have you two so happily settled, do you think we could turn our attention to my situation?"

"Yes, well, I meant to talk to you about that," Chloe stated resolutely with tilted chin. "Before I commit myself to your cause, I should like to ask you, just what are your intentions?"

This aggressive posture was too much for the rest of them and the three burst out laughing, but Chloe was not to be put down and soberly stood her ground, waiting for a serious reply.

The Duke composed himself and addressed Jonathan. "My friend, it seems that your Chloe is coming into her own. I am afraid we are both going to have to resign ourselves to being carried by a high hand."

"I am not dismayed by the prospect, David, and am happily committed, but you can still back off," Jonathan advised tauntingly.

For this helpful suggestion he was treated to a thoroughly disgusted look as the Duke stated caustically, "I may have shown myself to be a bungling idiot but I am not daft." He turned to Chloe. "My dear, I intend to marry your beloved sister and devote myself to her for the rest of my life."

"Exclusively?" Chloe pursued meaningfully with a slightly pugnacious expression.

"Yes," the Duke replied with a deep sigh. "But I do wish I stood a little higher in the eyes of the ladies in your family."

"It is your own fault if you do not," Chloe attested ruthlessly. "I mean, I think becoming engaged to me was one of the shabbiest most hurtful things you could have done to Andrea. It is no wonder she doesn't trust you."

The Duke winced at this relentless attack but took his medicine manfully as he admitted, "I know, Chloe. Do not think I haven't been reproaching myself. But I promise you, you need never worry that I would deceive Andrea.

I love her, you see—as much as you love Jonathan. If you could think of it in that light, perhaps you would understand."

"Oh," Chloe said in immediate comprehension as she looked at him searchingly. Being satisfied he was speaking with sincerity, she submitted, "Well, then, I suppose, if Andrea is in love with you as Jonathan believes, it would be a happy thing if you would marry."

"Thank you, Chloe," the Duke said with a relieved sigh. "I am pleased to have won my case with you. Now, I must decide how to face an even more difficult test."

"I have been thinking," Chloe mused as her mind followed another track. "When we announce that we are not to marry after all, and I immediately become engaged to Jonathan and then you pursue my sister, it will appear you are just in a miff. That would be terribly unfair to Andrea when you really wanted her all along."

"At first it might seem so, but it can't be helped now," David admitted resignedly.

"Yes, it can. I will not permit her to be so insulted," Chloe declared fiercely. "I shall tell everyone just how it was."

The Dowager was moved to object. "My dear, I don't think that would be at all advisable. Better to let it just blow over. A public announcement of the particulars would be much too discomposing."

"But Andrea should not be subjected to such an indignity," the young lady insisted stubbornly. "I know—I shall have a tea and invite those silly girls who helped lead me astray and I shall explain to them just how wrong we all were and warn them that they could find themselves in the briars, too, if they persist in getting carried away by romantic fantasies!"

Once again her friends were brought to a state of laughter as they envisioned this newly enlightened young miss attempting to instruct her benighted contemporaries.

Jonathan raised her hand to his lips and consented, "All right, Chloe. I don't see any harm in clearing the air. I know you will feel better for it, and we will all be leaving town shortly anyway. By the time we reconvene here in the autumn, it will be old hat."

She smiled, happy to be so well understood, but looked for confirmation from the Duke and his grandmother.

"If you wish, my dear, I will not object," David agreed, "if you do not fail to award me my share of the blame."

"We will both look pretty foolish, my lord Duke, but no more than we deserve," Chloe stated ruefully.

"I *do* have a favor to ask of you, however," the Duke ventured tentatively.

She looked at him warily. "What is it?"

He smiled at her suspicious face and responded, "I was hoping I could persuade you not to tell Andrea of these decisions just yet."

"Why?"

"Because I don't think an abrupt capitulation on my part will work to my advantage. I will have no leverage at all."

"You could just admit your blame and beg forgiveness," Chloe suggested bluntly.

"I have tried that before and have not had marked success," David remarked dourly. "Andrea does not exactly find me irresistible."

His woeful expression impressed Chloe favorably, and she looked questioningly at Jonathan. He asked, "What do you have in mind?"

"Just pretend things have not changed for a day or two and then, if I have not made any progress, we will set things straight."

The Duchess made a noise sounding suspiciously like a snort and she advised scornfully, "If you think you can pull the wool over anyone's eyes, especially Andrea's, with these two so obviously smelling of April and May, you are fair and far out."

The lovers looked at each other guiltily and David agreed with a benevolent eye, "Yes, I can see what you mean. Do you think you two could contrive to disguise your partiality for one another for just a very little while?"

Jonathan laughed and stood up, pulling Chloe with him. "Two days, my friend, that's all," he granted and hinted, "By the way, you are still indisposed this evening, are you not? I wish to take Chloe to the theater."

"As you say," David agreed, bowing mockingly. "But please try to be circumspect."

"Of course. You do realize," Jonathan reminded tauntingly, "that in order to play out this charade, you will have to keep to the house."

The Duke looked at his tormentor with a jaundiced eye and observed quellingly, "Sometimes I have serious reservations about getting myself involved with a family whose members and prospective members take such pleasure in adding to my discomfiture."

"You can still back off," Chloe reminded mischievously.

"Not a chance, my dear. You are stuck with me," David retorted with a grin. He apologetically held out the ring she had returned to him, which she reluctantly put back on her finger.

But, all things considered, she was well-satisfied with the way things had turned out. She gave the Duchess an affectionate embrace and raised herself to kiss David's cheek. He returned this mark of regard and then escorted her and Jonathan to the door, telling them dolefully that he supposed he would have to go to his library to find a good book, since he was forced to stay in for the evening.

On this whimsical note, the conspirators parted with every expectation that everything would be happily resolved in just a few days.

CHAPTER FIFTEEN

When Chloe and Jonathan arrived at Queen Anne's Gate, their euphoric mood was quickly dispelled by another disconcerting development. As they entered the hall, they quickly realized that something unusual had happened because of the obvious show of bustling about by the servants. The couple could hear Andrea giving instructions in the upper hall, and they started up the stairs to discover what had brought on this stepped-up activity. She stood on the landing waiting for them and announced mysteriously, "We have a surprise guest."

"Andy! Who is it?" Chloe demanded expectantly.

Andrea laughed and hugged her sister, replying, "Only Andrew, love—come to honor us with his presence."

"Andrew! Oh, no!" Chloe exclaimed in dismay and looked at Jonathan imploringly.

With difficulty he maintained a mildly interested expression as Andrea looked searchingly at Chloe and commented quizzically, "What do you mean, 'Oh, no!' That is not your usual reaction when he returns home."

"Oh, no!" Chloe said again in some confusion as she envisioned all sorts of inauspicious consequences. "I mean —it is just such a surprise, and I could not believe he would come. I wonder if he received my letter?" she asked guiltily in sudden unhappy comprehension of what had brought about this untimely visit.

"No doubt, my dear Chloe," Andrea replied tartly. "He obviously is in transports that his ill-conceived machinations have borne fruit, and he wishes to take part in the forthcoming celebrations. He arrived just a little while ago and is changing, so we will not see him for at least an hour if not longer. Will you stay for dinner, Jonathan?"

"That depends on Andrew's plans," he responded. "If he intends to remain at home this evening, I suppose Chloe and I will forego the theater. However, he may want to look in on Kensington, who is still a bit under the weather, so I had better disturb him to sound him out." He continued up the stairs to assure that the new arrival would not have any opportunity to complicate matters further, and the two girls went to join their mother in the drawing room, where Chloe tried to calm her disquieting thoughts by playing softly on the pianoforte.

Jonathan was admitted to the master bedroom, where Andrew was relaxing lazily in a tub of hot water. He looked up in surprise and greeted amiably, "Hello, Jonathan." Then, remembering the hopes his friend had cherished, added uncomfortably, "I am sorry that you are to be disappointed. I really did not mean to deal you a deliberate cut."

"I know, Drew. I have only myself to blame for being such a slowtop," Jonathan replied without rancor. "I came to inquire about your plans for the evening. I am engaged to take Chloe to the theater but I wonder if you intend to spend the night with the family?"

"No, just for dinner. Actually, I imagined I would toast the happily engaged couple. How is it David is not Chloe's escort?" Andrew asked, frowning slightly.

"He has been out of sorts for a couple of days, and I have been substituting. Chloe and I just came from a visit with him, and he plans to spend a quiet night at home so he would probably welcome your company," Jonathan suggested craftily.

"Right! I'll look in on him," Drew responded on cue. "He must be feeling pretty low to let himself be laid by the heels. I never once have known him to admit to any indisposition."

"Well, it can happen to any of us," he was advised cryptically. "I won't change our plans then, and I will leave you to your ministrations. Do you have a long leave?"

"Depends upon the wedding arrangements. Have they set a date yet?"

"No. Perhaps you can quiz Kensington on that," Jonathan suggested and then went back downstairs to inform the ladies that he would not stay for dinner but would return later to collect Chloe for the theater. He smiled reassuringly at his love and she acknowledged his message with a grateful nod. Andrea escorted him to the door, looking unusually dispirited as she mourned fatalistically, "We needed only this."

"Andrea," a faintly conscience-stricken young man said soothingly, "I do wish you would not worry yourself so. It will all work out. I promise you."

"I try to believe that, my friend, but it becomes more difficult every day, and now I am afraid Drew will try to push things along."

"He might, but I will put my money on Kensington's sense of accountability," Jonathan hinted obliquely.

The significance of this veiled intimation escaped Andrea and she regarded him with indignation. "I can't understand how you can deceive yourself into imagining him to have any moral principles at all, especially when you are one of the victims of his unscrupulous dealings!"

"You have an abnormally biased conception of the circumstances, my dear Andrea," her friend advised unsympathetically, "and I would wish that you could conquer your self-deceptive virulent persuasions and face up to the true nature of this affair. We would all be better served." With this unfeeling criticism he closed the door, leaving a thoroughly outraged young woman who believed herself unfairly judged. She reluctantly came to the conclusion that she alone stood between the devil and his nefarious designs.

When Jonathan arrived home, he scribbled a quick note and requested the footman to deliver it at once to Grosvenor Square. Having thus passed on the responsibility for Andrew's enlightenment to the Duke, he next stopped in to acquaint his mother with the newest developments, received her heartfelt congratulations, swore her to secrecy for a day or two, and finally, with a buoyant step continued on to his room to dress for dinner and his evening out.

The Duke was in his library reading some correspondence from the continent regarding a group of paintings that were expected to become available in a few months, when the butler brought him Jonathan's message. He read it almost gleefully. If there were anyone besides himself that he could blame for this unholy mess, it was certainly Andrew. He savored the thought that the agent provocateur had returned to be brought to book. The Dowager had retired to her room to rest, so David did not inform her of this latest turn of fortune until they sat down to dinner.

"Are you going out tonight?" he asked casually.

"No, I have no engagement this evening."

"Then you may be pleased to hear we are to have a visitor—a favorite of yours."

"Not Andrea!" the Duchess protested apprehensively.

"No—but you're close."

She looked at him for a moment, trying to decipher the meaning of his teasing eyes, and then cried out triumphantly, "Andrew! He's come home!"

"Yes, my love, so he has, and Jonathan has thoughtfully directed him to me," David remarked ruefully.

"Good Lord!" the old lady exclaimed, laughing irrepressibly. "Can anything else possibly happen to add to the confusion?"

"Let us hope not, but I don't propose to let Andrew aggravate the situation, and I must say I find his appearance extremely propitious. He is in for a rude awakening because I mean to inform him that he can no longer expect Andrea to shoulder responsibility for the management of their properties."

"Oh, oh," the Duchess said dubiously. "I can see you are going to have an extremely interesting interview. I will keep to my quarters while you advise him of all the shocking details and then you may bring him to me when he has recovered."

"I can't believe you are calling craven!"

"It isn't that, my boy. I expect there to be some gentlemanly disagreements, and my presence might be a trifle inhibiting."

"Only a trifle," David repeated with twinkling eyes, "but you are right. I have every intention of calling him down for his misrepresentation of Andrea and I may become a bit intemperate."

"Don't be too hard on him, David. You can't expect him to see her in the same light as you do."

"Now don't try to persuade me to back off," the Duke protested with a wry face. "I have been wanting to take out my frustrations on somebody and Drew is a prime candidate."

The Duchess looked at him reprovingly, but she knew he was only half-serious so she did not advance any further admonishments and left him to await his unsuspecting victim.

A short while later the butler announced Andrew's arrival and the dashingly handsome young man strode jauntily into the library and then stopped short.

"I expected to see you laid up," he said, almost accusingly, as he faced an elegantly attired gentleman who gave every appearance of being the very picture of health and vitality. "You don't look out of sorts to me."

"Hello, Drew," the Duke greeted affably with a grin. "Nice to see you."

"Don't try to fob me off," his visitor said suspiciously. "What kind of rig are you trying to run?"

"You know, my friend, I shudder to think what a pompous ass I might have become if I had not had the good fortune to meet up with the various members of your family. I am continually hard put to command any measure of respect from any of you. It is quite lowering to one's self-esteem."

"Cut line, David, and tell me what you're about," Andrew said impatiently.

"I intend to, Drew, but it's a long story so get off your high ropes and settle yourself comfortably," the Duke stated bluntly as he sat down in one of two leather lounge chairs and leaned forward with his elbows on his knees. When Andrew had placed himself across from him and waited for an explanation, he began. "First of all, I want you to know that all the trials and tribulations I have had to endure these past four months are a direct result of your damnable loose tongue and your totally deceptive description of Andrea."

Not being exactly prepared for such a sudden and, in his mind, unwarranted attack, Andrew sat up in surprise and demanded testily, "What trials and tribulations?! What the devil are you talking about?"

"I have, in a short period of time, committed a number of indiscretions, grassed myself with the only woman I have ever wanted to marry, miscalculated and misread the sweet, unselfish nature of a lovely young lady and, in general, have made a complete Jack Pudding of myself," the Duke caustically informed his friend.

Andrew narrowed his eyes and remarked speculatively, "All that self-reproach is immensely intriguing but hardly sufficient in the way of an explanation. What has my description of Andrea got to do with this?"

"Everything, my dear fellow," the Duke said vehemently, "because, with your help, I managed to get myself engaged to the wrong sister!"

Drew sat stunned for a moment and then declared as he suddenly understood what was the heart of the matter, "My God! So *that's* what has put you in such a temper. I can't believe it! You fell in love with Andrea!" and this realization of what to him seemed the height of the ridiculous sent him into a fit of laughter that was rekindled every time he looked at his friend's disapproving face.

The Duke did not appreciate the hilarity his revelation had aroused. From his viewpoint it was only another indication of Andrew's undervalued estimation of his twin. He had a strong desire to throttle this insensible fellow who had shirked his responsibilities to his family and then had the audacity to malign the sister who took them on her shoulders.

Andrew finally sensed his host's unsympathetic mood and, with as much sobriety as he could contrive, he protested, "I must say that I am not convinced all your problems can be laid at my door. You must have made a sad mull of it."

The Duke acknowledged his blame with a sheepish grin and admitted, "So I did. But the fact remains that you prejudiced her against me from the first and I have been fighting an uphill battle ever since."

"I suppose you are eventually going to tell me just how it is that you are engaged to Chloe," Andrew asked meaningfully with a faint antagonism.

"Well, actually, I'm not now," David was happy to relate, "and in a couple of days everything would have fallen into place—at least I hoped it would. I'll start from the beginning or you will never understand how the affair got so out of hand." He began to recount all the pertinent developments of the last few months, periodically being interrupted by a barbed comment or a disrespectful bout of laughter, all of which he determinedly ignored. When he had finished, Andrew looked at him quizzically and submitted, "After having been subjected to a few of Andrea's tirades. I don't see how you can censure me for the impression I gave you."

"You will have to admit you showed me only one side of the coin," the Duke charged and then said passionately, "Drew, I am mad about that ramshackle girl. I can't begin to tell you how much I love her, and I want her more than I have ever wanted anything in my life!"

"My God! You *are* in sad case!" Andrew exclaimed, shocked that this nonpareil of the footloose and fancy free had been reduced to such a state. "Are you sure you know what you are letting yourself in for? I wouldn't put anything past her if she caught you out."

"I expect she might shoot me," David surmised, grinning unconcernedly.

"Well, if *that* don't beat the Dutch! It's plain as pikestaff you've gone daft. Anyone who can laugh at being threatened by a crazy girl and want to marry her besides has got to be dicked in the nob!"

"Someday maybe you will understand, my friend. I shall hope for you. Now come pay your respects to my grandmother. She is probably becoming deucedly impatient."

They went upstairs to knock at the Duchess's door and were immediately admitted to find a still bright-eyed little old lady waiting for them.

Drew brazenly sat down on the bed and planted a resounding kiss on the Dowager's cheek, teasing, "My love, you look extremely fetching in that lace cap and are very brave to be entertaining two gentlemen in your bedroom."

"At least there is safety in numbers," she replied impishly.

This saucy retort drew a laugh from her guests and Andrew admired, "Still awake on every suit, aren't you?"

"Why shouldn't I be?" the Duchess challenged acerbically.

Drew grinned and remarked, "You know, if David had told me he was looking for a girl as malapert as his grandmother, we could have avoided this contretemps."

"Young man, you are an impertinent puppy!"

"I know, love. I have taken some pains to cultivate that posture. It goes over so well with the ladies."

The Duchess laughed indulgently and then shook her head in resignation as she remarked, "We can only hope you can address yourself to cultivating other, more constructive interests after you sell out."

"Sell out?" Andrew exclaimed. "Who's going to sell out?"

The Duchess turned to her grandson with raised brows, and David looked hard at Andrew as he stated succinctly, "You are."

"Now wait a minute, old man. Just because you have ambitions to marry my sister does not give you the right to order my life."

"I don't mean to, Drew, but think about it. After we

are married, Andrea is not going to have time to manage your estates, and you can't expect Jonathan to take over, especially with Lord Paxton urging him to assume control of some of his holdings. There won't be anyone to oversee the properties and, even though you have an excellent steward, it is never prudent to be an absentee landlord."

"Well, at least Ladyjane will be there part of the time. I know she has not been active in the management, but her presence will lend an appearance of patronage."

"I think Lord Howell might voice some objection on that score," the Duchess hinted significantly.

Andrew looked at her sharply and then at the Duke, who nodded affirmatively, and he queried unbelievingly, "Are you telling me that Ladyjane is going to marry Lord Howell?"

"She had not yet consented, but I don't think there's any doubt about it," David replied.

"So! I am to be completely deserted!"

"Yes. It seems the shoe is on the other foot," the Duke remarked pungently.

Andrew got up and walked around the room for a moment and then came back to lean against the bedpost. "Well, I suppose I don't really have much choice. It's odd, but now that it has been put to me, I don't find it as unsettling as I would have thought. The truth of the matter is that an Army of Occupation does not have the same allure as a fighting Army—gets rather boring, actually, once you've seen everything and have settled in."

The Duke clasped him on the shoulder and apologized. "My friend, I believe I have done you an injustice. I have been berating you for your underestimation of Andrea, and yet it is no worse than hers is of you."

"That sounds like a bit of gibberish, but I presume she has been cutting me down?" the young man asked with a long-suffering sigh.

"Not really. It's just that she has serious reservations about the prospects of you becoming a responsible citizen and a dutiful husband."

"Well, she has reason for it, if it comes to that," Andrew admitted fairly. "But, David, I must correct what I perceive is a false impression. Andrea and I are totally devoted and would fight to the death for the other. We have these lamentable impulses to criticize because we expect so much more of each other than we do of anyone else."

"I understand, Drew," David said affectionately. "I imagine that's an outcome of being twins. You have a tendency to view any imagined fault in the other as a reflection on yourself."

Andrew looked at him respectfully and then grinned crookedly as he agreed, "You could be right—sounds plausible anyway. Now that you have involved me in this mess with these confidences, do I have a special role?"

"No, just keep mum for a couple of days. I have to contrive some way to break down her defenses but it won't be easy. She has more fighting reserves than an army." The Duke turned to his grandmother and suggested, "I was hoping I could persuade you to ask her to call tomorrow."

"So you can badger her? That would hardly be seemly after I promised her you would remain invisible whenever she came."

"Please, Your Grace. This situation has got to be resolved," David pleaded humbly, knowing she would not be able to resist his importunities.

"Very well," the Duchess surrendered easily, satisfied with her token protest. "Andrew, I commission you to relay the message that I should be very much pleased to see her tomorrow afternoon anytime it is convenient. I am sure she will come for she never refuses me."

"All right," Andrew promised, and then, turning to David with a resolute expression, said, "but I must warn you that, if Andrea truly finds marriage to you abhorrent, I will stand her guardian."

The Duke appreciated this protective pose, but he would not give ground and stated firmly, "She does love me, Drew. I am sure of it and I will not be denied."

"Well, then, for the sake of our continued friendship,

let us hope you can command better success with your powers of persuasion," Drew taunted.

David grinned and concluded, "I think we have carried this discussion as far as is practical tonight, so let us leave the Duchess to her beauty sleep and challenge each other at the billiard table."

"Suits me," Drew agreed readily and he moved to kiss the old lady's hand. "Good night, love. Sweet dreams."

"Good night, Andrew. I shall hope to see more of you now."

"I shall probably haunt your doorstep," he promised mischievously.

The Duke also leaned to kiss his grandmother and then the two gentlemen retired to the game room where they spent the next several hours renewing their easy relationship.

CHAPTER SIXTEEN

The next morning Andrew sat down to breakfast at nine o'clock and Andrea joined him. She had risen earlier and had already eaten, but she wished to corner her twin early to express her unqualified disapproval of the disastrous results his meddling had inspired.

He greeted her pleasantly and remarked with an air of regret, "It seems I have missed an exciting Season. I had no idea of the stir my ladies would create when they stormed the *ton* en masse. Is it true Ladyjane is going to marry Lord Howell?"

"Yes! Isn't that the most famous thing?" Andrea exclaimed delightedly. "We had no idea they even knew each other, and when they renewed their acquaintance, it was the most natural thing in the world that they should find themselves so compatible. Actually, it appears to be deeper than that. I believe they truly love each other and I am so happy for them both."

Drew admitted, "At first it seemed perfectly incredible when the Duchess told me, because I have been used to thinking of our lady mother as incurably shy and a little frightened of the outside world. I never imagined her capable of accepting another man's attentions after her disillusioning experience with Father."

"I think Lady Fortune must be given credit because, you see, Ladyjane and Lord Leslie have known each other forever, since they were children, and she felt comfortable with him, so it just sort of went on from there. I hope you are not going to disapprove."

"Lord, no! I think it's an excellent match and certainly timely since Chloe is to leave the nest."

This reminder of the thorn in her side offered Andrea the opportunity to broach the distasteful subject and she assumed the offensive. "Yes, well, I wanted to talk to you about that, Drew. I know that this engagement gratifiies you tremendously—it is what you conceived, after all—but I hope to convince you it would be the gravest error to allow such a farce of a marriage. The Duke does not love Chloe and she does not love him. I don't know what possessed her to accept him except that she thought you wished it, but that is no reason to make a hash of her life because it is so apparent that she loves Jonathan. You have only to see them together to realize that. I beg you, Drew, do not press the issue, for I *cannot* permit your conniving, falsehearted friend to ruin the happiness of these two lovely people who are so important to me!"

This passionate appeal raised serious doubts in Andrew's mind about the Duke's estimation of Andrea's feelings toward him. If there were any affection behind these aspersions, it was certainly well-hidden. Nevertheless, he at least had the grace not to aggravate her anxiety and he said tactfully, "I think you are being a bit overzealous in your objections, but I see that you have taken an extremely strong stand on this matter, so I will hold my peace and let things develop as they will. Does that relieve your mind?"

"Immensely," she replied with a grateful sigh. "I was afraid you would push for an early wedding while you were home."

"No need to rush on that account. Fact is," Andrew advised casually, "I have decided to sell out."

"Drew! Are you serious?"

"Yes. What do you think about it?"

"I think it's marvelous! I have been wondering how I would manage with both Ladyjane and Chloe gone. I had visions of having to hire a companion, although I did consider asking Katherine Hanley to move in with me, but, if you are home, it will not be necessary."

"You would still need another lady to lend you countenance, my dear sister. It would be too much to expect me to bury myself in the country all the time."

Andrea giggled and acknowledged, "Oh, Drew, I know, but I don't doubt we will manage very well and make any adjustments we have to if you ever decide to marry."

Her brother feigned a look of alarm and warned, "Andrea, if you mean to work on getting me leg-shackled, I shall have second thoughts about coming home. There is nothing to say that my budding sense of responsibility will carry me to such extremes."

Andrea laughed again and placed her hand on his arm amicably. "Never fear, my dear Andrew. I would not wish you on anyone that I should be pleased to have for a sister."

This lightly spoken disparagement was received good-humoredly and the twins once again had reestablished their peculiarly disharmonious, yet affectionate, relationship. In the course of their conversation Andrew announced offhandedly, "Before I forget, the Duchess requested me to tell you that she would be pleased to see you this afternoon if you can spare a few moments."

"Oh. Well, I *am* promised to Charlotte for lunch—she is leaving town in a few days—but I can drop in after that."

Satisfied that he had played his part, Drew turned the discussion to matters concerning the estate. They were finishing their coffee when Lady Jane entered dressed smartly in her emerald-green riding habit. As usual, she was engaged to ride with Lord Howell and she left them shortly.

In his quiet way Lord Leslie had been keeping an interested eye on the proceedings, and with an occasional helpful hint from Jonathan, he had pretty well divined the underlying aspects of this complicated affair. Sensing that matters would soon be brought to a conclusion, he decided it was time to press his own suit. He asked Lady Jane if she would like to walk for a while, since it was an unusually fine morning. She agreed and they handed the reins of their mounts to the groom who had accompanied them. Lord Howell drew the lady's arm through his, placing his other hand over hers, and immediately made his proposal.

"My dearest Jane, I think we have come to the point of committing ourselves. You know that I love you very much and would be a happy man if you would only say you will marry me. You need not be afraid. I promise I would never dishonor you."

"Oh, Leslie," Lady Jane said reproachfully, "I know that. I am not the green girl I once was. And, if things were not so unsettled, I would not hesitate to accept you, but with Chloe engaged I cannot desert Andrea—I just cannot. You know she would never consent to live with us, and it would be unthinkable to let her fare for herself so far away in Devon."

"I understand, my love, and if things were precisely as you imagine, I would be forced to contrive some acceptable arrangement, but as it is, you really have nothing to worry about. Both of your daughters are going to be happily situated as new brides very shortly."

"Oh, no, Leslie, I'm sure you are wrong there because, in one case, Chloe is *not* going to be happy married to the Duke, and in the other, Andrea is not going to be married at all. She has definitely refused Charles Loudon and she would never accept Jeffrey."

"My love, would it be a terrible surprise to you if I told you that nothing you just said has any relevance whatsoever?"

Lady Jane looked bewildered and asked, "What do you mean, Leslie?"

"Well, first of all, Chloe *will* be happily wed, but to Jonathan, and Andrea—well—" he said, pausing as he looked at her quizzically, waiting for the light to dawn.

Lady Jane appeared skeptical but ventured bravely, "Andrea—and the Duke?"

"Yes, my dear."

"Oh, surely not! She detests him and he *did* propose to Chloe," she protested incredulously.

"All in the way of a monumental misunderstanding, Ladyjane."

She shook her head doubtfully and demurred, "I just can't credit it, Leslie. It is too bizarre."

"Nevertheless, presuming I am right and things go forward as I predicted, will you then marry me?" he persisted.

"Yes, Leslie," she responded softly. "I do love you and I would be proud to be your wife."

"Thank you, darling," he said gratefully. "You have made me very happy and I must apologize for having proposed in this public place. I wonder—do you think that large tree over there might afford some privacy?"

"Leslie! I don't think—" Lady Jane protested as her determined lover led her purposefully around a large beechwood. He took off her glove, placed an exquisite emerald on her finger, and then bent to kiss her warmly.

"Oh, dear—this is most improper," she objected weakly. "It is too soon but—how beautiful—well . . . are you really sure?"

"Yes, darling," he said, laughing at her. "Let us continue our ride and then go back to tell the family."

"All right," she agreed, smiling happily.

An hour or so later the newly engaged couple found brother and sisters in the drawing room. Lord Leslie proudly made his announcement, which was followed by squeals of delight, rounds of congratulations, and a short period of pandemonium. They all decided a proper celebration was in order, and Andrea was vexed that she had an appointment to keep, but she exacted a promise that they would all reconvene for dinner. Then she reluctantly left to change into a walking dress before leaving to meet her cousin at Retford House. As she walked out the door, she saw Jonathan coming toward her and she called to him, "Good news, Jonathan. Ladyjane has accepted Lord

Howell," and then waved her hand as she stepped into the waiting carriage.

Jonathan was received enthusiastically into the family circle and he proffered his good wishes, clasping Lord Howell's hand strongly and telling him that he was a lucky man to have won such a lovely lady.

Andrew presently informed the others, "It is convenient that we are all gathered here, and I propose that we plan to remain in council, because I expect there to be other pertinent developments this afternoon which will be of great interest to all of us."

"Is Andrea bound for Grosvenor Square?" Jonathan asked curiously.

"Later. After she lunches with cousin Charlotte. And, my sly friend, I now understand why you did not seem too perturbed about your apparent ill-fortune."

"I knew Kensington would set you straight soon enough so I did not see any point in dramatizing."

Lady Jane was looking totally confused and Chloe sat down next to her, stating purposefully, "Mama, I have something to tell you."

After the whole story had been unraveled and a merry group had rehashed all the particulars, they enjoyed a festive lunch, and then returned to the drawing room to take up various occupations to while away the hours as they waited for Andrea's return.

By the time she arrived at Kensington House, Andrea had talked herself into a very good mood, for she was sure everything was beginning to plan out very well. She was sincerely pleased that Ladyjane would have a chance for true happiness, and she had been noticing lately that Chloe seemed to be weakening in her resolve to become a duchess. Now that Andrew had agreed not to take an active part, she felt easier in her mind. With a light heart and a smiling face she blithely entered the Duchess's sitting room.

Even the presence of the Duke incited no more than a mild perturbation, and when he rose to greet her, she merely turned to the Duchess and said pointedly, "I am sorry, Your Grace. I should have sent word at what hour I would come."

The Duke laughed at this none too subtle hint that she found him definitely *de trop* and he quickly moved to the attack.

"Yes, my love, that was an unbecoming omission on your part because we have been waiting here for you for the past hour and a half."

She looked at him sharply and then turned accusing eyes on the Duchess.

"I'm sorry, Andrea," the old lady apologized with a guilty face, "but David persuaded me it was of the utmost importance that he have a chance to plead his case with you."

"He *has* no case," the girl exploded irritably, "and I am getting tired of having to correct his impression that he has only to snap his fingers to get what he wants."

"Snap my fingers! *That* is one of your most preposterous accusations yet! I have practically abjected myself at your feet and would do even that if I thought it would advance my suit," an outraged David fumed recklessly.

To ward off any such unwelcome prospect, Andrea protested hurriedly with an expression of distaste, "Please, my lord Duke, do not let yourself get carried away."

"No, darling," David said, grinning roguishly, "I know you would not like it," and then, before she could tear into him for his familiarity, he demanded, "Andrea, you must hear me out. You know that I haven't the slightest desire to marry Chloe. That proposal was meant to be a ruse to force your hand, but unfortunately, the strategy had serious pitfalls. Nevertheless, through all of this, nothing has changed. I want you, my love, as I have from the first day I saw you, and you have only to say you will marry me to put everything in order."

Andrea looked at him with a challenge in her eyes and asked menacingly, "Am I to understand that you are prepared to release Chloe from her commitment only if I agree to your proposition?"

"So it would seem," the Duke replied enigmatically.

"Well, Your Grace, let me repeat once more, since your memory is deplorably deficient, that I do not have to marry you to prevent Chloe's doing so. For one thing, it is becoming apparent that she has recognized her mistake and may withdraw herself, and beyond that, there is another alternative."

The Duke again found himself outmaneuvered and he said depressingly, "If you are referring to your outlandish threat to shoot me, may I remind you that murder, particularly of a peer, carries a very severe, even final, penalty."

"Murder!" she exclaimed with a contrived shocked expression. "Isn't it strange! I never thought of it like that. But, now that you mention it, I believe hanging is the usual sentence, is it not?"

"Yes," he confirmed, determined to play out the game.

"Well! I *do* think it exceedingly shabby of you to bring up such a macabre subject," she protested with an injured look.

"I only thought to offer some deterrent to the prospect of my premature demise," he apologized whimsically.

"I don't know why you should bother, since it is obvious that you do not care if you are not long for this world, or you would not be so unreasonable," she informed him flatly. "I, on the other hand, have been looking forward to living to a ripe old age, and now I have to consider that this ambition is certainly in jeopardy. I must admit the thought is quite unnerving. I have heard that death by hanging is particularly horrible," she mused, caught up in one of her dramatic flights, and tears began to run down her face as she launched into a graphic description of the spectacle. "As the rope tightens about the neck, the face turns a sickening purple, the eyes bulge grotesquely from the head and—"

"My God, Andrea!" the Duke groaned passionately, drawing her roughly into his arms. "Are you trying to drive me completely mad?" He kissed her eyes and her tear-stained cheeks and then brought his mouth down hard on hers. Taken by surprise, it was a moment before she could recover herself. She tried to break away, pounding on his chest. Finally he let her go and she stamped her foot angrily, raging, "How dare you! You are the most insolent, presumptous—"

David put up his hand and said in resignation, "All right, Andrea, you win. I withdraw my threats. I shall not marry Chloe but never, *never*, will I give up in my determination to make you my wife!"

Andrea had the most absurd desire to dance about the room or break into song. It *had* been all a hum. She had known it, of course. But she would not be bullied, and at last, she had won the battle of wills. It was a good omen. Still she was not quite ready to follow her inclinations. She would take a little time to savor her victory. With a galling kindness, which David recognized as a deliberate taunt, she said, "I am sorry you find yourself in such a cloud-borne state, beset by hallucinations, my lord Duke. Perhaps in time the mood will pass. I am glad to see that you do, after all, have some degree of sensibility, and I am persuaded you will find a sympathetic way of explaining to Chloe." She turned to the Duchess. "Now, I am sorry to rush off like this, but I wish to hurry home for we have something else to celebrate. Ladyjane has accepted Lord Howell."

"I am glad to hear it, my dear. I am sure they will deal very well together."

"Andrea," the Duke interrupted, "I will go with you. Do not leave without me," and before she could object, he went to change from his casual clothes.

During the contest of wills between Andrea and her grandson the Dowager had remained silent, though with some difficulty. She had found Andrea's dramatics extremely diverting. The girl was utterly lost to shame. David certainly had his work cut out for him and would likely enjoy every bit of it immensely. Now she laughed heartily and admonished, "Andrea, you are the most outrageous girl and a graceless imp besides to be standing there looking like the cat that has swallowed a mouse."

"But, Your Grace, it is hard not to seem pleased when one has been declared the victor," Andrea protested with a grin.

"It's a matter of degree, my dear. You do not have to turn the knife. Don't you think you have punished him enough?"

"I'm not sure I know what you mean," Andrea said cautiously.

"You know very well what I mean," she was told bluntly. "It is monstrously cruel of you to treat him so abominably when he loves you to distraction." In exasperation she noticed Andrea's withdrawal and she submitted, "Very well, I will not say more now, but I hope that you will at least examine your behavior honestly and ask yourself if you are not being more than a little arbitrary."

Andrea lowered her eyes and did not respond, so the Duchess leaned over to pat her hand affectionately. "Don't worry, my dear. I know you are having a serious difficulty about this, but it will work itself out." She looked up as her grandson reentered the room, dressed more formally in a dark blue superfine coat and a sparkling white shirt and cravat. She told him, "I am engaged for dinner and cards this evening, but I shall expect a full report from you in the morning."

"Yes, my love," he replied and moved to the door, waiting for Andrea to precede him. She took leave of the Duchess and then walked downstairs with the Duke to his carriage, feeling in especially fine feather.

They spoke freely and easily as they made their way through the crowded streets and were careful not to antagonize one another so that they had reached a state of truce by the time they arrived at Queen Anne's Gate.

Chloe had been playing the pianoforte and had just settled herself on the arm of Jonathan's chair, which encouraged him to put his arm around her and hold her hand in her lap. She smiled at him lovingly, and it was in this revealing position of intimacy that they were discovered as Andrea walked in, followed by the Duke.

Chloe looked at her sister guiltily and blushed tellingly as she started to get up. Jonathan held her fast, however, so she remained where she was, thoroughly compromised. Lady Jane and Lord Leslie were playing cribbage while Andrew was sprawled in a chair, reading a newspaper. They all waited expectantly for Andrea to speak, anticipating a happy announcement, and were dismayed at the signs of an impending explosion, which indicated only too clearly that David had not yet won his case.

Andrea regarded her sister with a frosty expression and asked ominously, "Just how long has this been going on?"

Chloe was not about to be intimidated, however, and she said defiantly, "Andy, you know that I have always loved Jonathan."

"*I* did, but I didn't know *you* did," Andrea advised caustically. "And don't you think you might have told the Duke?"

"I did—yesterday," Chloe blurted out without thinking.

"I see," Andrea remarked in a deceptively calm voice. "And how is it that you are still wearing his ring?"

"Well," a harassed young lady admitted uncomfortably, "David asked us not to tell you yet."

"Did he? *Naturally* his wishes were honored even though, it is obvious, I am the only one left out of your confidence," Andrea commented resentfully.

"Andy, you need not try to make me feel guilty because, if you had not been so secretive and had told me that the Duke had proposed to you several times, I would not have been so gullible as to think he had reformed for my sake and that it was my fate to marry him!" Chloe accused.

Andrea stared in disbelief at this artless confession and then broke into delighted laughter as she asked, "Is *that* what possessed you to be so impulsive?"

"Yes," giggled Chloe, and she and Andrea fell laughing into each other's arms with Andrea professing, "Chloe, you are the dearest little peagoose. I knew there was some odd explanation, but I couldn't for the life of me puzzle it out."

"Well," Chloe allowed impishly, "that's because you don't read enough romantic novels." Once again she took off the sapphire and handed it back to the Duke.

Andrea suddenly remembered the presence of her persecutor and, in one of her mercurial changes of mood, turned on him furiously, as she realized that her victory was not as perfect as she had supposed. "As for you!" she stormed, "how dare you let me rant and rave and make a perfect fool out of myself when you had already resolved the matter?"

"I have become a senselessly desperate man, my love, and I snatch at straws," David told her ruefully.

She ignored his pleading expression and charged, in one last extravagant barrage (no one could say she had not gone down fighting), "If you think a continuing program of deception and coercion will change my mind, you have become regrettably unsettled in your mind! I refuse to have anything to do with such a scurrilous, unprincipled, reprehensible—"

"Andrea," David said indulgently, "if you are going to engage in another of your lamentable attacks on my character, I insist you do it privately. There is no reason to subject the rest of the family to such a shocking display." He took her hand and pulled her across the hall to the library amid loud protests that included such derogatory expressions as dastardly, abhorrent, loathesome, and no doubt others, which were cut off by the thick library door.

Andrew closed the door of the drawing room, also, and the hard-pressed observers of this abbreviated scene gave way to their amusement and laughed until tears came to their eyes.

Meanwhile, across the hall, a persistent suitor had slowly drawn his recalcitrant lady into arms and was surprised to find that she was no longer putting up a stiff resistance. He decided to explore this unusual circumstance and held her more closely, saying softly, "I love you so much, Andrea, and I am glad that you have nearly reached the limit of your rejection."

"What makes you think I have?" she asked interestedly, a foolish question, considering her present position.

"Because, darling, I have noticed that you never call me the same thing twice and you must surely be close to exhausting your repertoire of invectives."

"Oh, what a perfectly hateful man you are," Andrea said with a shaky voice, "to make me laugh when I wish to rail at you."

"Again?" he protested incredulously. "I do hope, my love, that when we are married you can direct your energies into other channels. You *have* resigned yourself to becoming a duchess, haven't you?"

"David," came a small voice, "I can't."

"What?!" he exclaimed as he held her a little away. "How can you say that to me when you know very well you wish to?"

"I just cannot! You *know* I cannot!"

"Are you still laboring under the misapprehension that I would deceive you?" he asked reproachfully.

"I'm sorry, David. I don't seem to be able to conquer my fears about that."

"I understand, darling, but you are going to have to trust me. I have been unerringly faithful to you these last three months. Doesn't that tell you something? Besides," he said with a twinkling eye, "you could always carry out your threat."

"But—but that's just it," she wailed, "I don't think I could!"

"Andrea," the Duke said with a quivering voice, barely able to contain his amusement, "are you telling me that you are holding back on saying you will marry me because you are afraid you could not shoot me if I stepped out of line?"

She thought resentfully that it was just like him to make it sound ridiculous, but she lowered her eyes and gave an almost imperceptible nod.

A perfectly enchanted gentleman crushed her to him as he laughed and began to shower her with light kisses.

"Andrea, you little minx, do you know that that is the nicest thing you have ever said to me?"

This whimsical raillery had the effect of breaking down all her reservations and she uninhibitedly wrapped her arms tightly around his neck and confessed, "I *do* love you, David, I do truly love you. I don't want to but I can't help it."

"No need to apologize, love. It's what I've been wanting to hear these many months," he teased happily and began to demonstrate in earnest the full extent of his feelings, an extremely pleasant activity in which he received full cooperation, so much so in fact, that he felt compelled to call a halt and, still shaking from emotion, he disentangled himself as he admonished huskily, "My love, if you are going to behave so wantonly, I shall have to ask you to keep your distance until we are married. I have not played the pattern saint all this time only to have a relapse at the eleventh hour."

Andrea burst out laughing and complained, "Well, I must say you are hard to satisfy." He was gazing at her with a frankly warm expression and she was provoked to add doubtfully, "If you are going to make a practice of looking at me like that, I don't know how you expect me to follow your restrictions."

"Try to control yourself, darling. We will be married very soon and then you can attack me with every prerogative."

"How soon?" she asked with considerable interest.

"Tomorrow—next week," he answered sensuously.

"David! Be serious!"

"I am, love. I have waited long enough."

"But, darling, you know there are others to consider who came to this point earlier. Not only that, but I must have a wedding dress and other things."

"I will give you the week—no more. That is time enough for a wedding dress and you do not need many other things. I plan to spirit you away to my Berkshire estate, where we can be private for a few weeks. You can order new gowns before we go and have fittings later. As for the others, I have decided that there are some advantages to being a Duke, after all, and I mean to pull rank."

"Oh, what a shameless man you are!" Andrea accused even while smiling her approval.

David grinned and revealed smugly, "Besides, my heart's delight, I have still another argument which I hope will please you. Wellington has been asking me to go to Spain to elicit some kind of commitment from King Fernando about the unclaimed paintings. I have been putting him off with the excuse that I had a personal matter to resolve, but if you are agreeable, we will go to Spain for our honeymoon."

"David! How exciting! But—I should not like to miss the other weddings."

"Of course not. We'll work out an acceptable schedule for all of us."

Andrea smiled at him rapturously and felt moved to offer some sort of apology for her past behavior. "David, I am so happy that you did not give up on me. When I think of how I maligned you, I don't know why you didn't wish me to the devil."

"Well, I didn't mean to tell you," he responded with a suspiciously mischievous expression, "but, since you brought it up, I shall have to admit that I have been determined to use any ruse that was necessary to get into your bedroom, ever since you refused to let me see the portrait of your grandmother."

This bit of nonsense made her laugh and she asked, "Darling David, do you know why I love you?"

"I can think of several reasons why you should, the most important being that I am mad about you and mean to spoil you dreadfully, but I should be interested to hear your version."

"Because you are such fun. I mean, you make me laugh and I enjoy matching wits with you and talking to you and even fighting with you and, well, just everything. Always I feel alive when I am with you."

"I understand what you mean, love. We are a match. I have known it from the first, and I have been very aggrieved that you did not recognize it also."

"I did, David," she admitted candidly, pleasing him enormously, "but I was afraid."

"And you're not now?" he asked, looking at her keenly.

"No," she answered softly.

"And you are not going to turn on me if some revengeful female tries to make trouble?" he pursued, as he drew her to him once again.

"No, my love," she answered promptly and, wrapping her arms around his neck possessively, she vowed, "because, as you said, I could cut any one of them to pieces if I wanted to so they had better keep hands off."

As always, her impassioned declarations put a severe strain on his self-command. He easily convinced himself that under his new status he had every right to take certain liberties and so he proceeded to indulge himself quite freely until he felt her pushing lightly against his chest. He brought himself under control and whispered, "Sorry, darling, but I did warn you about this sort of thing."

"So you did. However, I do think you could make some effort. I don't know why the whole burden should fall on me," she said with a contrived resentment that was not at all convincing, considering the laughter in her sparkling eyes.

David grinned and put his arm around her waist. "Come on, you little vixen. Let us put our friends' minds at ease. They are probably ready to burst in on us wondering if we have come to blows or to an understanding."

They walked across the hall and, on entering the drawing room, were immediately engulfed by two jubilant ladies, which prompted David to note quizzically, "I don't suppose I have to tell you that I have finally won the hardest battle I ever fought in my life." Such a pungently expressed comment earned him heartfelt handclasps and rounds of congratulations.

After a long, sometimes heated discussion, all parties at last came to an amiable agreement on the sequence of happy events. All three engagements would be announced immediately, and Andrea and David would be married the following week. They would then retire to Berkshire until a few days before Lady Jane's marriage three weeks later. David and Andrea would then leave for Spain. In approximately one month they would return to participate in the preparations for Chloe and Jonathan's wedding. Having settled all matters to everyone's satisfaction, the group relaxed for an hour or so and then broke up for the evening.

After Andrew had bade his ladies good night, he sat for a time staring into space in the big chair in the library, wondering how all this had come about so suddenly. He had certainly not foreseen such a total disruption when he had insisted that Chloe be presented. If he felt a little out of it, he had only himself to blame. He realized he had some personal adjustments to make. Even so, he was sincerely pleased that things had turned out so happily. He reminded himself that Jeffrey would need some consolation and would no doubt spend a good part of his time in Devon. And one day—well, who could know—he might get riveted himself. This unbidden thought made him suddenly realize how benumbed he was, and in an exercise of rejection, he went out to ride in the cool night to remove the cobwebs from his head.

The next week the ladies were engaged in a flurry of activity to prepare Andrea for her wedding. True to her promise, Chloe revealed the ludicrous origins of the confusion and her story was confirmed when Andrea appeared publicly with the Newbury betrothal ring on her finger.

At last at nine o'clock on a bright Wednesday morning, Andrea and David were married at St. George's in Hanover Square, attended by their family and friends. Afterward, they were toasted at a lavish breakfast on Grosvenor Square but left their well-wishers very quickly, as it was a six- or seven-hour drive to the Duke's Berkshire estate.

It was still light when they arrived and Andrea was delighted with the lovely grounds and stately Palladian mansion. David ordered a light supper for them and then retired to his private apartment to bathe and change, while Andrea did the same. They joined each other for an elegant meal in an intimate parlor and then David took her on a short tour through some of the exquisitely decorated chambers. Presently he slipped his arm around her waist and murmured provocatively, "I don't want to wait any longer, darling. Run along and get ready for bed. I'll join you very soon."

"Yes, Your Grace," the new Duchess replied demurely and then, with an impish smile, blew him a kiss and ran lightly up the stairs.

Andrea was standing by the window when she heard David enter and she turned slowly to face him. He had never seen her other than elegantly and perfectly groomed and the sight of her in the filmy gown with her dark hair hanging almost to her waist took his breath away. He gazed at her for a moment and then said softly, "All right, darling. Now it is perfectly proper for you to attack me."

She gave a ripple of laughter and ran into his arms, saying, "Devil!" to which he promptly responded, "Witch!"—words of endearment that were a fitting prelude to more satisfying expressions of love. Very soon David concluded that he really had no inclination to be a pattern saint after all and gave up all pretense in the matter—a fall from grace Andrea had reason to applaud.

*Author's note: The paintings referred to in this book were presented to the Duke of Wellington by King Fernando and may be seen at Apsley House, the Wellington Museum in London.

Love—the way you want it!

Candlelight Romances

		TITLE NO.	
☐ **A MAN OF HER CHOOSING** by Nina Pykare	$1.50	#554	(15133-3)
☐ **PASSING FANCY** by Mary Linn Roby	$1.50	#555	(16770-1)
☐ **THE DEMON COUNT** by Anne Stuart	$1.25	#557	(11906-5)
☐ **WHERE SHADOWS LINGER** by Janis Susan May	$1.25	#556	(19777-5)
☐ **OMEN FOR LOVE** by Esther Boyd	$1.25	#552	(16108-8)
☐ **MAYBE TOMORROW** by Marie Pershing	$1.25	#553	(14909-6)
☐ **LOVE IN DISGUISE** by Nina Pykare	$1.50	#548	(15229-1)
☐ **THE RUNAWAY HEIRESS** by Lillian Cheatham	$1.50	#549	(18083-X)
☐ **HOME TO THE HIGHLANDS** by Jessica Eliot	$1.25	#550	(13104-9)
☐ **DARK LEGACY** by Candace Connell	$1.25	#551	(11771-2)
☐ **LEGACY OF THE HEART** by Lorena McCourtney	$1.25	#546	(15645-9)
☐ **THE SLEEPING HEIRESS** by Phyllis Taylor Pianka	$1.50	#543	(17551-8)
☐ **DAISY** by Jennie Tremaine	$1.50	#542	(11683-X)
☐ **RING THE BELL SOFTLY** by Margaret James	$1.25	#545	(17626-3)
☐ **GUARDIAN OF INNOCENCE** by Judy Boynton	$1.25	#544	(11862-X)
☐ **THE LONG ENCHANTMENT** by Helen Nuelle	$1.25	#540	(15407-3)
☐ **SECRET LONGINGS** by Nancy Kennedy	$1.25	#541	(17609-3)

At your local bookstore or use this handy coupon for ordering:

Dell | **DELL BOOKS**
P.O. BOX 1000, PINEBROOK, N.J. 07058

Please send me the books I have checked above. I am enclosing $ _____
(please add 75¢ per copy to cover postage and handling). Send check or money order—no cash or C.O.D.'s. Please allow up to 8 weeks for shipment.

Mr/Mrs/Miss _____

Address _____

City _____ State/Zip _____

INTRODUCING...

Romantique

The Romance Magazine For The 1980's

Each exciting issue contains a full-length romance novel — the kind of first-love story we all dream about...

PLUS

other wonderful features such as a travelogue to the world's most romantic spots, advice about your romantic problems, a quiz to find the ideal mate for you and much, much more.

ROMANTIQUE: A complete novel of romance, plus a whole world of romantic features.

ROMANTIQUE: Wherever magazines are sold. Or write Romantique Magazine, Dept. C-1, 41 East 42nd Street, New York, N.Y. 10017

Romantique

INTERNATIONALLY DISTRIBUTED BY DELL DISTRIBUTING, INC.